THE DELUGE
PART ONE
AN HISTORICAL NOVEL
OF POLAND, SWEDEN, AND
RUSSIA

Schegge Runte

AUTHOR: **Henryk Sienkiewicz**
(Wola Okrzejska, 5 maggio 1846 – Vevey, 15 novembre 1916)
Publisher: **Francesco Tosi**

Editio Princeps: THE DELUGE. Vol. I. An Historical Novel OF POLAND, SWEDEN, AND RUSSIA. A SEQUEL TO "WITH FIRE AND SWORD." BY HENRYK SIENKIEWICZ. AUTHORIZED AND UNABRIDGED TRANSLATION FROM THE POLISH BY JEREMIAH CURTIN. IN TWO VOLUMES.; Vol. II., BOSTON: LITTLE, BROWN, AND COMPANY 1915.

Jeremiah Curtin (6 September 1835 – 14 December 1906)

"Schegge Riunite",

ISBN edizione cartacea: 9781983377389

THE DELUGE
PART ONE

Sir,--I beg to dedicate to you this translation of a remarkable work, touching a period eventful in the history of the Poles, and the Slav race in general. You will appreciate the pictures of battle and trial contained in these volumes, for you know great events not from books merely but from personal contact. You receive pleasure from various literatures, and from considering those points of character by which nations and men are distinguished; hence, as I think, The Deluge will give you some mental enjoyment, and perhaps turn your attention to a new field of history.

JEREMIAH CURTIN.

Smithsonian Institution, Bureau of Ethnology, November 25, 1891.

INTRODUCTION.

The wars described in The Deluge are the most complicated and significant in the whole career of the Commonwealth, for the political motives which came into play during these wars had their origin in early and leading historical causes.

The policy of the Teutonic Knights gave the first of its final results in the war of 1655, between Sweden and Poland, since it made the elector independent in Prussia, where soon after, his son was crowned king. The war with Great Russia in 1654, though its formal cause came, partly at least, from the struggle of 1612, in which the Poles had endeavored to subjugate Moscow, was really roused by the conflict of Southern Russian with Poland to win religious and material equality.

The two fundamental events of Polish history are the settlement of the Teutonic Knights in Prussia, through the action of the Poles themselves; and the union of Poland with Lithuania and Russia by the marriage of Yadviga, the Polish princess, to Yagyello, Grand Prince of Lithuania.

Before touching on the Teutonic Knights, a few words may be given to the land where they began that career which cut off Poland from the sea, took from the Poles their political birthplace, and gave its name and territory to the chief kingdom of the new German Empire, the kingdom which is in fact the creator and head of that Empire.

Prussia in the thirteenth century extended from the Vistula eastward to the Niemen, and from the Baltic southward about as far as it does at present. In this territory lived the Prussians. East of the Niemen lived the Lithuanians, another division of the same stock of people. West of the Vistula lay Pomorye,[1] now Pomerania, occupied at that time exclusively by Slavs under Polish dominion.

The Prussians, a people closely related to the Slavs, were still Pagans, as were also the Lithuanians; and having a more highly developed religion than either the pre-Christian Slavs or the Germans, their conversion was likely to be of a more difficult nature.

At the end of the tenth and in the beginning of the thirteenth centuries attempts were made to convert the Prussians; but the only result was the death of the missionaries, who seem to have been too greatly filled with zeal to praise their own faith and throw contempt on that of the people among whom they were really only guests and sojourners.

Finally, a man appeared more adroit and ambitious than others,-- Christian, a monk of Olivka, near Dantzig. This monk, we are told, had a knowledge of the weak points of men, spoke Prussian as well as Polish, was not seeking the crown of martyrdom, and never made light of things held sacred by those to whom he was preaching. After a few years his success was such as to warrant a journey to Rome, where he explained to Innocent III. the results of his labor. The Pope encouraged the missionary, and in 1211 instructed the Archbishop of Gnezen to aid Christian with his co-workers and induce secular princes to help them.

Christian returned from Rome with renewed zeal; but instead of being helped he was hindered, for tribute and labor were imposed on his converts by the secular power. Since the new religion was coupled with servitude, the Prussians were roused greatly against it.

Christian strove to obtain relief for his converts, but in vain. Then, taking two native followers, he made a second journey to Rome, was created first Bishop of Prussia, and returned again to the field.

The great body of Prussians now considered all converts as traitors. The priests of the native religion roused the people, and attacked those persons as renegades who had deserted the ancient faith and were bringing slavery to the country. They went farther and fell upon Mazovia, whence the propaganda had issued. Konrad, unable to defend himself, bought them off with rich presents. The newly made converts were killed, captured, or driven to deep forests.

Christian turned to the Pope a third time, and implored him to direct against Prussia those Poles who were going to the Holy Land.

The Archbishop of Gnezen was instructed from Rome to make this change, and the Poles were summoned against Prussia for the following year. The crusade was preached also in Germany.

Warriors arrived from both countries in fairly large numbers, and during their presence ruined villages and churches were rebuilt in the district of Culm, where the conversions had taken place mainly. In a couple of seasons the majority of the warriors found their way home again. A second crusade was proclaimed, and men responded freely. All these forces were simply guarding the missionaries and the converts,--a position which could not endure.

Christian, seeing this, formed the plan of founding an order of armed monks in Poland like the Knights of the Sword in Livonia. Konrad gave his approval at once.

The Bishop of Modena, at that time papal legate in Poland, hastened the establishment of the order; for to him it seemed the best agent to bend the stiff necks of idolaters. Permission to found the order was obtained from the Pope, and a promise of means to maintain it from Konrad.

Christian, who had interested Rome and the West in his work, now gave great praise before the world to the Prince of Mazovia, who thereupon rewarded him with a gift of twelve castles and one hundred villages, reserving merely sovereign rights without income. This gift was confirmed to the Bishop of Prussia by Honorius III.

Christian labored so zealously that in 1225 he consecrated twenty-five superior knights in his new order, which received the same rules as the Livonian Knights of the Sword,--that is, the rules of the Templars.

The new knights were called Brothers of Dobjin, from the castle of Dobjin, which Konrad gave them as a residence, adding the district of Leslin near Inovratslav as a means of support.

As soon as the Brothers had settled in their castle, they attacked the Prussians, ruined villages, and brought in plunder. The enraged Prussians collected large forces, and attacked the land of Culm, with the intent to raze Dobjin. On hearing this, Konrad with his own troops and a general levy hastened to the relief of the order.

A bloody and stubborn battle of two days' duration was fought with great loss on both sides. Konrad, despairing of victory, left the field, thus causing the complete overthrow of the Poles. The surviving Brothers of Dobjin took refuge in the castle, which the Prussians were unable to capture. The order, shattered at its very inception, hoped for reinforcements from abroad; but the Pope at that juncture was sending a crusade to Palestine, and would not permit a division in the forces of the West. The Prussians, elated with victory, plundered at pleasure the lands bordering on their own.

In this disaster Christian conceived the idea of calling in the Teutonic Knights against Prussia. This idea, suicidal from a Polish point of view, was accepted by the Prince of Mazovia.

The Teutonic Order was founded in Palestine near the end of the twelfth century to succeed some German hospitallers who had resided in Jerusalem till the capture of the city by Saracens in 1187.

In a few years the new order became military, and under the patronage of Frederick, Duke of Suabia, afterward the Emperor Frederick II., acquired much wealth, with great imperial and papal favor. Under Herman Von Salza, who was grand master from 1210 to 1239, the future of the order was determined, its main scene of action transferred to the West, and that career begun which made the Teutonic Order the most remarkable of the weapon-bearing monks of Europe. Herman Von Salza--a keen, crafty man, of great political astuteness and ambition--had determined to win separate territory for the order, and the dignity of Prince of the Empire for the grand master.

Nothing therefore could be more timely for his plans than the invitation from the Prince of Mazovia, who in 1225 sent envoys to Herman; especially since the order had just been deprived in Transylvania of lands given to support it while warding off heathen Kumanians.

The envoys offered the Teutonic master Culm and some adjoining lands for the order, in return for curbing the Prussians. Herman resolved to accept, should the Emperor prove friendly to the offer. He hastened to Frederick at Rimini, explained the whole question, received a grant in which Konrad's endowment was confirmed; besides the order was given all the land it could conquer and make subject to the Emperor alone. The grand master's next care was to obtain papal approval.

Two envoys from Herman were sent to Poland, where they obtained, as the chronicles of the order relate, a written title to Culm and the neighboring land as well as to all Prussia which they could conquer. Near Torun (Thorn) a wooden fortress was built, called in German Fogelsang (Bird-song). This fortress was the first residence of the knights, who later on had so much power and such influence in the history of Poland.

Only two years later did Herman send his knights to Culm. One of the first acts was to purchase for various considerations, from the Bishop of Plotsk and from Christian, the Bishop of Prussia, their rights over the lands granted them in Culm. The labor of conversion began, and soon the grand master prevailed on the Pope to proclaim throughout Europe a crusade against Prussia.

From Poland alone came twenty thousand men, and many more from other parts of Europe. When the knights had made a firm beginning of work, their design of independence was revealed. They wished to be rid of even a show of submission to the Prince of Mazovia. They raised the question by trying to incorporate the remaining Brothers of Dobjin, and thus acquire the grant given them by Konrad. They had disputes also with Bishop Christian and the Bishop of Plotsk. In 1234 the Bishop of Modena was sent as papal legate to settle the disputes. The legate decided, to the satisfaction of the bishops, that of all lands won from the Pagans two thirds were to be retained by the knights and one third given to the bishops, the church administration being under the order in its own two thirds. For the Prince of Mazovia nothing was left, though he asserted sovereign rights in Culm and Prussia, and would not permit the order to acquire the grant given the Brothers of Dobjin by incorporating the remaining members of that body.

The Teutonic Order would not recognize the sovereignty of the Polish prince, and insisted on incorporating the Brothers of Dobjin. The order, knowing that Konrad would yield only under constraint, placed its possessions at the feet of the Pope, made them the property of the Holy See. This action found success; the Pope declared Culm and all the acquisitions of the order the property of Saint Peter, which the church for a yearly tax then gave in feudal tenure to the Teutonic Knights, who therefore could not recognize in those regions the sovereignty of any secular prince. In August, 1234, the Pope informed Konrad in a special bull of the position of the order, and enjoined on him to aid it with all means in his power. The Polish prince could do nothing; he could not even prevent the incorporation of the majority of the remaining Brothers of Dobjin, and of the lands and property given for their use he was able to save nothing but the castle of Dobjin.

Konrad now found himself in a very awkward position; he had introduced of his own will a foreign and hostile power which had all Western Europe and the Holy See to support it, which had unbounded means of discrediting the Poles and putting them in the wrong before the world; and these means the order never failed to use. In half a century after their coming the knights, by the aid of volunteers and contributions from all Europe, had converted Prussia, and considered Poland and the adjoining parts of Lithuania as sure conquests to be made at their own leisure and at the expense of all Western Christendom.

The first Polish territory acquired was Pomerania. The career of the knights was easy and successful till the union of Poland and Lithuania in 1386. In 1410, at the battle called by the names both of Grünwald and Tannenberg, the power of the order was broken. Some years later Pomerania was returned to Poland, and the order was allowed to remain in East Prussia in the position of a vassal to the Commonwealth. In this reduced state the knights lived for a time, tried to gain allies, but could not; the most they did--and that was the best for the German cause--was to induce Albert, a member of the Franconian branch of the Hohenzollerns, to become grand master. He began to reorganize the order, and tried to shake off allegiance to Poland; but finding no aid in the Empire or elsewhere, he acted on Luther's advice to introduce Protestantism and convert Prussia into a secular and hereditary duchy. This he did in 1525. Poland, with a simplicity quite equal to that of Konrad, who called in the order at first, permitted the change. The military monks married, and were converted into hereditary nobles. Albert became Duke of Prussia, and took the oath of allegiance to Poland. Later the Hohenzollerns of Brandenburg inherited the duchy, became feudatories of Poland as well as electors at home. This was the position during the war between Sweden and Poland described in THE DELUGE. Frederick William, known as the Great Elector, was ruling at that time in Brandenburg and Prussia. He acted with great adroitness and success; paying no attention to his oath as vassal, he took the part of one side, and then of the other when he saw fit. He fought on the Swedish side in the three days' battle around Warsaw in which Yan Kazimir was defeated. This service was to be rewarded by the independence of Prussia.

Hardly had the scale turned in favor of Poland when the Great Elector assisted Yan Kazimir against Sweden; and in the treaty of Wehlau (1657) Poland relinquished its rights over Prussia, which thus became sovereign and independent in Europe. This most important change was confirmed three years later at the peace of Oliva.

Frederick, son of the Great Elector, was crowned "King in Prussia" at Königsberg in 1701. The Elector of Brandenburg became king in that territory in which he had no suzerain.

At the first division of Poland, Royal Prussia of The Deluge, the territory lying between the Vistula and Brandenburg, went to the new kingdom; and Brandenburg, Pomerania, and Prussia became continuous territory.

The early success of the Teutonic Knights was so great that in the third half century of their rule on the Baltic their power overshadowed Poland, which was thus seriously threatened. Toward the end of the fourteenth century, however (1386), the Poles escaped imminent danger by their union with Lithuania and Russia. Through this most important connection they rose at once from a position of peril to one of safety and power.

This union, brought about through the marriage of the Polish princess Yadviga to Yagyello, Grand Prince of Lithuania, and by exceedingly adroit management on the part of the Polish nobles and clergy, opened to the Poles immense regions of country and the way to vast wealth. Before the union their whole land was composed of Great and Little Poland, with Mazovia (see map); after the union two thirds of the best lands of pre-Tartar Russia formed part of the Commonwealth.

Since Poland managed to place and maintain itself at the head of affairs, though this roused at all times opposition of varying violence in the other two parts of the Commonwealth, the social ideals and political structure of Poland prevailed in Lithuania and Russia, so far as the upper classes were concerned. In Lithuania, by the terms of the union, all were obliged to become Catholic; in different parts of Russia, which was Orthodox, the people were undisturbed in their religion at first; but after a time the majority of the nobles became Catholic in religion, and Poles in language, name, manners, and ideas. To these was added a large immigration of Polish nobles seeking advancement and wealth. All Russia found itself after a time under control of an upper class which was out of all sympathy with the great mass and majority of the people.

During the Yagyellon dynasty, which lasted from 1386 to 1572, the religious question was not so prominent for any save nobles; but ownership of their own land and their own labor was gradually slipping away from the people. During the reign of Sigismund III. (1587-1632), religion was pushed to the foreground, the United Church was brought into Russia; and land and religion, which raise the two greatest problems in a State, the material and the spiritual, were the main objects of thought throughout Russia.

Under Vladislav in 1648 the storm burst forth in Southern Russia. There was a popular uprising, the most wide-spread and stubborn in history, during which the Poles lost many battles and gained one great victory, that of Berestechko; the Southern Russians turned to the North, and selected the Tsar Alexai Mihailovich as sovereign.

Jan. 8, 1654, there was a great meeting in Pereyaslav, [2] at which Bogdan Hmelnitski, hetman of the Zaporojian army and head of all

Southern Russia, after he had consulted with the Cossacks, took his place in the centre of the circle, and in presence of the army, the people, and Buturlin, the envoy of Alexai Mihailovich, said:--

"Gentlemen, Colonels, Essauls, Commanders of hundreds, the whole Zaporojian army, and all Orthodox Christians,--You know how the Lord delivered us from the hands of our enemies who persecuted the Church of God and were envenomed against all Christians of our Eastern Orthodoxy. We have lived six years without a sovereign, in endless battles against our persecutors and enemies who desire to root out the church of God, so that the Russian name may not be heard in our land. This position has grown unendurable, and we cannot live longer without a sovereign. Therefore we have assembled a council before the whole people, so that you with us may choose from four sovereigns that one whom you wish. The first is the Sovereign of Turkey, who has invited us under his authority many times through his envoys; the second is the Khan of the Crimea; the third the King of Poland, who, if we wish, may receive us into former favor; the fourth is the Orthodox sovereign, the Tsar and Grand Prince Alexai Mihailovich, the sole ruler of all Russia, whom we have been imploring six years with unceasing petitions. Choose whom you like. The Sovereign of Turkey is a Mussulman; you all know how our brethren, the Greeks, Orthodox Christians, suffer, and what persecution they endure from godless men. A Mussulman also is the Khan of the Crimea, whom we took into friendship of necessity, by reason of the unendurable woes which we passed through. Of persecutions from Polish lords it is needless to speak; you know yourselves that they esteemed a Jew and a dog more than a Christian, our brother. But the great Orthodox sovereign of the East is of one faith with us, one confession of the Greek rite; we are one spiritual body with the Orthodoxy of Great Russia, having Jesus Christ for our head. This great sovereign, this Christian Tsar, taking pity on the suffering of our Orthodox church in Little Russia, giving ear to our six years' entreating, has inclined his heart to us graciously, and was pleased to send with his favor dignitaries from near his person. If we love him earnestly, we shall not find a better refuge than his lofty hand. If any man is not agreed with us, let him go whither he pleases; the road is free--"

Here the whole people shouted: "We choose to be under the Orthodox sovereign; better to die in our Orthodox faith than to go to a hater of Christ, to a Pagan!"

Then the Pereyaslav colonel, Teterya, passed around in the circle, and asked in every direction: "Are all thus agreed?"

"All with one spirit," was the answer.

The hetman now said: "May the Lord our God strengthen us under the strong hand of the Tsar."

The people shouted back in one voice: "God confirm us! God give us strength to be one for the ages!"

The hetman, the army, and the representatives of Southern Russia took the oath of allegiance to the Tsar. The result of this action was a war between the Commonwealth on one side, and Northern and Southern Russia on the other. The Commonwealth being thus occupied on the east, Sweden decided to attack on the west.

The war between Russia and the Commonwealth lasted thirteen years, and ended with a truce of thirteen years more, made at Andrusovo. By this agreement the city and province of Smolensk went to Russia, and all the left bank of the Dnieper, while Kieff was to be occupied by Poland after two years. This truce became a treaty during the reign of

Sobyeski. Kieff remained with the Russians, and peace was unbroken till the second half of the following century, when all Russia west of the Dnieper was restored to the East in nearly the same limits which it had before the Tartar invasion; excepting the territory included in Galicia, and known as Red Russia.

Jeremiah Curtin.

Smithsonian Institution, Bureau of Ethnology,

November 25, 1891.

REMARKS ON PERSONAGES IN "THE DELUGE."

Yan Kazimir was a son of Sigismund III., who was a son of King John of Sweden and Catherine, daughter of Sigismund I. of Poland.

John of Sweden was succeeded by his son Sigismund, who under the name of Sigismund III. was elected King of Poland in 1587 to succeed his mother's brother, Sigismund Augustus, the last descendant of Yagyello in the male line.

Sigismund III. was dethroned by the Swedes, and his issue excluded from the succession. Duke Charles, the ablest of Gustavus Vasa's sons, and uncle of Sigismund, was made king as Charles IX.

This Charles IX. was father of Gustavus Adolphus. Gustavus Adolphus was succeeded by his only daughter, Christina, who would not marry, and who after reigning for a time resigned in favor of her cousin Karl Gustav of Zweibrücken, [3] son of the only sister of Gustavus Adolphus. Gustavus Vasa was therefore the great-grandfather of both

Yan Kazimir and Karl Gustav, who were thus second cousins. The Polish Vasas laid claim to the Swedish crown, thereby causing the Commonwealth during sixty years much loss in money and men. Yan Kazimir relinquished this claim when he made peace with Sweden.

Before his election Yan Kazimir, being a cardinal, was dispensed from his vows by the Pope. Chosen king, he married Louise Marie, daughter of the Duke of Nevers, a woman of strong will and much beauty.

Discouraged and wearied by many wars and reverses, and more than all by the endless dissensions of magnates, Yan Kazimir resigned the kingly office in 1668, and retired to France. Being now a widower, he became Abbot of St. Germain and St. Martin, and lived on his stipend from these foundations, for the Poles refused to continue his pension. It seems, however, that he did not remain in seclusion till the end, for he is mentioned as marrying in secret a widow who had once been a laundress. He died in 1672, remembering the world much more than the world remembered him.

Yan Zamoyski, one of the most celebrated nobles in Polish history, was the grandfather of Sobiepan Zamoyski. The time of Zamoyski's success was during the reign of Stephen Batory, who gave him more offices and power than any citizen of the Commonwealth had ever enjoyed. As castellan of Cracow, he was the first among lay senators; as starosta of the same territory, he had extensive jurisdiction over criminals in Little Poland; as hetman, he was commander of all the military forces of the kingdom; as chancellor, he held the seals, without which no official act of the king had validity.

Perhaps the most notable action in Zamoyski's career as a civilian during Batory's reign was his treatment of the Zborovskis, one of whom he had beheaded, and another condemned to decapitation and infamy. The hatred of the Zborovskis for Zamoyski became so intense that later on they tried to seat their candidate, Maximilian of Austria, in opposition to Sigismund III., Zamoyski's choice and that of the majority. The Zborovski party brought their candidate to the gate of Cracow, intending to enthrone him with armed hand. Zamoyski repulsed and pursued them to Silesia, where he defeated and made Maximilian prisoner. The Austrian Archduke was held in captivity till he renounced all claim to the throne. This is the captivity to which Sobiepan refers on page 324, Vol. II.

Zamoyski had Sigismund impeached in 1592, not to condemn him, but to give him a lesson. Zamoyski's course in this affair, and his last speech in the Diet of 1605 are his most prominent acts during a reign in which he was first in opposition, as he had been first on the king's side during Batory's time. Zamoyski died in 1605, alarmed, as Lelevel says, for the future of his country.

Sobiepan Zamoyski, who conceived such a friendship for Zagloba, married the daughter of Henri de la Grange, a captain in the guard of Philip, Duke of Orleans. After Zamoyski's death, his widow, a woman of great beauty and ambition, married Sobyeski, subsequently elected king to succeed Michael Vishnyevetski, who is mentioned on page 253, Vol. II.

Kmita, the hero of THE DELUGE, was probably of the Kmitas of Little Poland, and of those who inherited lands granted Poles in Lithuania and Russia after the union.

Kmitsits, which means "son of Kmita," as "starostsits" means "son of a starosta," is the name used by Sienkiewicz; but as that word would baffle most English readers, I have taken Kmita, the original form of the family name. Kmita is mentioned in Solovyóff's Russian history as co-operating with Sapyeha and Charnyetski against Hovanski and Dolgoruki; in that connection he is called Kmitich.

NOTES.

POLISH ALPHABET.

Since the Polish alphabet has many peculiar phonetic combinations which are difficult to one who does not know the language, it was decided to transliterate the names of persons and places in which such combinations occur in this book. The following are the letters and combinations which are met with most frequently;--

Polish Letters. English Sounds.

c	ts
ch	h
cz	ch
rz	*r* followed by the French *j*
sz	sh
szcz	shch
w	v
ż	j

In this transliteration *ch* retains its ordinary English sound. *J* is the French *j*; the vowels *e, i, u*, are, respectively, *ai* in "bait," *ee* in "beet," *oo* in "pool," when long; when short, "bet," "bit," "put" would represent their values. *I*, when unaccented and followed by a vowel, is sounded as *y*.

The following names will illustrate the method of this transliteration:--

Polish Form of Name. Form in Transliteration.

Potocki	Pototski
Chudzynski	Hudzynski
Czarnkowski	Charnkovski
Rzendzian	Jendzian
Bleszynski	Bleshyuski
Szandarowski	Shandarovski
Wlostowski	Vlostovski
Żyromski	Jyromski

In Jendzian and Jechytsa,--only names, as I believe, beginning in Polish with *rz* in this work,--the initial *r* has been omitted in the transliteration on account of the extreme difficulty, for any one not a Pole, of pronouncing *r* followed by the French *j*.

ACCENT.

All Polish words, with few exceptions, are accented on the syllable next the last, the penult. The exceptions are foreign names, some compounds, some words with enclitics. Polish names of men and places are generally accented on the penult.

MAP OF THE POLISH COMMONWEALTH.

This map, though diminutive, contains data through which the reader may see, at least in part, the historical course of the Commonwealth.

The territory is indicated which was lost to the Teutonic Knights, and which became later the kingdom of Prussia. On the east are indicated the Russian lands which became connected with Poland, and which rose against Polish rule in 1618. These lands are included between the lines running north and south on the map, and which are designated, respectively, "Western limit of Russia before the Tartar invasion," "Eastern limit of the Polish Commonwealth at the accession of Yan Kazimir."

The names of more important places mentioned in Fire and Sword and The Deluge appear also on the map. A few of these names are not so familiar in their Polish forms, which I have preserved; therefore the German is given, as follows:--

Polish.	German.
Elblang	Elbing
Glogov	Glogau
Gnyezno	Gnesen
Taurogi	Tauroggen
Tyltsa	Tilsit
Opol	Oppeln
Poznan	Posen

TITLES OF RANK AND ADDRESS.

The highest military rank in Poland was grand hetman; next in order came field-hetman, which has appeared inadvertently in these volumes as full hetman. "Your worthiness," so frequently used, would be better translated "your dignity," "dignity" being used in the sense of "office." The terms Pan, Pani, and Panna are applied, respectively, to a gentleman, a married lady, and an unmarried lady; they are now equivalent to Mr., Mrs. or Madame, and Miss.

Map of the Polish Commonwealth at the accession of Yan Kazimir
Map of the Polish Commonwealth at the accession of Yan Kazimir.

THE DELUGE
PART ONE

CHAPTER I.

There was in Jmud a powerful family, the Billeviches, descended from Mendog, connected with many, and respected, beyond all, in the district of Rossyeni. The Billeviches had never risen to great offices, the highest they had filled were provincial; but in war they had rendered the country unsurpassed services, for which they were richly rewarded at various times. Their native nest, existing to this day, was called Billeviche; but they possessed many other estates, both in the neighborhood of Rossyeni and farther on toward Krakin, near Lauda, Shoi, Nyevyaja, and beyond Ponyevyej. In later times they branched out into a number of houses, the members of which lost sight of one another. They all assembled only when there was a census at Rossyeni of the general militia of Jmud on the plain of the invited Estates. They met also in part under the banners of the Lithuanian cavalry and at provincial diets; and because they were wealthy and influential, even the Radzivills, all powerful in Lithuania and Jmud, had to reckon with them.

In the reign of Yan Kazimir, the patriarch of all the Billeviches, was Heraclius, colonel of light-horse and under-chamberlain of Upita. He did not dwell in the ancestral nest, which was rented at that time by Tomash, the sword-bearer of Rossyeni; Heraclius Billevich owned also Vodokty, Lyubich, and Mitruny, situated near Lauda, surrounded, as if with a sea, by agriculturists of the petty nobility.

Besides the Billeviches there were only a few of the more considerable families in the neighborhood, such as the Sollohubs, the Montvills, the Schyllings, the Koryznis, the Sitsinskis,--though there was no lack of smaller nobility of these names; finally, the whole river region of Lauda was thickly studded with so-called "neighborhoods," or, in common parlance, *zastsianki*,[4] occupied by the nobility of Lauda, renowned and celebrated in the history of Jmud.

In other neighborhoods of the region the families took their names from the places, or the places from the families, as was customary in Podlyasye; but along the river region of Lauda it was different. In Morezi dwelt the Stakyans, whom Batory in his time settled there for bravery at Pskoff; in Volmontovichi, on good land, swarmed the Butryms, the bulkiest fellows in all Lauda, noted for few words and heavy hands,-- men who in time of provincial diets, raids on property, or wars were wont to go in close rank and in silence. The lands in Drojeykani and Mozgi were managed by the numerous Domasheviches, famed hunters; these men tramped through the wilderness of Zyelonka as far as Wilkomir on bear-trails. The Gashtovts occupied Patsuneli; their women were famous for beauty, so that finally all pretty girls around Krakin, Ponyevyej, and Upita were known as Patsuneli girls. The Sollohubs Mali were rich in horses and excellent cattle, bred in forest pastures. The Gostsyeviches in Goshchuni made tar in the woods, from which occupation they were called Gostsyevichi Charni (Black) or Dymni (Smoky),--the Black or Smoky Gostsyeviches.

There were other villages and families also. The names of many of them are still extant; but these villages are not situated as before, and men call them by other names. Wars came too with misfortunes and fires, villages were not always rebuilt on the ruins; in a word, much has changed. But in that time old Lauda was still flourishing in its primeval estate; and the nobles had reached their highest repute a few years before, when, fighting at Loyovo against the uprisen Cossacks, they covered themselves with great glory under the lead of Yanush Radzivill.

All the Lauda men served in the regiment of old Heraclius Billevich,--the richer with two horses, the poorer with one, and the poorest as attendants. In general, these nobles were warlike, and especially enamoured of a knightly career; but in questions which formed the ordinary subjects of discussion at a provincial diet they were less skilled. They knew that there was a king in Warsaw; that Radzivill and Pan Hlebovich were starostas in Jmud, and Pan Billevich at Vodokty in Lauda. That was sufficient for them; and they voted as Pan Billevich instructed them, convinced that he wanted the same as Pan Hlebovich, and that the latter went hand in hand with Radzivill. Radzivill was the king's arm in Lithuania and Jmud; the king was the consort of the Commonwealth, the father of the legion of nobles.

Pan Billevich was, in fact, a friend rather than a client of the powerful oligarchs in Birji, and a greatly esteemed one at that; for at every call he had a thousand voices and a thousand Lauda sabres,--and sabres in the hands of the Stakyans, the Butryms, the Domasheviches, or the Gashtovts were despised at that period by no man on earth. It was only later that everything changed, just at the time when Pan Heraclius Billevich was no more.

This father and benefactor of the nobles of Lauda died in 1654. In that year a terrible war [5] flamed forth along the whole eastern line of the Commonwealth; Pan Billevich did not go to it, for his age and his deafness did not permit; but the Lauda men went. When tidings came that Radzivill was defeated at Shklov, and the Lauda regiment in an attack on the hired infantry of France was cut almost to pieces, the old colonel, stricken by apoplexy, yielded his soul.

These tidings were brought by a certain Pan Michael Volodyovski, a young but very famous warrior, who instead of Heraclius had led the Lauda regiment by appointment of Radzivill. The survivors came with him to their inherited fields, wearied, weighed down, and famished; in common with the whole army, they complained that the grand hetman, trusting in the terror of his name and the spell of victory, had rushed with small forces on a power ten times greater than his own, and thus had overwhelmed the army and the whole country.

But amid the universal complaining not one voice was raised against Volodyovski. On the contrary, those who had escaped lauded him to the skies, relating wonders of his skill and his deeds. And the only solace left the survivors was the memory of the exploits performed under the young colonel's leadership,--how in the attack they had burst through the first line of reserves as through smoke; how later they fell on the French mercenaries and cut to pieces with their sabres the foremost regiment, on which occasion Pan Volodyovski with his own hand killed the colonel; how at last, surrounded and under fire from four sides, they saved themselves from the chaos by desperate fighting, falling in masses, but breaking the enemy.

Those of the Lauda men who, not serving in the Lithuanian quota, were obliged to form a part of the general militia, listened in sorrow but with pride to these narratives. It was hoped on all sides that the general militia, the final defence of the country, would soon be called. It was agreed already that Volodyovski would be chosen captain of Lauda in that event; for though not of the local residents, there was no man among them more celebrated than he. The survivors said, besides, that he had rescued the hetman himself from death. Indeed, all Lauda almost bore him in its arms, and one neighborhood seized him from another. The Butryms, the Domasheviches, and the Gashtovts disputed as to whose guest he should be for the longest period. He pleased that valiant nobility so much that when the remnant of Radzivill's troops marched to Birji so as to be brought to some order after the defeat, he did not go with others, but passing from village to village took up his abode at last in Patsuneli with the Gashtovts, at the house of Pakosh Gashtovt, who had authority over all in that place.

In fact, Pan Volodyovski could not have gone to Birji in any event, for he was so ill as to be confined to the bed. First an acute fever came on him; then from the contusion which he had received at Tsybihovo he lost the use of his right arm. The three daughters of his host, who were noted for beauty, took him into their tender care, and vowed to bring back to his original health such a celebrated cavalier. The nobility to the last man were occupied with the funeral of their former chief, Heraclius Billevich.

After the funeral the will of the deceased was opened, from which it transpired that the old colonel had made his granddaughter, Aleksandra Billevich, daughter of the chief hunter of Upita, the heiress of all his property with the exception of the village of Lyubich. Guardianship over her till her marriage he confided to the entire nobility of Lauda--

"who, as they were well wishing to me," continued he in the will, "and returned kindness for kindness, let them do the same too for the orphan in these times of corruption and wickedness, when no one is safe from the license of men or free of fear; let them guard the orphan from mischance, through memory of me.

"They are also to see that she has safe use of her property with the exception of the village of Lyubich, which I give, present, and convey to the young banneret of Orsha, so that he may meet no obstacle in entering into possession of it. Should any man wonder at this my affection for Andrei Kmita, or see in it injustice to my own granddaughter Aleksandra, he must and should know that I held in friendship and true brotherly love from youthful years till the day of his death the father of Andrei Kmita. I was with him in war, he saved my life many times; and when the malice and envy of the Sitsinskis strove to wrest from me my fortune, he lent me his aid to defend it. Therefore I, Heraclius Billevich, under-chamberlain of Upita, and also an unworthy sinner standing now before the stern judgment of God, went four years ago, while alive and walking upon the earthly vale, to Pan Kmita, the father, the sword-bearer of Orsha, to vow gratitude and steady friendship. On that occasion we made mutual agreement, according to ancient noble and Christian custom, that our children-- namely his son Andrei and my granddaughter Aleksandra--were to be married, so that from them posterity might rise to the praise of God and the good of the State, which I wish most earnestly; and by the will here written I bind my granddaughter to obedience unless the banneret of Orsha (which God forbid) stain his reputation with evil deeds and be despoiled of honor. Should he lose his inheritance near Orsha, which may easily happen, she is to take him as husband with blessing; and even should he lose Lyubich, to pay no heed to the loss.

"However, if by the special favor of God, my granddaughter should wish in praise of Him to make an offering of her virginity and put on the habit of a nun, it is permitted her to do so, for I know that the praise of God is to precede that of man."

In such fashion did Pan Heraclius Billevich dispose of his fortune and his granddaughter, at which no one wondered much. Panna Aleksandra had been long aware of what awaited her, and the nobles had heard from of old of the friendship between Billevich and the Kmitas; besides, in time of defeat the thoughts of men were occupied with other things, so that soon they ceased to talk of the will.

But they talked of the Kmitas continually in the house at Vodokty, or rather of Pan Andrei, for the old sword-bearer also was dead. The younger Kmita had fought at Shklov with his own banner and with volunteers from Orsha. Then he vanished from the eye; but it was not admitted that he had perished, since the death of so noted a cavalier would surely not have escaped notice. The Kmitas were people of birth in Orsha, and lords of considerable fortune; but the flame of war had ruined those regions. Districts and entire lands were turned into deserts, fortunes were devoured, and people perished. After the crushing of Radzivill no one offered firm resistance. Gosyevski, full hetman, had no troops; the hetmans of the Crown with their armies in the Ukraine were struggling with what strength they had left and could not help him, exhausted as well as the Commonwealth by the Cossack wars. The deluge covered the land more and more, only breaking here and there against fortified walls; but the walls fell one after another, as had fallen Smolensk. The province of Smolensk, in which lay the fortune of the Kmitas, was looked on as lost. In the universal chaos, in the general terror, people were scattered like leaves in a tempest, and no man knew what had become of the banneret of Orsha.

But war had not reached Jmud yet. The nobles of Lauda returned to their senses by degrees. "The neighborhoods" began to assemble, and discuss both public and private affairs. The Butryms, readiest for battle, muttered that it would be necessary to go to Rossyeni to the muster of the general militia, and then to Gosyevski, to avenge the defeat of Shklov; the Domasheviches, the hunters, had gone through the wilderness of Rogovo by the forests till they found parties of the enemy and brought back news; the Smoky Gostsyeviches smoked meat in their huts for a future expedition. In private affairs it was decided to send tried and experienced men to find Pan Andrei Kmita.

The old men of Lauda held these deliberations under the presidency of Pakosh Gashtovt and Kassyan Butrym, two neighborhood patriarchs. All the nobility, greatly flattered by the confidence which the late Pan Billevich had placed in them, swore to stand faithfully by the letter of the will, and to surround Panna Aleksandra with well-nigh fatherly care. This was in time of war, when even in places to which war had not come disturbance and suffering were felt. On the banks of the Lauda all remained quiet, there were no disputes, there was no breaking through boundaries on the estates of the young heiress, landmarks were not shifted, no ditches were filled, no branded pine-trees were felled on forest borders, no pastures were invaded. On the contrary, the heiress was aided with provisions,--whatever the neighborhood had; for instance, the Stakjans on the river sent salt-fish, wheat came from the surly Butryms at Voimontovichi, hay from the Gashtovts, game from the Domasheviches (the hunters), tar and pitch from the Gostsyeviches. Of Panna Aleksandra no one in the villages spoke otherwise than as "our lady," and the pretty girls of Patsuneli waited for Pan Kmita perhaps as impatiently as she.

Meanwhile came the summons calling the nobility. The Lauda men began to move. He who from being a youth had grown to be a man, he whom age had not bent, had to mount his horse. Yan Kazimir arrived at Grodno, and fixed that as the place of general muster. There, then, they mustered. The Butryms in silence went forth; after them others, and the Gashtovts last,--as they always did, for they hated to leave the Patsuneli girls. The nobles from other districts appeared in scant numbers only, and the country was left undefended; but God-fearing Lauda had appeared in full quota.

Pan Volodyovski did not march, for he was not able yet to use his arm; he remained therefore as if district commander among the women. The neighborhoods were deserted, and only old men and women sat around the fires in the evening. It was quiet in Ponycvyej and Upita; they were waiting on all sides for news.

Panna Aleksandra in like manner shut herself in at Vodokty, seeing no one but servants and her guardians of Lauda.

CHAPTER II.

The new year 1655 came. January was frosty, but dry; a stern winter covered sacred Jmud with a white coat three feet thick, the forests were bending and breaking under a wealth of snow bunches, snow dazzled the eyes during days of sunshine, and in the night by the moon there glittered as it were sparks vanishing on a surface stiffened by frost; wild beasts approached the dwellings of men, and the poor gray birds hammered with their beaks the windows covered with hoar frost and snow-flowers.

On a certain evening Panna Aleksandra was sitting in the servants' hall with her work-maidens. It was an old custom of the Billeviches, when there were no guests, to spend evenings with the servants singing hymns and edifying simple minds by their example. In this wise did Panna Aleksandra; and the more easily since among her house-maidens were some really noble, very poor orphans. These performed every kind of work, even the rudest, and were servants for ladies; in return they were trained in good manners, and received better treatment than simple girls. But among them were peasants too, differing mainly in speech, [6] for many did not know Polish.

Panna Aleksandra, with her relative Panna Kulvyets, sat in the centre, and the girls around on benches; all were spinning. In a great chimney with sloping sides pine-logs were burning, now dying down and now flaming freshly with a great bright blaze or with sparks, as the youth standing near the chimney threw on small pieces of birch or pitch-pine. When the flame shot upward brightly, the dark wooden walls of the great hall were to be seen, with an unusually low ceiling resting on cross-beams. From the beams hung, on threads, many-colored stars, made of wafers, trembling in the warm air; behind, from both sides of the beams, were bunches of combed flax, hanging like captured Turkish horse-tail standards. Almost the whole ceiling was covered with them. On the dark walls glittered, like stars, tin plates, large and small, standing straight or leaning on long oaken shelves.

In the distance, near the door, a shaggy-haired man of Jmud was making a great noise with a hand-mill, and muttering a song with nasal monotone. Panna Aleksandra slipped her beads through her fingers in silence; the spinners spun on, saying nothing the one to the other.

The light of the flame fell on their youthful, ruddy faces. They, with both hands raised,--with the left feeding the soft flax, with the right turning the wheel,--spun eagerly, as if vying with one another, urged on by the stern glances of Panna Kulvyets. Sometimes, too, they looked at one another with quick eye, and sometimes at Panna Aleksandra, as if in expectation that she would tell the man to stop grinding, and would begin the hymn; but they did not cease working. They spun and spun on; the threads were winding, the wheel was buzzing, the distaff played in the hand of Panna Kulvyets, the shaggy-haired man of Jmud rattled on with his mill.

But at times he stopped his work. Evidently something was wrong with the mill, for at those times was heard his angry voice: "It's down!"

Panna Aleksandra raised her head, as if roused by the silence which followed the exclamations of the man; then the blaze lighted up her face and her serious blue eyes looking from beneath black brows. She was a comely lady, with flaxen hair, pale complexion, and delicate features. She had the beauty of a white flower. The mourning robes added to her dignity. Sitting before the chimney, she seemed buried in thought, as in a dream; doubtless she was meditating over her own lot, for her fates were in the balance. The will predestined her to be the wife of a man whom she had not seen for ten years; and as she was now almost twenty, there remained to her but unclear childhood reminiscences of a certain boisterous boy, who at the time when he with his father had come to Vodokty, was more occupied with racing through the swamps with a gun than in looking at her. "Where is he, and what manner of man is he now?" These were the questions which thrust themselves on the mind of the dignified lady. She knew him also, it is true, from the narratives of the late under-chamberlain, who four years before had undertaken the long journey to Orsha. According to those narratives, he was a cavalier "of great courage, though very quick-tempered." By the contract of marriage for their descendants concluded between old Billevich and Kmita the father, Kmita the son was to go at once to Vodokty and be accepted by the lady; but a great war broke out just then, and the cavalier, instead of going to the lady, went to the fields of Berestechko. Wounded at Berestechko, he recovered at home; then he nursed his sick father, who was near death; after that another war broke out, and thus four years passed. Since the death of the old colonel considerable time had elapsed, but no tidings of Kmita.

Panna Aleksandra therefore had something to meditate upon, and perhaps she was pining for the unknown. In her pure heart, especially because it knew not love as yet, she bore a great readiness for that feeling. A spark only was needed to kindle on that hearth a flame quiet but bright, and as steady as the undying sacred fire of Lithuania.

Disquiet then seized her,--at times pleasant, at times bitter; and her soul was ever putting questions to which there was no answer, or rather the answer must come from distant fields. The first question was whether he would marry her with good-will and respond with readiness to her readiness. In those days contracts by parents for the marriage of their children were usual; and if the parents died the children, held by the blessing, observed in most cases the contract. In the engagement itself the young lady saw nothing uncommon; but good pleasure does not always go hand in hand with duty; hence the anxiety that weighed down the blond head of the maiden. "Will he love me?" And then a flock of thoughts surrounded her, as a flock of birds surround a tree standing alone in spacious fields: "Who art thou? What manner of person? Art walking alive in the world, or perhaps thou hast fallen? Art thou distant or near?" The open heart of the lady, like a door open to a precious guest, called involuntarily to distant regions, to forests and snow-fields covered with night: "Come hither, young hero; for there is naught in the world more bitter than waiting."

That moment, as if in answer to the call, from outside, from those snowy distances covered with night, came the sound of a bell.

The lady trembled, but regaining her presence of mind, remembered that almost every evening some one came to Vodokty to get medicine for the young colonel.

Panna Kulvyets confirmed that idea by saying, "Some one from the Gashtovts for herbs."

The irregular sound of the bell shaken by the shaft rang more distinctly each moment; at last it stopped on a sudden. Evidently the sleigh had halted before the door.

"See who has come," said Panna Kulvyets to the man of Jmud who was turning the mill.

The man went out of the servants' hall, but soon returned, and taking again the handle of the mill, said phlegmatically, "Panas Kmitas." [7]

"The word is made flesh!" cried Panna Kulvyets.

The spinners sprang to their feet; the flax and the distaffs fell to the floor.

Panna Aleksandra rose also. Her heart beat like a hammer; a flush came forth on her face, and then pallor; but she turned from the chimney, lest her emotion might be seen.

Then in the door appeared a certain lofty figure in a fur mantle and fur-bound cap. A young man advanced to the middle of the room, and seeing that he was in the servants' hall, inquired in a resonant voice, without removing his cap, "Hei! but where is your mistress?"

"I am the mistress," said Panna Billevich, in tones sufficiently clear.

Hearing this, the newly arrived removed his cap, cast it on the floor, and inclining said, "I am Andrei Kmita."

The eyes of Panna Aleksandra rested with lightning-like swiftness on the face of Kmita, and then dropped again to the floor; still during that time the lady was able to see the tuft shaven high, yellow as wheat, an embrowned complexion, blue eyes, looking quickly to the front, dark mustache, a face youthful, eagle-like, but joyous and gallant.

He rested his left hand on his hip, raised his right to his mustache, and said: "I have not been in Lyubich yet, for I hastened here like a bird to bow down at the feet of the lady, the chief hunter's daughter. The wind--God grant it was a happy one!--brought me straight from the camp."

"Did you know of the death of my grandfather?" asked the lady.

"I did not; but I bewailed with hot tears my benefactor when I learned of his death from those rustics who came from this region to me. He was a sincere friend, almost a brother, of my late father. Of course it is well known to you that four years ago he came to us at Orsha. Then he promised me your ladyship, and showed a portrait about which I sighed in the night-time. I wished to come sooner, but war is not a mother: she makes matches for men with death only."

This bold speech confused the lady somewhat. Wishing to change the subject, she said, "Then you have not seen Lyubich yet?"

"There will be time for that. My first service is here; and here the dearest inheritance, which I wish to receive first. But you turned from the hearth, so that to this moment I have not been able to look you in the eye--that's the way! Turn, and I will stand next the hearth; that's the way!"

Thus speaking, the daring soldier seized by the hand Olenka,[8] who did not expect such an act, and brought her face toward the fire, turning her like a top. She was still more confused, and covering her eyes with her long lashes, stood abashed by the light and her own beauty. Kmita released her at last, and struck himself on the doublet.

"As God is dear to me, a beauty! I'll have a hundred Masses said for my benefactor because he left you to me. When the betrothal?"

"Not yet awhile; I am not yours yet," said Olenka.

"But you will be, even if I have to burn this house! As God lives, I thought the portrait flattered. I see that the painter aimed high, but missed. A thousand lashes to such an artist, and stoves to paint, not beauties, with which eyes are feasted! Oh, 'tis a delight to be the heir to such an inheritance, may the bullets strike me!"

"My late grandfather told me that you were very hot-headed."

"All are that way with us in Smolensk; not like your Jmud people. One, two! and it must be as we want; if not, then death."

Olenka laughed, and said with a voice now more confident, raising her eyes to the cavalier, "Then it must be that Tartars dwell among you?"

"All one! but you are mine by the will of parents and by your heart."

"By my heart? That I know not yet."

"Should you not be, I would thrust myself with a knife!"

"You say that laughing. But we are still in the servants' hall; I beg you to the reception-room. After a long road doubtless supper will be acceptable. I beg you to follow me."

Here Olenka turned to Panna Kulvyets. "Auntie, dear, come with us."

The young banneret glanced quickly. "Aunt?" he inquired,--"whose aunt?"

"Mine,--Panna Kulvyets."

"Then she is mine!" answered he, going to kiss her hand. "I have in my company an officer named Kulvyets-Hippocentaurus. Is he not a relative?"

"He is of the same family," replied the old maid, with a courtesy.

"A good fellow, but a whirlwind like myself," added Kmita.

Meanwhile a boy appeared with a light. They went to the antechamber, where Pan Andrei removed his shuba; then they passed to the reception-room.

Immediately after their departure the spinners gathered in a close circle, and one interrupted another, talking and making remarks. The stately young man pleased them greatly; therefore they did not spare words on him, vying with one another in praises.

"Light shines from him," said one; "when he came I thought he was a king's son."

"And he has lynx eyes, so that he cuts with them," said another; "do not cross such a man."

"That is worst of all," said a third.

"He met the lady as a betrothed. It is easily seen that she pleased him greatly, for whom has she not pleased?"

"But he is not worse than she, never fear! Could you get his equal, you would go even to Orsha, though likely that is at the end of the world."

"Ah, lucky lady!"

"It is always best for the rich in the world. Ei, ei, that's gold, not a knight."

"The Patsuneli girls say that that cavalry captain who is stopping with old Pakosh is a handsome cavalier."

"I have not seen him; but how compare him with Pan Kmita! Such another as Pan Kmita surely there is not in the world!"

"It's down!" cried the man of Jmud on a sudden, when something broke again in the mill.

"Go out, shaggy head, with thy freaks! Give us peace, for we cannot hear.--True, true; hard to find better than Pan Kmita in the whole world; surely in Kyedani there is none such."

"Dream of one like him!"

"May his like come in a dream!"

In such fashion did the girls talk among themselves in the servants' hall. Meanwhile in the dining-room the table was laid in all haste, while in the drawing-room Panna Aleksandra conversed face to face with Kmita, for Aunt Kulvyets had gone to bustle about the supper.

Pan Andrei did not remove his gaze from Olenka, and his eyes shot sparks more and more every moment; at last he said,--

"There are men to whom land is dearer than all things else; there are others who chase after plunder in war, others love horses; but I would not give you for any treasure. As God lives, the more I look the more I wish to marry; so that even if it were to-morrow-- Oh, that brow,--just as if painted with burned cork!"

"I hear that some use such strange things, but I am not of that kind."

"And eyes as from heaven! From confusion, words fail me."

"You are not greatly confused, if in my presence you can be so urgent that I am wonder-stricken."

"That is our way in Smolensk,--to go boldly at women as we do into battle. You must, my queen, grow accustomed to this, for thus will it ever be."

"You must put it aside, for thus it cannot be."

"Perhaps I may yield, may I be slain! Believe, believe me not, but with gladness would I bend the skies for you. For you, my queen, I am ready to learn other manners; for I know myself that I am a simple soldier, I have lived more in camps than in chambers of castles."

"Oh, that harms nothing, for my grandfather was a soldier; but I give thanks for the good-will," said Olenka; and her eyes looked with such sweetness on Pan Andrei that his heart melted like wax in a moment, and he answered,--

"You will lead me on a thread."

"Ah, you are not like those who are led on threads; to do that is most difficult with men who are unsteady."

Kmita showed in a smile teeth as white as a wolf's teeth, "How is that?" asked he. "Are the rods few that the fathers broke on me in the monastery to bring me to steadiness and make me remember various fair maxims for guidance in life--"

"And which one do you remember best?"

"'When in love, fall at the feet,'--in this fashion."

When he had spoken, Kmita was already on his knees. The lady screamed, putting her feet under the table.

"For God's sake! they did not teach that in the monastery. Leave off, or I shall be angry--my aunt will come this minute--"

Still on his knees, he raised his head and looked into her eyes. "Let a whole squadron of aunts come; I shall not forbid their pleasure."

"But stand up!"

"I am standing."

"Sit down!"

"I am sitting."

"You are a traitor, a Judas!"

"Not true, for when I kiss 'tis with sincerity,--will you be convinced?"

"You are a serpent!"

Panna Aleksandra laughed, however, and a halo of youth and gladness came from her. His nostrils quivered like the nostrils of a young steed of noble blood.

"Ai! ai!" said he. "What eyes, what a face! Save me, all ye saints, for I cannot keep away!"

"There is no reason to summon the saints. You were absent four years without once looking in here; sit still now!"

"But I knew only the counterfeit. I will have that painter put in tar and then in feathers, and scourge him through the square of Upita. I will tell all in sincerity,--forgive, if it please you; if not, take my head. I thought to myself when looking at that portrait: 'A pretty little rogue, pretty; but there is no lack of pretty ones in the world. I have time.' My late father urged me hither, but I had always one answer: 'I have time! The little wife will not vanish; maidens go not to war and do not perish.' I was not opposed at all to the will of my father, God is my witness; but I wanted first to know war and feel it on my own body. This moment I see my folly. I might have married and gone to war afterward; and here every delight was waiting for me. Praise be to God that they did not hack me to death! Permit me to kiss your hand."

"Better, I'll not permit."

"Then I will not ask. In Orsha we say, 'Ask; but if they don't give, take it thyself.'"

Here Pan Andrei clung to the hand of the lady and began to kiss it; and the lady did not resist too greatly, lest she might exhibit ill-will.

Just then Panna Kulvyets came in. When she saw what was going on, she raised her eyes. That intimacy did not please her, but she dared not scold. She gave invitation to supper.

Both went to the supper-room, holding each the other's hand as if they were related. In the room stood a table covered, and on it an abundance of all kinds of food, especially choice smoked meats and a mouldy thick bottle of strength-giving wine. It was pleasant for the young people with each other, gladsome, vivacious. The lady had supped already; therefore Kmita sat alone, and began to eat with animation equal to that with which he had just been conversing.

Olenka looked at him with sidelong glance, glad that he was eating and drinking. When he had appeased his first hunger, she began again to inquire,--

"Then you are not direct from Orsha?"

"Scarcely do I know whence I come,--here to-day, tomorrow in another place. I prowled near the enemy as a wolf around sheep, and what was possible to seize I seized."

"And how had you daring to meet such a power, before which the grand hetman himself had to yield?"

"How had I daring? I am ready for all things, such is the nature within me."

"That is what my grandfather said. Great luck that you were not killed!"

"Ai, they covered me with cap and with hand as a bird is covered on the nest; but I, whom they covered, sprang out and bit them in another place. I made it so bitter for them that there is a price on my head-- A splendid half-goose!"

"In the name of the Father and the Son!" cried Olenka, with unfeigned wonder, gazing with homage on that young man who in the same moment mentions the price on his head and the half-goose. "Had you many troops for defence?"

"I had, of course, my poor dragoons,--very excellent men, but in a month they were all kicked to bits. Then I went with volunteers whom I gathered wherever I could without question. Good fellows for battle, but knave upon knave! Those who have not perished already will sooner or later be meat for the crows."

Pan Andrei laughed, emptied his goblet of wine, and added: "Such plunderers you have not seen yet. May the hangman light them! Officers,--all nobles from our parts, men of family, worthy people, but against almost every one of them is a sentence of outlawry. They are now in Lyubich, for where else could I send them?"

"So you have come to us with the whole squadron?"

"I have. The enemy took refuge in towns, for the winter is bitter. My men too are as ragged as brooms after long sweeping. The prince voevoda assigned me winter quarters in Ponyevyej. God knows the breathing-spell is well earned!"

"Eat, I beg you."

"I would eat poison for your sake! I left a part of my ragged fellows in Ponyevyej, a part in Upita, and the most worthy officers I invited to Lyubich as guests. These men will come to beat to you with the forehead."

"But where did the Lauda men find you?"

"They found me on the way to winter quarters in Ponyevyej. Had I not met them I should have come here."

"But drink."

"I would drink even poison for you!"

"Were the Lauda men the first to tell you of my grandfather's death and the will?"

"They told of the death.--Lord, give light to the soul of my benefactor!--Did you send those men to me?"

"Think not such a thing! I had nothing but mourning and prayer on my mind."

"They too said the same. They are an arrogant set of homespuns. I wanted to give them a reward for their toil; instead of accepting it, they rose against me and said that the nobility of Orsha might take drink-money, but the Lauda men never. They spoke very foully to me; while listening, I thought to myself: 'If you don't want money, then I'll command to give you a hundred lashes.'"

Panna Aleksandra seized her head. "Jesus Mary! and did you do that?"

Kmita looked at her in astonishment. "Have no fears! I did not, though my soul revolts within me at such trashy nobility, who pretend to be the equal of us. But I thought to myself, 'They will cry me down without cause in those parts, call me tyrant, and calumniate me before you!'"

"Great is your luck," said Olenka, drawing a deep breath of relief, "for I should not have been able to look you in the eyes."

"But how so?"

"That is a petty nobility, but ancient and renowned. My dear grandfather always loved them, and went with them to war. He served all his life with them. In time of peace he received them in his house. That is an old friendship of our family which you must respect. You have moreover a heart, and will not break that sacred harmony in which thus far we have lived."

"I knew nothing of them at that moment,--may I be slain if I did!--but yet I confess that this barefooted nobledom somehow cannot find place in my head. With us a peasant is a peasant, and nobles are all men of good family, who do not sit two on one mare. God knows that such scurvy fellows have nothing to do with the Kmitas nor with the Billeviches, just as a mudfish has nothing to do with a pike, though this is a fish and that also."

"My grandfather used to say that blood and honor, not wealth, make a man; and these are honorable people, or grandfather would not have made them my guardians."

Pan Andrei was astonished and opened wide his eyes, "Did your grandfather make all the petty nobility of Lauda guardians over you?"

"He did. Do not frown, for the will of the dead is sacred. It is a wonder to me that the messengers did not mention this."

"I should have-- But that cannot be. There is a number of villages. Will they all discuss about you? Will they discuss me,--whether I am to their thinking or not? But jest not, for the blood is storming up in me."

"Pan Andrei, I am not jesting; I speak the sacred and sincere truth. They will not debate about you; but if you will not repulse them nor show haughtiness, you will capture not only them, but my heart. I, together with them, will thank you all my life,--all my life, Pan Andrei."

Her voice trembled as if in a beseeching request; but he did not let the frown go from his brow, and was gloomy. He did not burst into anger, it is true, though at moments there flew over his face as it were lightnings; but he answered with haughtiness and pride,--

"I did not look for this! I respect the will of the dead, and I think the under-chamberlain might have made those petty nobles your guardians till the time of my coming; but when once I have put foot here, no other, save me, will be guardian. Not only those gray coats, but the Radzivills of Birji themselves have nothing in this place to do with guardianship."

Panna Aleksandra grew serious, and answered after a short silence: "You do ill to be carried away by pride. The conditions laid down by my late grandfather must be either all accepted or all rejected. I see no other way. The men of Lauda will give neither trouble nor annoyance, for they are worthy people and peaceful. Do not suppose that they will be disagreeable. Should any trouble arise, they might say a word; but it is my opinion that all will pass in harmony and peace, and then the guardianship will be as if it had not been."

Kmita held silence a moment, then waved his hand and said: "It is true that the marriage will end everything. There is nothing to quarrel about. Let them only sit quietly and not force themselves on me; for God knows I will not let my mustache be blown upon. But no more of them. Permit an early wedding; that will be best."

"It is not becoming to mention that now, in time of mourning."

"Ai, but shall I be forced to wait long?"

"Grandfather himself stated that no longer than half a year."

"I shall be as dried up as a chip before that time. But let us not be angry. You have begun to look on me as sternly as on an offender. God be good to you, my golden queen! In what am I to blame if the nature within me is such that when anger against a man takes me I would tear him to pieces, and when it passes I would sew him together again."

"'Tis a terror to live with such a man," answered Olenka, more joyously.

"Well, to your health! This is good wine; for me the sabre and wine are the basis. What kind of terror to live with me? You will hold me ensnared with your eyes, and make a slave of me,--a man who hitherto would endure no superior. At the present time I chose to go with my own little company in independence rather than bow to the hetman. My golden queen, if anything in me does not please you, overlook it; for I learned manners near cannon and not among ladies, in the tumult of soldiers and not at the lute. Our region is restless, the sabre is never let go from the hand. There, though some outlawry rests on a man, though he be pursued by sentences, 'tis nothing! People respect him if he has the daring of a warrior. For example, my companions who in some other place would have long been in prison are in their fashion worthy persons. Even women among us go in boots, and with sabres lead parties,--like Pani Kokosinski, the aunt of my lieutenant. She died a heroes death; and her nephew in my command has avenged her, though in life he did not love her. Where should we, even of the greatest families, learn politeness? But we know when there is war how to fight, when there is a diet how to talk; and if the tongue is not enough, then the sabre. That's the position; as a man of such action did the late chamberlain know me, and as such did he choose me for you."

"I have always followed the will of my grandfather willingly," answered the lady, dropping her eyes.

"Let me kiss your hand once again, my dear girl! God knows you have come close to my heart. Feeling has so taken hold of me that I know not how I can find that Lyubich which I have not yet seen."

"I will give you a guide."

"Oh, I shall find the way. I am used to much pounding around by night. I have an attendant from Ponyevyej who must know the road. And there Kokosinski and his comrades are waiting for me. With us the Kokosinskis are a great family, who use the seal of Pypka. This one was outlawed without reason because he burned the house of Pan Orpishevski, carried off a maiden, and cut down some servants. A good comrade!-- Give me your hand once more. I see it is time to go."

Midnight began to beat slowly on the great Dantzig clock standing in the hall.

"For God's sake! 'tis time, 'tis time!" cried Kmita. "I may not stay longer. Do you love me, even as much as would go around your finger?"

"I will answer another time. You will visit me, of course?"

"Every day, even if the ground should open under me! May I be slain!"

Kmita rose, and both went to the antechamber. The sleigh was already waiting before the porch; so he enrobed himself in the shuba, and began to take farewell, begging her to return to the chamber, for the cold was flying in from the porch.

"Good-night, my dear queen," said he, "sleep sweetly, for surely I shall not close an eye thinking of your beauty."

"May you see nothing bad! But better, I'll give you a man with a light, for there is no lack of wolves near Volmontovichi."

"And am I a lamb to fear wolves? A wolf is a friend to a soldier, for often has he profit from his hand. We have also firearms in the sleigh. Good-night, dearest, good-night."

"With God."

Olenka withdrew, and Pan Kmita went to the porch. But on the way, through the slightly open door of the servants' hall he saw a number of pairs of eyes of maidens who waiting to see him once more had not yet lain down to sleep. To them Pan Andrei sent, soldier-fashion, kisses from his mouth with his hand, and went out. After a while the bell began to jingle, at first loudly, then with a continually decreasing sound, ever fainter and fainter, till at last it was silent.

It grew still in Vodokty, till the stillness amazed Panna Aleksandra. The words of Pan Andrei were sounding in her ears; she heard his laughter yet, heartfelt, joyous; in her eyes stood the rich form of the young man; and now after that storm of words, mirth, and joyousness, such marvellous silence succeeded. The lady bent her ear,--could she not hear even one sound more from the sleigh? But no! it was sounding somewhere off in the forest, near Volmontovichi. Therefore a mighty sadness seized the maiden, and never had she felt so much alone in the world.

Taking the light, slowly she went to her chamber, and knelt down to say the Lord's Prayer. She began five times before she could finish with proper attention; and when she had finished, her thoughts, as if on wings, chased after that sleigh and that figure sitting within. On one side were pine-woods, pine-woods on the other, in the middle a broad road, and he driving on,--Pan Andrei! Here it seemed to Olenka that she saw as before her the blond foretop, the blue eyes, the laughing mouth in which are gleaming teeth as white as the teeth of a young dog. For this dignified lady could hardly deny before her own face that this wild cavalier had greatly pleased her. He alarmed her a little, he frightened her a little, but he attracted her also with that daring, that joyous freedom and sincerity, till she was ashamed that he pleased her, especially with his haughtiness when at mention of the guardians he reared his head like a Turkish war-horse and said, "Even the Radzivills of Birji themselves have nothing to do here with guardianship."

"That is no dangler around women; that is a true man," said the lady to herself. "He is a soldier of the kind that my grandfather loved most of all,--and he deserved it!"

So meditated the lady; and a happiness undimmed by anything embraced her. It was an unquiet; but that unquiet was something dear. Then she began to undress; the door creaked, and in came Panna Kulvyets, with a candle in her hand.

"You sat terribly long," said she. "I did not wish to interfere with young people, so that you might talk your fill the first time. He seems a courteous cavalier. But how did he please you?"

Panna Aleksandra gave no answer at first, but barefooted ran up to her aunt, threw herself on her neck, and placing her bright head on her bosom, said with a fondling voice, "Auntie, oh, Auntie!"

"Oho!" muttered the old maid, raising her eyes and the candle toward heaven.

CHAPTER III.

When Pan Andrei drove up to the mansion at Lyubich, the windows were gleaming, and bustle reached the front yard. The servants, hearing the bell, rushed out through the entrance to greet their lord, for they had learned from his comrades that he would come. They greeted him with submission, kissing his hands and seizing his feet. The old land-steward, Znikis, stood in the entrance holding bread and salt, and beating worship with the forehead; all gazed with uneasiness and curiosity,--how would their future lord look? Kmita threw a purse full of thalers on the tray, and asked for his comrades, astonished that no one of them had come forth to meet his proprietary mightiness.

But they could not come forth, for they were then the third hour at the table, entertaining themselves at the cup, and perhaps in fact they had not taken note of the sounding of the bell outside. But when he entered the room, from all breasts a loud shout burst forth: "The heir, the heir has come!" and all his comrades, springing from their places, started toward him with their cups. But he placed his hands on his hips, and laughed at the manner in which they had helped themselves in his house, and had gone to drinking before his arrival. He laughed with increasing heartiness when he saw them advance with tipsy solemnity.

Before the others went the gigantic Pan Yaromir Kokosinski, with the seal of Pypka, a famous soldier and swaggerer, with a terrible scar across his forehead, his eye, and his cheek, with one mustache short, the other long, the lieutenant and friend of Kmita, the "worthy comrade," condemned to loss of life and honor in Smolensk for stealing a maiden, for murder and arson. At that time war saved him, and the protection of Kmita, who was of the same age; and their lands were adjoining in Orsha till Pan Yaromir had squandered his away. He came up holding in both hands a great-eared bowl filled with dembniak.

Next came Ranitski, whose family had arms,--Dry Chambers (Suche Komnaty). He was born in the province of Mstislavsk, from which he was an outlaw for killing two noblemen, landowners. One he slew in a duel, the other he shot without an encounter. He had no estate, though he inherited his step-mother's land on the death of his father. War saved him, too, from the executioner. He was an incomparable hand-to-hand sword-slasher.

The third in order was Rekuts-Leliva, on whom blood did not weigh, save the blood of the enemy. But he had played away, drunk away his substance. For the past three years he had clung to Kmita.

With him came the fourth, also from Smolensk, Pan Uhlik, under sentence of death and dishonor for breaking up a court. Kmita protected him because he played beautifully on the flageolet.

Besides them was Pan Kulvyets-Hippocentaurus, in stature the equal of Kokosinski, in strength even his superior; and Zend, a horse-trainer, who knew how to imitate wild beasts and all kinds of birds,--a man of uncertain descent, though claiming to be a noble of Courland; being without fortune he trained Kmita's horses, for which he received an allowance.

These then surrounded the laughing Pan Andrei. Kokosinski raised the eared bowl and intoned:--

"Drink with us, dear host of ours,

Dear host of ours!

With us thou mightst drink to the grave,

Drink to the grave!"

Others repeated the chorus; then Kokosinski gave Kmita the eared bowl, and Zend gave Kokosinski a goblet.

Kmita raised high the eared bowl and shouted, "Health to my maiden!"

"Vivat! vivat!" cried all voices, till the window-panes began to rattle in their leaden fittings. "Vivat! the mourning will pass, the wedding will come!"

They began to pour forth questions: "But how does she look? Hei! Yendrus,[9] is she very pretty, or such as you pictured her? Is there another like her in Orsha?"

"In Orsha?" cried Kmita. "In comparison with her you might stop chimneys with our Orsha girls! A hundred thunders! there's not another such in the world."

"That's the kind we wanted for you," answered Ranitski. "Well, when is the wedding to be?"

"The minute the mourning is over."

"Oh, fie on the mourning! Children are not born black, but white."

"When the wedding comes, there will be no mourning. Hurry, Yendrus!"

"Hurry, Yendrus!" all began to exclaim at once.

"The little bannerets of Orsha are crying in heaven for the earth," said Kokosinski.

"Don't make the poor little things wait!"

"Mighty lords," added Rekuts-Leliva, with a thin voice, "at the wedding we'll drink ourselves drunk as fools."

"My dear lambs," said Kmita, "pardon me, or, speaking more correctly, go to a hundred devils, let me look around in my own house."

"Nonsense!" answered Uhlik. "To-morrow the inspection, but now all to the table; there is a pair of demijohns there yet with big bellies."

"We have already made inspection for you. This Lyubich is a golden apple," said Ranitski.

"A good stable!" cried Zend; "there are two ponies, two splendid hussar horses, a pair of Jmud horses, and a pair of Kalmuks,--all in pairs, like eyes in the head. We will look at the mares and colts to-morrow."

Here Zend neighed like a horse; they wondered at his perfect imitation, and laughed.

"Is there such good order here?" asked Kmita, rejoiced.

"And how the cellar looks!" piped Rekuts; "resinous kegs and mouldy jugs stand like squadrons in ranks."

"Praise be to God for that! let us sit down at the table."

"To the table! to the table!"

They had barely taken their places and filled their cups when Ranitski sprang up again: "To the health of the Under-chamberlain Billevich!"

"Stupid!" answered Kmita, "how is that? You are drinking the health of a dead man."

"Stupid!" repeated the others. "The health of the master!"

"Your health!"

"May we get good in these chambers!"

Kmita cast his eyes involuntarily along the dining-hall, and he saw on the larch wood walls, blackened by age, a row of stern eyes fixed on him. Those eyes were gazing out of the old portraits of the Billeviches, hanging low, within two ells of the floor, for the wall was low. Above the portraits in a long unbroken row were fixed skulls of the aurochs, of stags, of elks, crowned with their antlers: some, blackened, were evidently very old; others were shining with whiteness. All four walls were ornamented with them.

"The hunting must be splendid, for I see abundance of wild beasts," said Kmita.

"We will go to-morrow or the day after. We must learn the neighborhood," answered Kokosinski. "Happy are you, Yendrus, to have a place to shelter your head!"

"Not like us," groaned Ranitski.

"Let us drink for our solace," said Rekuts.

"No, not for our solace," answered Kulvyets-Hippocentaurus, "but once more to the health of Yendrus, our beloved captain. It is he, my mighty lords, who has given here in Lyubich an asylum to us poor exiles without a roof above our heads."

"He speaks justly," cried a number of voices; "Kulvyets is not so stupid as he seems."

"Hard is our lot," piped Rekuts. "Our whole hope is that you will not drive us poor orphans out through your gates."

"Give us peace," said Kmita; "what is mine is yours."

With that all rose from their places and began to take him by the shoulders. Tears of tenderness flowed over those stern drunken faces.

"In you is all our hope, Yendrus," cried Kokosinski, "Let us sleep even on pea straw; drive us not forth."

"Give us peace," repeated Kmita.

"Drive us not forth; as it is, we have been driven,--we nobles and men of family," said Uhlik, plaintively.

"To a hundred fiends with you, who is driving you out? Eat, drink! What the devil do you want?"

"Do not deny us," said Ranitski, on whose face spots came out as on the skin of a leopard. "Do not deny us, Andrei, or we are lost altogether."

Here he began to stammer, put his finger to his forehead as if straining his wit, and suddenly said, looking with sheepish eyes on those present, "Unless fortune changes."

And all blurted out at once in chorus, "Of course it will change."

"And we will yet pay for our wrongs."

"And come to fortune."

"And to office."

"God bless the innocent! Our prosperity!"

"Your health!" cried Pan Andrei.

"Your words are holy, Yendrus," said Kokosinski, placing his chubby face before Kmita. "God grant us improvement of fortune!"

Healths began to go around, and tufts to steam. All were talking, one interrupting the other; and each heard only himself, with the exception of Rekuts, who dropped his head on his breast and slumbered. Kokosinski began to sing, "She bound the flax in bundles," noting which Uhlik took a flageolet from his bosom and accompanied him.

Ranitski, a great fencer, fenced with his naked hand against an unseen opponent, repeating in an undertone, "You thus, I thus; you cut, I strike,--one, two, three, check!"

The gigantic Kulvyets-Hippocentaurus stared fixedly for some time at Ranitski; at last he waved his hand and said: "You're a fool! Strike your best, but still you can't hold your own before Kmita with a sabre."

"For no one can stand before him; but try yourself."

"You will not win against me with a pistol."

"For a ducat a shot."

"A ducat! But where and at what?"

Ranitski cast his eyes around; at last he cried out, pointing at the skulls, "Between the antlers, for a ducat!"

"For what?" asked Kmita.

"Between the antlers, for two ducats, for three! Bring the pistols!"

"Agreed!" cried Kmita. "Let it be three. Zend, get the pistols!"

All began to shout louder and louder, and bargain among themselves; meanwhile Zend went to the antechamber, and soon returned with pistols, a pouch of bullets, and a horn with powder.

Ranitski grasped for a pistol. "Is it loaded?" asked he.

"Loaded."

"For three, four, five ducats!" blustered Kmita, drunk.

"Quiet! you will miss, you will miss."

"I shall hit at that skull between the antlers--one! two!"

All eyes were turned to the strong elk-skull fixed in front of Ranitski. He straightened his arm; the pistol turned in his palm.

"Three!" cried Kmita.

The shot sounded; the room was filled with powder smoke.

"He has missed, he has missed! See where the hole is!" cried Kmita, pointing with his hand at the dark wall from which the bullet had torn out a brighter chip.

"Two shots each time!"

"No; give it to me," cried Kulvyets.

At that moment the astonished servants ran in at the sound of the shot.

"Away! away!" called Kmita. "One! two! three!"

Again the roar of a shot; this time the pieces fell from the bone.

"But give us pistols too!" shouted all at the same time.

And springing up, they began to pound on the shoulders of their attendants, urging them to hurry. Before a quarter of an hour had passed, the whole room was thundering with shots. The smoke hid the light of the candles and the forms of the men shooting. The report of discharges was accompanied by the voice of Zend, who croaked like a raven, screamed like a falcon, howled like a wolf, bellowed like an aurochs. The whistle of bullets interrupted him; bits flew from the skulls, chips from the wall, and portraits from their frames; in the disorder the Billeviches were shot, and Ranitski, falling into fury, slashed them with his sabre.

The servants, astonished and terrified, stood as if bereft of their senses, gazing with startled eyes on that sport which resembled a Tartar invasion. The dogs began to howl and bark. All in the house were on their feet; in the yard groups of people assembled. The girls of the house ran to the windows, and putting their faces to the panes, flattening their noses, gazed at what was passing within.

Zend saw them at last; he whistled so piercingly that it rang in the ears of all, and then shouted, "Mighty lords! titmice are under the window,--titmice!"

"Titmice! titmice!"

"Now for a dance!" roared dissonant voices.

The drunken crowd sprang through the anteroom to the porch. The frost did not sober their steaming heads. The girls, screaming in voices that rose to the sky, ran in every direction through the yard; but the men chased them, and brought each one they seized to the room. After a while they began dancing in the midst of smoke, bits of bone, and chips around the table on which spilled wine lay in pools.

In such fashion did Pan Kmita and his wild company revel in Lyubich.

CHAPTER IV.

For a number of subsequent days Pan Andrei was at Vodokty daily; and each time he returned more in love, and admired more and more his Olenka. He lauded her to the skies, too, before his companions, till on a certain day he said to them,--

"My dear lambs, you will go to-day to beat with the forehead; then, as we have stipulated with the maiden, we will go to Mitruny to have a sleigh-ride through the forests and look at the third estate. She will entertain us there, and do you bear yourselves decently; for I would cut into hash the man who offended her in anything."

The cavaliers hurried willingly to prepare, and soon four sleighs were bearing the eager young men to Vodokty. Kmita sat in the first sleigh, which was highly ornamented and had the form of a silvery bear. This sleigh was drawn by three captured Kalmuk horses in variegated harness, in ribbons and peacock feathers, according to the Smolensk fashion, borrowed from more distant neighbors. A young fellow sitting in the neck of the bear drove the horses. Pan Andrei was dressed in a green velvet coat buttoned on golden cords and trimmed with sable, and wore a sable cap with a heron's feather. He was gladsome, joyous, and spoke to Kokosinski sitting at his side,--

"Listen, Kokoshko! I suppose we played tricks wild beyond measure on two evenings, and especially the first, when the skulls and the portraits suffered. But the case of the girls was still worse. The Devil always pushes forward that Zend, and then on whom does he pound out the punishment? On me. I am afraid that people will talk, for in this place my reputation is at stake."

"Hang yourself on your reputation; it is good for nothing else, just like ours."

"And who is to blame for that, if not you men? Remember, Kokoshko, they held me for a disturbing spirit in Orsha, and tongues were sharpened on me like knives on a whetstone."

"But who dragged Pan Tumgrat out in the frost with a horse; who cut up that official, who asked whether men walked on two feet in Orsha or on four? Who hacked the Vyzinskis, father and son? Who broke up the last provincial Diet?"

"I broke up the Diet in Orsha, not somewhere else; that was a home affair. Pan Tumgrat forgave me when he was dying; and as to the others, speak not, for a duel may happen to the most innocent."

"I have not told all yet; I have not spoken of the trials in the army, of which two are still waiting for you."

"Not for me, but for you men; for I am to blame only for letting you rob the people. But no more of this! Shut your mouth, Kokoshko, and say nothing to Olenka about the duels, and especially nothing of that shooting at the portraits and of the girls. If it is told, I shall lay the blame on you. I have informed the servants and the girls that if a word is said, I will order belts taken out of their skins."

"Have yourself shod like a horse, Yendrus, if you are in such dread of your maiden. You were another man in Orsha. I see already that you will go in leading-strings, and there is no good in that. Some ancient philosopher says, 'If you will not manage Kahna, Kahna will manage you.' You have given yourself to be tied up in all things."

"You are a fool, Kokoshko! But as to Olenka you will stand on one foot and then on the other when you put eyes on her, for another woman with such proper intent is not to be found. What is good she will praise in a moment, but the bad she will blame without waiting; for she judges according to virtue, and has in herself a ready measure. The late under-chamberlain reared her in that way. Should you wish to boast of warlike daring before her, and say that you trampled on justice, you will soon be ashamed; for at once she will say, 'An honorable citizen should not do that; it is against the country.' She will speak so to you that it will be as if some one had slapped you on the face, and you'll wonder that you did not know these things yourself. Tfu! shame! We have raised fearful disorder, and now must stand open-eyed before virtue and innocence. The worst was those girls--"

"By no means the worst. I have heard that in the villages there are girls of the petty nobility like blood and milk, and probably not stubborn at all."

"Who told you?" asked Kmita, quickly.

"Who told me? Who, if not Zend? Yesterday while trying the roan steed he rode to Volmontovichi; he merely rode along the highway, but he saw many titmice, for they were coming from vespers. 'I thought,' said he, 'that I should fly off the horse, they were so handsome and pretty.' And whenever he looked at any one of them she showed her teeth directly. And no wonder! for all the grown men of the nobles have gone to Rossyeni, and it is dreary for the titmice alone."

Kmita punched his companion in the side with his fist. "Let us go, Kokoshko, some time in the evening,--pretend we are astray,--shall we?"

"But your reputation?"

"Oh, to the Devil! Shut your mouth! Go alone, if that is the way; but better drop the matter. It would not pass without talk, and I want to live in peace with the nobles here, for the late under-chamberlain made them Olenka's guardians."

"You have spoken of that, but I would not believe it. How did he have such intimacy with homespuns?"

"Because he went with them to war, and I heard of this in Orsha, when he said that there was honorable blood in those Lauda men. But to tell the truth, Kokoshko, it was an immediate wonder to me, for it is as if he had made them guards over me."

"You will yield to them and bow to your boots before dish-cloths."

"First may the pestilence choke them! Be quiet, for I am angry! They will bow to me and serve me. Their quota is ready at every call."

"Some one else will command this quota. Zend says that there is a colonel here among them--I forget his name--Volodyovski or something? He led them at Shklov. They fought well, it appears, but were combed out there."

"I have heard of a Volodyovski, a famous warrior--But here is Vodokty in sight."

"Hei, it is well for people in Jmud; for there is stern order. The old man must have been a born manager. And the house,--I see how it looks. The enemy brought fire here seldom, and the people could build."

"I think that she cannot have heard yet of that outburst in Lyubich," said Kmita, as if to himself. Then he turned to his comrade: "My Kokoshko, I tell you, and do you repeat it to the others, that you must bear yourselves decently here; and if any man permits himself anything, as God is dear to me, I will cut him up like chopped straw."

"Well, they have saddled you!"

"Saddled, saddled not, I will cut you up!"

"Don't look at my Kasia or I'll cut you to pieces," said Kokosinski, phlegmatically.

"Fire out thy whip!" shouted Kmita to the driver.

The youth standing in the neck of the silvery bear whirled his whip, and cracked it very adroitly; other drivers followed his example, and they drove with a rattling, quick motion, joyous as at a carnival.

Stepping out of the sleighs, they came first to an antechamber as large as a granary, an unpainted room; thence Kmita conducted them to the dining-hall, ornamented as in Lyubich with skulls and antlers of slain beasts. Here they halted, looking carefully and with curiosity at the door of the adjoining room, by which Panna Aleksandra was to enter. Meanwhile, evidently keeping in mind Kmita's warning, they spoke with one another in subdued tones, as in a church.

"You are a fellow of speech," whispered Uhlik to Kokosinski, "you will greet her for us all."

"I was arranging something to say on the road," answered Kokosinski, "but I know not whether it will be smooth enough, for Yendrus interrupted my ideas."

"Let it be as it comes, if with spirit. But here she is!"

Panna Aleksandra entered, halting a little on the threshold, as if in wonder at such a large company. Kmita himself stood for a while as if fixed to the floor in admiration of her beauty; for hitherto he had seen her only in the evening, and in the day she seemed still more beautiful. Her eyes had the color of star-thistles; the dark brows above them were in contrast to the forehead as ebony with white, and her yellow hair shone like a crown on the head of a queen. Not dropping her eyes, she had the self-possessed mien of a lady receiving guests in her own house, with clear face seeming still clearer from the black dress trimmed with ermine. Such a dignified and exalted lady the warriors had not seen; they were accustomed to women of another type. So they stood in a rank as if for the enrolling of a company, and shuffling their feet they also bowed together in a row; but Kmita pushed forward, and kissing the hand of the lady a number of times, said,--

"See, my jewel, I have brought you fellow soldiers with whom I fought in the last war."

"It is for me no small honor," answered Panna Billevich, "to receive in my house such worthy cavaliers, of whose virtue and excellent qualities I have heard from their commander, Pan Kmita."

When she had said this she took her skirt with the tips of her fingers, and raising it slightly, courtesied with unusual dignity. Kmita bit his lips, but at the same time he was flushed, since his maiden had spoken with such spirit.

The worthy cavaliers continuing to shuffle their feet, all nudged at the same moment Pan Kokosinski: "Well, begin!"

Kokosinski moved forward one step, cleared his throat, and began as follows: "Serene great mighty lady, under-chamberlain's daughter--"

"Chief-hunter's daughter," corrected Kmita.

"Serene great mighty lady, chief-hunter's daughter, but to us right merciful benefactress," repeated Kokosinski,--"pardon, your ladyship, if I have erred in the title--"

"A harmless mistake," replied Panna Aleksandra, "and it lessens in no wise such an eloquent cavalier--"

"Serene great mighty lady, chief-hunter's daughter, benefactress, and our right merciful lady, I know not what becomes me in the name of all Orsha to celebrate more,--the extraordinary beauty and virtue of your ladyship, our benefactress, or the unspeakable happiness of the captain and our fellow-soldier, Pan Kmita; for though I were to approach the clouds, though I were to reach the clouds themselves--I say, the clouds--"

"But come down out of those clouds!" cried Kmita.

With that the cavaliers burst into one enormous laugh; but all at once remembering the command of Kmita, they seized their mustaches with their hands.

Kokosinski was confused in the highest degree. He grew purple, and said, "Do the greeting yourselves, pagans, since you confuse me."

Panna Aleksandra took again, with the tips of her fingers, her skirt. "I could not follow you gentlemen in eloquence," said she, "but I know that I am unworthy of those homages which you give me in the name of all Orsha."

And again she made a courtesy with exceeding dignity, and it was somehow out of place for the Orsha roisterers in the presence of that courtly maiden. They strove to exhibit themselves as men of politeness, but it did not become them. Therefore they began to pull their mustaches, to mutter and handle their sabres, till Kmita said,--

"We have come here as if in a carnival, with the thought to take you with us and drive to Mitruny through the forest, as was the arrangement yesterday. The snow-road is firm, and God has given frosty weather."

"I have already sent Aunt Kulvyets to Mitruny to prepare dinner. But now, gentlemen, wait just a little till I put on something warm."

Then she turned and went out.

Kmita sprang to his comrades. "Well, my dear lambs, isn't she a princess? Now, Kokosinski, you said that she had saddled me, and why were you as a little boy before her? Where have you seen her like?"

"There was no call to interrupt me; though I do not deny that I did not expect to address such a person."

"The late under-chamberlain," said Kmita, "lived with her most of the time in Kyedani, at the court of the prince voevoda, or lived with the Hleboviches; and there she acquired those high manners. But her beauty,--what of that? You cannot let your breath go yet."

"We have appeared as fools," said Ranitski, in anger; "but the biggest fool was Kokosinski."

"Traitor! why punch me with your elbow? You should have appeared yourself, with your spotted mouth."

"Harmony, lambs, harmony!" said Kmita; "I will let you admire, but not wrangle."

"I would spring into the fire for her," said Rekuts. "Hew me down, Yendrus, but I'll not deny that."

Kmita did not think of cutting down; he was satisfied, twisted his mustache, and gazed on his comrades with triumph. Now Panna Aleksandra entered, wearing a marten-skin cap, under which her bright face appeared still brighter. They went out on the porch.

"Then shall we ride in this sleigh?" asked the lady, pointing to the silvery bear. "I have not seen a more beautiful sleigh in my life."

"I know not who has used it hitherto, for it was captured. It suits me very well, for on my shield is a lady on a bear. There are other Kmitas who have banners on their shield, but they are descended from Filon

Kmita of Charnobil; he was not of the same house from which the great Kmitas are descended."

"And when did you capture this bear sleigh?"

"Lately, in this war. We poor exiles who have fallen away from fortune have only what war gives us in plunder. But as I serve that lady faithfully, she has rewarded me."

"May God grant a better; for war rewards one, but presses tears from the whole dear fatherland."

"God and the hetmans will change that."

Meanwhile Kmita wrapped Panna Aleksandra in the beautiful sleigh robe of white cloth lined with white wolfskin; then taking his own seat, he cried to the driver, "Move on!" and the horses sprang forward at a run.

The cold wind struck their faces with its rush; they were silent, therefore, and nothing was heard save the wheezing of frozen snow under the runners, the snorting of the horses, their tramp, and the cry of the driver.

At last Pan Andrei bent toward Olenka. "Is it pleasant for you?"

"Pleasant," answered she, raising her sleeve and holding it to her mouth to ward off the rush of air.

The sleigh dashed on like a whirlwind. The day was bright, frosty; the snow sparkled as if some one were scattering sparks on it. From the white roofs of the cottages, which were like piles of snow, rosy smoke curled in high columns. Flocks of crows from among the leafless trees by the roadside flew before the sleighs with shrill cawing.

About eighty rods from Vodokty they came out on a broad road into dark pine-woods which stood gloomy, hoary, and silent as if sleeping under the thick snow-bunches. The trees flitted before the eye, appeared to be fleeing to some place in the rear of the sleigh; but the sleigh flew on, every moment swiftly, more swiftly, as if the horses had wings. From such driving the head turns, and ecstasy seizes one; it seized Panna Aleksandra. She leaned back, closed her eyes, and yielded completely to the impetus. She felt a sweet powerlessness, and it seemed to her that that boyar of Orsha had taken her by violence: that he is rushing away like a whirlwind, and she growing weak has no strength to oppose or to cry,--and they are flying, flying each moment more swiftly. Olenka feels that arms are embracing her; then on her cheek as it were a hot burning stamp. Her eyes will not open, as if in a dream; and they fly, fly.

An inquiring voice first roused the sleeping lady: "Do you love me?"

She opened her eyes. "As my own soul."

"And I for life and death."

Again the sable cap of Kmita bent over the marten-skin cap of Olenka. She knew not herself which gave her more delight,--the kisses or the magic ride.

And they flew farther, but always through pine-woods, through pine-woods. Trees fled to the rear in whole regiments. The snow was wheezing, the horses snorting; but the man and the maiden were happy.

"I would ride to the end of the world in this way," cried Kmita.

"What are we doing? This is a sin!" whispered Olenka.

"What sin? Let us commit it again."

"Impossible! Mitruny is not far."

"Far or near, 'tis all one!"

And Kmita rose in the sleigh, stretched his arms upward, and began to shout as if in a full breast he could not find place for his joy: "Hei-ha! hei-ha!"

"Hei-hop! hoop-ha!" answered the comrades from the sleighs behind.

"Why do you shout so?" asked the lady.

"Oh, so, from delight! And shout you as well!"

"Hei-ha!" was heard the resonant, thin alto voice.

"O thou, my queen! I fall at thy feet."

"The company will laugh."

After the ecstasy a noisy joyousness seized them, as wild as the driving was wild. Kmita began to sing,--

"Look thou, my girl! look through the door,

To the rich fields!

Oh, knights from the pine-woods are coming, my mother,

Oh, that's my fate!

Look not, my daughter! cover thy eyes,

With thy white hands,

For thy heart will spring out of thy bosom

With them to the war."

"Who taught you such lovely songs?" asked Panna Aleksandra.

"War, Olenka. In the camp we sang them to one another to drive away sadness."

Further conversation was interrupted by a loud calling from the rear sleighs: "Stop! stop! Hei there--stop!"

Pan Andrei turned around in anger, wondering how it came to the heads of his comrades to call and stop him. He saw a few tens of steps from the sleigh a horseman approaching at full speed of the horse.

"As God lives, that is my sergeant Soroka; what can have happened?" said Pan Andrei.

That moment the sergeant coming up, reined his horse on his haunches, and began to speak with a panting voice: "Captain!--"

"What is the matter, Soroka?"

"Upita is on fire; they are fighting!"

"Jesus Mary!" screamed Olenka.

"Have no fear!--Who is fighting?"

"The soldiers with the townspeople. There is a fire on the square! The townspeople are enraged, and they have sent to Ponyevyej for a garrison. But I galloped here to your grace. I can barely draw breath."

During this conversation the sleighs behind caught up; Kokosinski, Ranitski, Kulvyets-Hippocentaurus, Uhlik, Rekuts, and Zend, springing out on the snow, surrounded the speakers with a circle.

"What is the matter?" asked Kmita.

"The townspeople would not give supplies for horses or men, because there was no order for it; the soldiers began to take by force. We besieged the mayor and those who barricaded themselves in the square. Firing was begun, and we burned two houses; at present there is terrible violence, and ringing of bells--"

Kmita's eyes gleamed with wrath.

"We must go to the rescue!" shouted Kokosinski.

"The rabble are oppressing the army!" cried Ranitski, whose whole face was covered at once with red, white, and dark spots. "Check, check! mighty lords!"

Zend laughed exactly as a screech-owl hoots, till the horses were frightened; and Rekuts raised his eyes and piped, "Strike, whoso believes in God! smoke out the ruffians!"

"Be silent!" roared Kmita, till the woods echoed, and Zend, who stood nearest, staggered like a drunken man. "There is no need of you there, no need of slashing! Sit all of you in two sleighs, leave me the third. Drive back to Lyubich; wait there unless I send for succor."

"How is that?" asked Ranitski, opposing.

But Pan Andrei laid a hand on his throat, and his eyes gleamed more terribly. "Not a breath out of you!" said he, threateningly.

They were silent; evidently they feared him, though usually on such familiar footing.

"Go back, Olenka, to Vodokty," said Kmita, "or go for your Aunt Kulvyets to Mitruny. Well, our party was not a success. But it will be quieter there soon; only a few heads will fly off. Be in good health and at rest; I shall be quick to return."

Having said this, he kissed her hand, and wrapped her in the wolf-skin; then he took his seat in the other sleigh, and cried to the driver, "To Upita!"

CHAPTER V.

A number of days passed, and Kmita did not return; but three men of Lauda came to Vodokty with complaints to the lady. Pakosh Gashtovt from Patsuneli came,--the same who was entertaining at his house Pan Volodyovski. He was the patriarch of the village, famed for wealth and six daughters, of whom three had married Butryms, and received each one hundred coined dollars as dowry, besides clothing and cattle. The second who came was Kassyan Butrym, who remembered Batory well, and with him the son-in-law of Pakosh, Yuzva Butrym; the latter, though in the prime of life,--he was not more than fifty years old,--did not go to Rossyeni to the registry of the general militia, for in the Cossack wars a cannon-ball had torn off his foot. He was called on this account Ankle-foot, or Yuzva Footless. He was a terrible man, with the strength of a bear, and great sense, but harsh, surly, judging men severely. For this reason he was feared somewhat in the capitals, for he could not pardon either himself or others. He was dangerous also when in liquor; but that happened rarely.

These men came, then, to the lady, who received them graciously, though she divined at once that they had come to make complaints, and wanted to hear something from her regarding Pan Kmita.

"We wish to pay our respects to Pan Kmita, but perhaps he has not come back yet from Upita," said Pakosh; "so we have come to inquire, our dear darling, when it will be possible to see him."

"I think the only hindrance is that he is not here," answered the lady. "He will be glad with his whole soul to see you, my guardians, for he has heard much good concerning you,--in old times from my grandfather, and lately from me."

"If only he does not receive us as he received the Domasheviches when they went to him with tidings of the colonel's death," muttered Yuzva, sullenly.

The lady listened to the end, and answered at once with animation: "Be not unjust about that. Perhaps he did not receive them politely enough, but he has confessed his fault in this house. It should be remembered too that he was returning from a war in which he endured much toil and suffering. We must not wonder at a soldier, even if he snaps at his own, for warriors have tempers like sharp swords."

Pakosh Gashtovt, who wished always to be in accord with the whole world, waved his hand and said: "We did not wonder, either. A beast snaps at a beast when it sees one suddenly; why should not a man snap at a man? We will go to old Lyubich to greet Pan Kmita, so that he may live with us, go to war and to the wilderness, as the late under-chamberlain used to do."

"Well, tell us, dear darling, did he please you or did he not please you?" asked Kassyan Butrym. "It is our duty to ask this."

"God reward you for your care. Pan Kmita is an honorable cavalier, and even if I had found something against him it would not be proper to speak of it."

"But have you not seen something, our dearest soul?"

"Nothing! Besides, no one has the right to judge him here, and God save us from showing distrust. Let us rather thank God."

"Why thank too early? When there will be something to thank for, then thank; if not, then not thank," answered the sullen Yuzva, who, like a genuine man of Jmud, was very cautious and foreseeing.

"Have you spoken about the marriage?" inquired Kassyan.

Olenka dropped her eyes: "Pan Kmita wishes it as early as possible."

"That's it! and why shouldn't he wish it?" muttered Yuzva; "he is not a fool! What bear is it that does not want honey from a tree? But why hurry? Is it not better to see what kind of man he is? Father Kassyan, tell what you have on your tongue; do not doze like a hare at midday under a ridge."

"I am not dozing, I am only turning in my head what to say," answered the old man. "The Lord Jesus has said, 'As Kuba [Jacob] is to God, so will God be to Kuba.' We wish no ill to Pan Kmita, if he wishes no ill to us,--which God grant, amen."

"If he will be to our thinking," said Yuzva.

Panna Billevich frowned with her falcon brows, and said with a certain haughtiness: "Remember that we are not receiving a servant. He will be master here; and his will must have force, not ours. He will succeed you in the guardianship."

"Does that mean that we must not interfere?" asked Yuzva.

"It means that you are to be friends with him, as he wishes to be a friend of yours. Moreover he is taking care of his own property here, which each man manages according to his wish. Is not this true, Father Pakosh?"

"The sacred truth," answered the old man of Patsuneli.

Yuzva turned again to old Butrym. "Do not doze, Father Kassyan!"

"I am not dozing, I am only looking into my mind."

"Then tell what you see there."

"What do I see? This is what I see: Pan Kmita is a man of great family, of high blood, and we are small people. Moreover he is a soldier of fame; he alone opposed the enemy when all had dropped their hands,--God give as many as possible of such men! But he has a company that is worthless. Pan Pakosh, my neighbor, what have you heard about them from the Domasheviches? That they are all dishonored men, against whom outlawry has been declared, infamous and condemned, with declarations and trials hanging over them, children of the hangman. They were grievous to the enemy, but more grievous to their own people. They burned, they plundered, they rioted; that is what they did. They may have slain people in duels or carried out executions,--that happens to honest men; but they have lived in pure Tartar fashion, and long ago would have been rotting in prison but for the protection of Pan Kmita, who is a powerful lord. He favors and protects them, and they cling to him just as flies do in summer to a horse. Now they have come hither, and it is known to all what they are doing. The first day at Lyubich they fired out of pistols,--and at what?--at the portraits of the dead Billeviches, which Pan Kmita should not have permitted, for the Billeviches are his benefactors."

Olenka covered her eyes with her hands. "It cannot be! it cannot be!"

"It can, for it has been. He let them shoot at his benefactors, with whom he was to enter into relationship; and then they dragged the girls of the house into the room for debauchery. Tfu! an offence against God! That has never been among us! The first day they began shooting and dissoluteness,--the first day!"

Here old Kassyan grew angry, and fell to striking the floor with his staff. On Olenka's face were dark blushes, and Yuzva said,--

"And Pan Kmita's troops in Upita, are they better? Like officers, like men. Some people stole Pan Sollohub's cattle; it is said they were Pan Kmita's men. Some persons struck down on the road peasants of Meizagol who were drawing pitch. Who did this? They, the same soldiers. Pan Sollohub went to Pan Hlebovich for satisfaction, and now there is violence in Upita again. All this is in opposition to God. It used to be quiet here as in no other place, and now one must load a gun for the night and stand guard; but why? Because Pan Kmita and his company have come."

"Father Yuzva, do not talk so," cried Olenka.

"But how must I talk? If Pan Kmita is not to blame, why does he keep such men, why does he live with such men? Great mighty lady, tell him to dismiss them or give them up to the hangman, for otherwise there will be no peace. Is it a thing heard of to shoot at portraits and commit open debauchery? Why, the whole neighborhood is talking of nothing else."

"What have I to do?" asked Olenka. "They may be evil men, but he fought the war with them. If he will dismiss them at my request?"

"If he does not dismiss them," muttered Yuzva, in a low voice, "he is the same as they."

With this the lady's blood began to boil against those men, murderers and profligates.

"Let it be so. He must dismiss them. Let him choose me or them. If what you say is true,--and I shall know to-day if it is true,--I shall not forgive them either the shooting or the debauchery. I am alone and a weak orphan, they are an armed crowd; but I do not fear them."

"We will help you," said Yuzva.

"In God's name," continued Olenka, more and more excited, "let them do what they like, but not here in Lyubich. Let them be as they like,--that is their affair, their necks' answer; but let them not lead away Pan Kmita to debauchery. Shame and disgrace! I thought they were awkward soldiers, but now I see that they are vile traitors, who stain both themselves and him. That's the truth! Wickedness was looking out of their eyes; but I, foolish woman, did not recognize it. Well, I thank you, fathers, for opening my eyes on these Judases. I know what it beseems me to do."

"That's it!" said old Kassyan. "Virtue speaks through you, and we will help you."

"Do not blame Pan Kmita, for though he has offended against good conduct he is young; and they tempt him, they lead him away, they urge him to license with example, and bring disgrace to his name. This is the condition; as I live, it will not last long."

Wrath roused Olenka's heart more and more, and indignation at the comrades of Pan Kmita increased as pain increases in a wound freshly given; for terribly wounded in her were the love special to woman and that trust with which she had given her whole unmixed feeling to Pan Andrei. She was ashamed, for his sake and for her own, and anger and internal shame sought above all guilty parties.

The nobles were glad when they saw their colonel's granddaughter so terrible and ready for unyielding war against the disturbers from Orsha.

She spoke on with sparkling eyes: "True, they are to blame; and they must leave not only Lyubich, but the whole country-side."

"Our heart, we do not blame Pan Kmita," said old Kassyan. "We know that they tempt him. Not through bitterness nor venom against him have we come, but through regret that he keeps near his person revellers. It is evident, of course, that being young he is foolish. Even Pan Hlebovich the starosta was foolish when he was young, but now he keeps us all in order."

"And a dog," said the mild old man from Patsuneli, with a voice of emotion,--"if you go with a young one to the field, won't the fool instead of running after the game fall about your feet, begin to play, and tug you by the skirts?"

Olenka wanted to say something, but suddenly she burst into tears.

"Do not cry," said Yuzva Butrym.

"Do not cry, do not cry," repeated the two old men.

They tried to comfort her, but could not. After they had gone, care, anxiety, and as it were an offended feeling against them and against Pan Andrei remained. It pained the proud lady more and more deeply that she had to defend, justify, and explain him. But the men of that company! The delicate hands of the lady clinched at thought of them. Before her eyes appeared as if present the faces of Pan Kokosinski, Uhlik, Zend, Kulvyets-Hippocentaurus, and the others; and she discovered what she had not seen at first, that they were shameless faces, on which folly, licentiousness, and crime had all fixed their stamps in common. A feeling of hatred foreign to Olenka began to seize her as a rattling fire seizes fuel; but together with this outburst offence against Pan Kmita increased every minute.

"Shame, disgrace," whispered the maiden, with pallid lips, "that yesterday he went from me to house-wenches!" and she felt herself overborne. A crushing burden stopped the breath in her breast.

It was growing raw out of doors. Panna Aleksandra walked in the room with hurried step, but anger was seething in her soul without ceasing. Hers was not the nature to endure the persecutions of fate without defending herself against them. There was knightly blood in the girl. She wanted straightway to begin a struggle with that band of evil spirits,--straightway. But what remained to her? Nothing, save tears and the prayer that Pan Andrei would send to the four winds those shame-bringing comrades. But if he will not do that--And she did not dare to think more of the question.

The meditations of the lady were interrupted by a youth who brought an armful of juniper sticks to the chimney, and throwing them down at the side of the hearth, began to pull out the coals from under the smouldering ashes. Suddenly a decision came to Olenka's mind.

"Kostek!" said she, "sit on horseback for me at once, and ride to Lyubich. If the master has returned, ask him to come here; but if he is not there, let the manager, old Znikis, mount with thee and come straight to me, and quickly."

The youth threw some bits of pitch on the coals and covered them with clumps of dry juniper. Bright flames began to crackle and snap in the chimney. It grew somewhat lighter in Olenka's mind.

"Perhaps the Lord God will change this yet," thought she to herself, "and maybe it is not so bad as the guardians have said."

After a while she went to the servants' room to sit, according to the immemorial custom of the Billeviches, with the maidens to oversee the spinning and sing hymns.

In two hours Kostek entered, chilled from cold. "Znikis is in the antechamber," said he. "The master is not in Lyubich."

The lady rose quickly. The manager in the antechamber bowed to her feet. "But how is your health, serene heiress? God give you the best."

They passed into the dining-hall; Znikis halted at the door.

"What is to be heard among you people?" asked the lady.

The peasant waved his hand. "Well, the master is not there."

"I know that, because he is in Upita. But what is going on in the house?"

"Well!--"

"Listen, Znikis, speak boldly; not a hair will fall from thy head. People say that the master is good, but his companions wild?"

"If they were only wild, serene lady!--"

"Speak candidly."

"But, lady, if it is not permitted me--I am afraid--they have forbidden me."

"Who has forbidden?"

"My master."

"Has he?" asked the lady.

A moment of silence ensued. She walked quickly in the room, with compressed lips and frowning brow. He followed her with his eyes. Suddenly she stopped before him.

"To whom dost thou belong?"

"To the Billeviches. I am from Vodokty, not from Lyubich."

"Thou wilt return no more to Lyubich; stay here. Now I command thee to tell all thou knowest."

The peasant cast himself on his knees at the threshold where he was standing. "Serene lady, I do not want to go back; the day of judgment is there. They are bandits and cut-throats; in that place a man is not sure of the day nor the hour."

Panna Billevich staggered as if stricken by an arrow. She grew very pale, but inquired calmly, "Is it true that they fired in the room, at the portraits?"

"Of course they fired! And they dragged girls into their rooms, and every day the same debauchery. In the village is weeping, at the house Sodom and Gomorrah. Oxen are killed for the table, sheep for the table. The people are oppressed. Yesterday they killed the stable man without cause."

"Did they kill the stable-man?"

"Of course. And worst of all, they abused the girls. Those at the house are not enough for them; they chase others through the village."

A second interval of silence followed. Hot blushes came out on the lady's face, and did not leave it.

"When do they look for the master's return?"

"They do not know, my lady. But I heard, as they were talking to one another, that they would have to start to-morrow for Upita with their whole company. They gave command to have horses ready. They will come here and beg my lady for attendants and powder, because they need both there."

"They are to come here? That is well. Go now, Znikis, to the kitchen. Thou wilt return to Lyubich no more."

"May God give you health and happiness!"

Panna Aleksandra had learned what she wanted, and she knew how it behooved her to act.

The following day was Sunday. In the morning, before the ladies had gone to church, Kokosinski, Uhlik, Kulvyets-Hippocentaurus, Ranitski, Rekuts, and Zend arrived, followed by the servants at Lyubich, armed and on horseback, for the cavaliers had decided to march to Upita with succor for Kmita.

The lady went out to meet them calmly and haughtily, altogether different from the woman who had greeted them for the first time a few days before. She barely motioned with her head in answer to their humble bows; but they thought that the absence of Pan Kmita made her cautious, and took no note of the real situation.

Kokosinski stepped forward more confidently than the first time, and said,--

"Serene great mighty lady, chief-hunter's daughter, benefactress; we have come in here on our way to Upita to fall at the feet of our lady benefactress and beg for assistance, such as powder, and that you would permit your servants to mount their horses and go with us. We will take Upita by storm, and let out a little blood for the basswood-barks."

"It is a wonder to me," answered Panna Billevich, "that you are going to Upita, when I heard myself how Pan Kmita commanded you to remain quietly in Lyubich, and I think that it beseems him to command and you to obey, as subordinates."

The cavaliers hearing these words looked at one another in astonishment. Zend pursed out his lips as if about to whistle in bird fashion. Kokosinski began to draw his broad palm over his head.

"As true as life," said he, "a man would think that you were speaking to Pan Kmita's baggage-boys. It is true that we were to sit at home; but since the fourth day is passing and Yendrus has not come, we have reached the conviction that some serious tumult may have risen, in which our sabres, too, would be of service."

"Pan Kmita did not go to a battle, but to punish turbulent soldiers, and punishment may meet you also if you go against orders. Besides, a tumult and slashing might come to pass more quickly if you were there."

"It is hard to deliberate with your ladyship. We ask only for powder and men."

"Men and powder I will not give. Do you hear me, sirs!"

"Do I hear correctly?" asked Kokosinski. "How is this? You will not give? You will spare in the rescue of Kmita, of Yendrus? Do you prefer that some evil should meet him?"

"The greatest evil that can meet him is your company."

Here the maiden's eyes began to flash lightning, and raising her head she advanced some steps toward the cutthroats, and they pushed back before her in astonishment.

"Traitors!" said she, "you, like evil spirits, tempt him to sin; you persuade him on. But I know you,--your profligacy, your lawless deeds. Justice is hunting you; people turn away from you, and on whom does the shame fall? On him, through you who are outlaws, and infamous."

"Hei, by God's wounds, comrades, do you hear?" cried Kokosinski. "Hei, what is this? Are we not sleeping, comrades?"

Panna Billevich advanced another step, and pointing with her hand to the door, said, "Be off out of here!"

The ruffians grew as pale as corpses, and no one of them found a word in answer. But their teeth began to gnash, their hands to quiver toward their sword-hilts, and their eyes to shoot forth malign gleams. After a moment, however, their spirits fell through alarm. That house too was under the protection of the powerful Kmita; that insolent lady was his betrothed. In view of this they gnawed their rage in silence, and she stood unflinchingly with flashing eyes pointing to the door with her finger.

At last Kokosinski spoke in a voice broken with rage: "Since we are received here so courteously, nothing remains to us but to bow to the polished lady and go--with thanks for the entertainment."

Then he bowed, touching the floor with his cap in purposed humility; after him all the others bowed, and went out in order. When the door closed after the last man, Olenka fell exhausted into the armchair, panting heavily, for she had not so much strength as daring.

They assembled in counsel in front of the entrance near their horses, but no man wanted to speak first. At last Kokosinski said, "Well, dear lambs, what's that?"

"Do you feel well?"

"Do you?"

"Ei! but for Kmita," said Ranitski, rubbing his hands convulsively, "we would revel with this lady here in our own fashion."

"Go meet Kmita," piped Rekuts.

Ranitski's face was covered completely with spots, like the skin of a leopard. "I'll meet him and you too, you reveller, wherever it may please you!"

"That's well!" cried Rekuts.

Both rushed to their sabres, but the gigantic Kulvyets-Hippocentaurus thrust himself between. "See this fist!" said he, shaking as it were a loaf of bread; "see this fist!" repeated he. "I'll smash the head of the first man who draws his sabre." And he looked now at one and now at the other, as if asking in silence who wished to try first; but they, addressed in such fashion, were quiet at once.

"Kulvyets is right," said Kokosinski. "My dear lambs, we need agreement now more than ever. I would advise to go with all speed to Kmita, so that she may not see him first, for she would describe us as devils. It is well that none of us snarled at her, though my own hands and tongue were itching. If she is going to rouse him against us, it is better for us to rouse him first. God keep him from leaving us! Straightway the people here would surround us, hunt us down like wolves."

"Nonsense!" said Ranitski. "They will do nothing to us. There is war now; are there few men straggling through the world without a roof, without bread? Let us collect a party for ourselves, dear comrades, and let all the tribunals pursue us. Give your hand, Rekuts, I forgive you."

"I should have cut off your ears," piped Rekuts; "but let us be friends, a common insult has met us."

"To order out cavaliers like us!" said Kokosinski.

"And me, in whom is senatorial blood!" added Ranitski.

"Honorable people, men of good birth!"

"Soldiers of merit!"

"And exiles!"

"Innocent orphans!"

"I have boots lined with wool, but my feet are freezing," said Kulvyets. "Shall we stand like minstrels in front of this house? They will not bring us out heated beer. We are of no use here; let us mount and ride away. Better send the servants home, for what good are they without guns and weapons? We will go on alone."

"To Upita!"

"To Yendrus, our worthy friend! We will make complaint before him."

"If only we do not miss him."

"To horse, comrades, to horse!"

They mounted, and moved on at a walk, chewing their anger and shame. Outside the gate Ranitski, whom rage still held as it were by the throat, turned and threatened the house with his fist. "Ei! I want blood! I want blood!"

"If we can only raise a quarrel between her and Kmita," said Kokosinski, "we shall go through this place yet with fire."

"That may happen."

"God aid us!" added Uhlik.

"Oh, pagan's daughter, mad heath-hen!"

Railing thus, and enraged at the lady, snarling sometimes too at themselves, they reached the forest. They had barely passed the first trees when an enormous flock of crows whirled above their heads. Zend began at once to croak in a shrill voice; thousands of voices answered him from above. The flock came down so low that the horses began to be frightened at the sound of their wings.

"Shut your mouth!" cried Ranitski to Zend. "You'll croak out misfortune on us yet. Those crows are circling over us as over carrion."

The others laughed. Zend croaked continually. The crows came down more and more, and the party rode as if in the midst of a storm. Fools! they could not see the ill omen.

Beyond the forest appeared Volmontovichi, toward which the cavaliers moved at a trot, for the frost was severe; they were very cold, and it was still a long way to Upita, but they had to lessen their speed in the village itself. In the broad road of the village the space was full of people, as is usual on Sundays. The Butryms, men and women, were returning on foot and in sleighs from Mitruny after receiving indulgence. The nobles looked on these unknown horsemen, half guessing who they were. The young women, who had heard of their license in Lyubich and of the notorious public sinners whom Pan Kmita had brought, looked at them with still greater curiosity. But they rode proudly in imposing military posture, with velvet coats which they had captured, in panther-skin caps, and on sturdy horses. It was to be seen that they were soldiers by profession,--their gestures frequent and haughty, their right hands resting on their hips, their heads erect. They gave the way to no man, advancing in a line and shouting from time to time, "Out of the road!" One or another of the Butryms looked at them with a frown, but yielded; the party chatted among themselves about the village.

"See, gentlemen," said Kokosinski, "what sturdy fellows there are here; one after another like an aurochs, and each with the look of a wolf."

"If it were not for their stature and swords, they might be taken for common trash."

"Just look at those sabres,--regular tearers, as God is dear to me!" remarked Ranitski. "I would like to make a trial with some of those fellows." Here he began to fence with his hand: "He thus, I thus! He thus, I thus--and check!"

"You can easily have that delight for yourself," said Rekuts. "Not much is needed with them for a quarrel."

"I would rather engage with those girls over there," said Zend, all at once.

"They are candles, not girls!" cried Rekuts, with enthusiasm.

"What do you say,--candles? Pine-trees! And each one has a face as if painted with crocus."

"It is hard to sit on a horse at such a sight."

Talking in this style, they rode out of the village and moved on again at a trot. After half an hour's ride they came to a public house called Dola, which was half-way between Volmontovichi and Mitruny. The Butryms, men and women, generally stopped there going to and returning from church, in order to rest and warm themselves in frosty weather. So the cavaliers saw before the door a number of sleighs with pea-straw spread in them, and about the same number of saddle-horses.

"Let us drink some gorailka, for it is cold," said Kokosinski.

"It wouldn't hurt," answered the others, in a chorus.

They dismounted, left their horses at the posts, and entered the drinking-hall, which was enormous and dark. They found there a crowd of people,--nobles sitting on benches or standing in groups before the water-pail, drinking warmed beer, and some of them a punch made of mead, butter, vudka, and spice. Those were the Butryms themselves, stalwart and gloomy; so sparing of speech that in the room scarcely any conversation was heard. All were dressed in gray overcoats of home-made or coarse cloth from Rossyeni, lined with sheepskin; they had leather belts, with sabres in black iron scabbards. By reason of that uniformity of dress they had the appearance of soldiers. But they were old men of sixty or youths under twenty. These had remained at home for the winter threshing; the others, men in the prime of life, had gone to Rossyeni.

When they saw the cavaliers of Orsha, they drew back from the water-bucket and began to examine them. Their handsome soldierly appearance pleased that warlike nobility; after a while, too, some one dropped the word,--

"Are they from Lyubich?"

"Yes, that is Pan Kmita's company!"

"Are these they?"

"Of course."

The cavaliers drank gorailka, but the punch had a stronger odor. Kokosinski caught it first, and ordered some. They sat around a table then; and when the steaming kettle was brought they began to drink, looking around the room at the men and blinking, for the place was rather dark. The snow had blocked the windows; and the broad, low opening of the chimney in which the fire was burning was hidden completely by certain figures with their backs to the crowd.

When the punch had begun to circulate in the veins of the cavaliers, bearing through their bodies an agreeable warmth, their cheerfulness, depressed by the reception at Vodokty, sprang up again; and all at once

Zend fell to cawing like a crow, so perfectly that all faces were turned toward him.

The cavaliers laughed, and the nobles, enlivened, began to approach, especially the young men,--powerful fellows with broad shoulders and plump cheeks. The figures sitting at the chimney turned their faces to the room, and Rekuts was the first to see that they were women.

Zend closed his eyes and cawed, cawed. Suddenly he stopped, and in a moment those present heard the cry of a hare choked by a dog; the hare cried in the last agony, weaker and lower, then screamed in despair, and was silent for the ages; in place of it was heard the deep bellow of a furious stag as loud as in spring-time.

The Butryms were astonished. Though Zend had stopped, they expected to hear something again; but they heard only the piping voice of Rekuts,--

"Those are titmice sitting near the chimney!"

"That is true!" replied Kokosinski, shading his eyes with his hand.

"As true as I live!" added Uhlik, "but it is so dark in the room that I could not see them."

"I am curious. What are they doing?"

"Maybe they have come to dance."

"But wait; I will ask," said Kokosinski. And raising his voice, he asked, "My dear women, what are you doing there at the chimney?"

"We are warming our feet," answered thin voices.

Then the cavaliers rose and approached the hearth. There were sitting at it, on a long bench, about ten women, old and young, holding their bare feet on a log lying by the fire. On the other side of the log their shoes wet from the snow were drying.

"So you are warming your feet?" asked Kokosinski.

"Yes, for they are cold."

"Very pretty feet," piped Rekuts, inclining toward the log.

"But keep at a distance," said one of the women.

"I prefer to come near. I have a sure method, better than fire, for cold feet; which is,--only dance with a will, and the cold flies away."

"If to dance, then dance," said Uhlik. "We want neither fiddles nor bass-viols. I will play for you on the flageolet."

Taking from its leather case which hung near his sabre the ever-present flageolet, he began to play; and the cavaliers, pushing forward with dancing movement to the maidens, sought to draw them from the benches. The maidens appeared to defend themselves, but more with their voices than their hands, for in truth they were not greatly opposed. Maybe the men, too, would have been willing in their turn; for against dancing on Sunday after Mass and during the carnival no one would protest greatly. But the reputation of the "company" was already too well known in Volmontovichi; therefore first the gigantic Yuzva Butrym, he who had but one foot, rose from the bench, and approaching Kulvyets-Hippocentaurus, caught him by the breast, held him, and said with sullen voice,--

"If your grace wants dancing, then dance with me."

Kulvyets-Hippocentaurus blinked, and began to move his mustaches convulsively. "I prefer a girl," said he; "I can attend to you afterward."

Meanwhile Ranitski ran up with face already spotted, for he sniffed a quarrel. "Who are you, road-blocker?" asked he, grasping his sabre.

Uhlik stopped playing, and Kokosinski shouted, "Hei, comrades! together, together!"

But the Butryms were already behind Yuzva; sturdy old men and great youths began to assemble, growling like bears.

"What do you want? Are you looking for bruises?" asked Kokosinski.

"No talk! Be off out of here!" said Yuzva, stolidly.

Then Ranitski, whose interest it was that an hour should not pass without a fight, struck Yuzva with the hilt of his sword in the breast, so that it was heard in the whole room, and cried, "Strike!"

Rapiers glittered; the scream of women was heard, the clatter of sabres, uproar and disturbance. Then the gigantic Yuzva pushed out of the crowd, took a roughly hewn bench from beside a table, and raising it as though it were a light strip of wood, shouted, "Make way! make way!"

Dust rose from the floor and hid the combatants; but in the confusion groans were soon heard.

CHAPTER VI.

In the evening of that same day Pan Kmita came to Vodokty, at the head of a hundred and some tens of men whom he had brought from Upita so as to send them to Kyedani; for he saw himself that there were no quarters in such a small place for a large number of soldiers, and when the townspeople had been brought to hunger the soldiers would resort to violence, especially soldiers who could be held in discipline only by fear of a leader. A glance at Kmita's volunteers was enough to convince one that it would be difficult to find men of worse character in the whole Commonwealth. Kmita could not have others. After the defeat of the grand hetman, the enemy deluged the whole country. The remnants of the regular troops of the Lithuanian quota withdrew for a certain time to Birji and Kyedani, in order to rally there. The nobility of Smolensk, Vityebsk, Polotsk, Mstislavsk, and Minsk either followed the army or took refuge in the provinces still unoccupied. Men of superior courage among the nobility assembled at Grodno around the under-treasurer, Pan Gosyevski; for the royal proclamation summoning the general militia appointed that as the place of muster. Unfortunately few obeyed the proclamation, and those who followed the voice of duty assembled so negligently that for the time being no one offered real resistance save Kmita, who fought on his own account, animated more by knightly daring than patriotism. It is easy to understand that in the absence of regular troops and nobility he took such men as he could find, consequently men who were not drawn by duty to the hetmans and who had nothing to lose. Therefore there gathered around him vagrants without a roof and without a home, men of low rank, runaway servants from the army, foresters grown wild, serving-men from towns, or scoundrels pursued by the law. These expected to find protection under a flag and win profit from plunder. In the iron hands of Kmita they were turned into daring soldiers, daring even to madness; and if Kmita had been prudent he might have rendered high service to the Commonwealth. But Kmita was insubordinate himself, his spirit was always seething; besides, whence could he take provisions and arms and horses, since being a partisan he did not hold even a commission, and could not look for any aid from the treasury of the Commonwealth? He took therefore with violence,--often from the enemy, often from his own,--could suffer no opposition, and punished severely for the least cause.

In continual raids, struggles, and attacks he had grown wild, accustomed to bloodshed in such a degree that no common thing could move the heart within him, which however was good by nature. He was in love with people of unbridled temper who were ready for anything. Soon his name had an ominous sound. Smaller divisions of the enemy did not dare to leave the towns and the camps in those regions where the terrible partisan was raging. But the townspeople ruined by war feared his men little less than they did the enemy, especially when the eye of Kmita in person was not resting on them. When command was taken by his officers, Kokosinski, Uhlik, Kulvyets, Zend, and particularly by Ranitski,--the wildest and most cruel of them all, though a man of high lineage,--it might always be asked, Are those defenders or ravagers? Kmita at times punished his own men without mercy when something happened not according to his humor; but more frequently he took their part, regardless of the rights, tears, and lives of people. His companions with the exception of Rekuts, on whom innocent blood was not weighing, persuaded the young leader to give the reins more and more to his turbulent nature. Such was Kmita's army. Just then he had taken his rabble from Upita to send it to Kyedani.

When they stopped in front of the house at Vodokty, Panna Aleksandra was frightened as she saw them through the window, they were so much like robbers. Each one had a different outfit: some were in helmets taken from the enemy; others in Cossack caps, in hoods and Polish caps; some in faded overcoats, others in sheep-skin coats; their arms were guns, spears, bows, battle-axes; their horses, poor and worn, were covered with trappings, Polish, Russian, or Turkish.

Olenka was set at rest only when Pan Andrei, gladsome and lively as ever, entered the room and rushed straight to her hands with incredible quickness.

And she, though resolved in advance to receive him with dignity and coldness, was still unable to master the joy which his coming had caused her. Feminine cunning too may have played a certain part, for it was necessary to tell Pan Andrei about turning his comrades out of doors; therefore the clever girl wished to incline him first to her side. And in addition he greeted her so sincerely, so lovingly that the remnant of her offended feeling melted like snow before a blaze.

"He loves me! there is no doubt about that," thought she.

And he said: "I so longed for you that I was ready to burn all Upita if I could only fly to you the sooner. May the frost pinch them, the basswood barks!"

"I too was uneasy lest it might come to a battle there. Praise be to God that you have returned!"

"And such a battle! The soldiers had begun to pull around the basswood barks a little--"

"But you quieted them?"

"This minute I will tell you how it all happened, my jewel; only let me rest a little, for I am wearied. Ei! it is warm here. It is delightful in this Vodokty, just as in paradise. A man would be glad to sit here all his life, look in those beautiful eyes, and never go away--But it would do no harm, either, to drink something warm, for there is terrible frost outside."

"Right away I will have wine heated, with eggs, and bring it myself."

"And give my gallows' birds some little keg of gorailka, and give command to let them into the stable, so that they may warm themselves a little even from the breath of the cattle. They have coats lined with wind, and are terribly chilled."

"I will spare nothing on them, for they are your soldiers."

While speaking she smiled, so that it grew bright in Kmita's eyes, and she slipped out as quietly as a cat to have everything prepared in the servants' hall.

Kmita walked up and down in the room, rubbing the top of his head, then twirling his young mustache, thinking how to tell her of what had been done in Upita.

"The pure truth must be told," muttered he; "there is no help for it, though the company may laugh because I am here in leading-strings." And again he walked, and again he pushed the foretop on his forehead; at last he grew impatient that the maiden was so long in returning.

Meanwhile a boy brought in a light, bowed to the girdle, and went out. Directly after the charming lady of the house entered, bringing with both hands a shining tin tray, and on it a small pot, from which rose the fragrant steam of heated Hungarian, and a goblet of cut glass with the escutcheon of the Kmitas. Old Billevich got this goblet in his time from Andrei's father, when at his house as a guest.

Pan Andrei when he saw the lady sprang toward her. "Hei!" cried he, "both hands are full, you will not escape me."

He bent over the tray, and she drew back her head, which was defended only by the steam which rose from the pot. "Traitor! desist, or I will drop the drink."

But he feared not the threat; afterward he cried, "As God is in heaven, from such delight a man might lose his wits!"

"Then you lost your wit long ago. Sit down."

He sat down obediently; she poured the drink into the goblet.

"Tell me how you sentenced the guilty in Upita."

"In Upita? Like Solomon!"

"Praise to God for that! It is on my heart that all in this region should esteem you as a steady and just man. How was it then?"

Kmita took a good draught of the drink, drew breath, and began,--

"I must tell from the beginning. It was thus: The townspeople with the mayor spoke of an order for provisions from the grand hetman or the under-treasurer. 'You gentlemen,' said they to the soldiers, 'are volunteers, and you cannot levy contributions. We will give you quarters for nothing, and provisions we will give when it is shown that we shall be paid.'"

"Were they right, or were they not?"

"They were right according to law; but the soldiers had sabres, and in old fashion whoever has a sabre has the best argument. They said then to the basswood barks, 'We will write orders on your skins immediately.' And straightway there rose a tumult. The mayor and the people barricaded themselves in the street, and my men attacked them; it did not pass without firing. The soldiers, poor fellows, burned a couple of barns to frighten the people, and quieted a few of them also."

"How did they quiet them?"

"Whoso gets a sabre on his skull is as quiet as a coward."

"As God lives, that is murder!"

"That is just why I went there. The soldiers ran to me at once with complaints and outcries against the oppression in which they were living, being persecuted without cause. 'Our stomachs are empty,' said they, 'what are we to do?' I commanded the mayor to appear. He hesitated long, but at last came with three other men. They began: 'Even if the soldiers had not orders, why did they beat us, why burn the place? We should have given them to eat and to drink for a kind word; but they wanted ham, mead, dainties, and we are poor people, we have not these things for ourselves. We will seek defence at law, and you will answer before a court for your soldiers.'"

"God will bless you," cried Olenka, "if you have rendered justice as was proper."

"If I have." Here Pan Andrei wriggled like a student who has to confess his fault, and began to collect the forelock on his forehead with his hand. "My queen!" cried he at last, in an imploring voice, "my jewel, be not angry with me!"

"What did you do then?" asked Olenka, uneasily.

"I commanded to give one hundred blows apiece to the mayor and the councillors," said Kmita, at one breath.

Olenka made no answer; she merely rested her hands on her knees, dropped her head on her bosom, and sank into silence.

"Cut off my head!" cried Kmita, "but do not be angry! I have not told all yet!"

"Is there more?" groaned the lady.

"There is, for they sent then to Ponyevyej for aid. One hundred stupid fellows came with officers. These men I frightened away, but the officers--for God's sake be not angry!--I ordered to be chased and flogged with braided whips, naked over the snow, as I once did to Pan Tumgrat in Orsha."

Panna Billevich raised her head; her stern eyes were flashing with indignation, and purple came out on her cheeks. "You have neither shame nor conscience!" said she.

Kmita looked at her in astonishment, he was silent for a moment, then asked with changed voice, "Are you speaking seriously or pretending?"

"I speak seriously; that deed is becoming a bandit and not a cavalier. I speak seriously, since your reputation is near my heart; for it is a shame to me that you have barely come here, when all the people look on you as a man of violence and point at you with their fingers."

"What care I for the people? One dog watches ten of their cabins, and then has not much to do."

"There is no infamy on those modest people, there is no disgrace on the name of one of them. Justice will pursue no man here except you."

"Oh, let not your head ache for that. Every man is lord for himself in our Commonwealth, if he has only a sabre in his hand and can gather any kind of party. What can they do to me? Whom fear I here?"

"If you fear not man, then know that I fear God's anger, and the tears of people; I fear wrongs also. And moreover I am not willing to share disgrace with any one; though I am a weak woman, still the honor of my name is dearer to me than it is to a certain one who calls himself a cavalier."

"In God's name, do not threaten me with refusal, for you do not know me yet."

"I think that my grandfather too did not know you."

Kmita's eyes shot sparks; but the Billevich blood began to play in her.

"Oh, gesticulate and grit your teeth," continued she, boldly; "but I fear not, though I am alone and you have a whole party of robbers,--my innocence defends me. You think that I know not how you fired at the portraits in Lyubich and dragged in the girls for debauchery. You do not know me if you suppose that I shall humbly be silent. I want honesty from you, and no will can prevent me from exacting it. Nay, it was the will of my grandfather that I should be the wife of only an honest man."

Kmita was evidently ashamed of what had happened at Lyubich; for dropping his head, he asked in a voice now calmer, "Who told you of this shooting?"

"All the nobles in the district speak of it."

"I will pay those homespuns, the traitors, for their good will," answered Kmita, sullenly. "But that happened in drink,--in company,--

for soldiers are not able to restrain themselves. As for the girls I had nothing to do with them."

"I know that those brazen ruffians, those murderers, persuade you to everything."

"They are not murderers, they are my officers."

"I commanded those officers of yours to leave my house."

Olenka looked for an outburst; but she saw with greatest astonishment that the news of turning his comrades out of the house made no impression on Kmita; on the contrary, it seemed to improve his humor.

"You ordered them to go out?" asked be.

"I did."

"And they went?"

"They did."

"As God lives, you have the courage of a cavalier. That pleases me greatly, for it is dangerous to quarrel with such people. More than one man has paid dearly for doing so. But they observe manners before Kmita! You saw they bore themselves obediently as lambs; you saw that,--but why? Because they are afraid of me."

Here Kmita looked boastfully at Olenka, and began to twirl his mustache. This fickleness of humor and inopportune boastfulness enraged her to the last degree; therefore she said haughtily and with emphasis, "You must choose between me and them; there is no other way."

Kmita seemed not to note the decision with which she spoke, and answered carelessly, almost gayly: "But why choose when I have you and

I have them? You may do what you like in Vodokty; but if my comrades have committed no wrong, no license here, why should I drive them away? You do not understand what it is to serve under one flag and carry on war in company. No relationship binds like service in common. Know that they have saved my life a thousand times at least. I must protect them all the more because they are pursued by justice. They are almost all nobles and of good family, except Zend, who is of uncertain origin; but such a horse-trainer as he there is not in the whole Commonwealth. And if you could hear how he imitates wild beasts and every kind of bird, you would fall in love with him yourself."

Here Kmita laughed as if no anger, no misunderstanding, had ever found place between them; and she was ready to wring her hands, seeing how that whirlwind of a nature was slipping away from her grasp. All that she had said of the opinions of men, of the need of sedateness, of disgrace, slipped along on him like a dart on steel armor. The unroused conscience of this soldier could give no response to her indignation at every injustice and every dishonorable deed of license. How was he to be touched, how addressed?

"Let the will of God be done," said she at last; "since you will resign me, then go your way. God will remain with the orphan."

"I resign you?" asked Kmita, with supreme astonishment.

"That is it!--if not in words, then in deeds; if not you me, then I you. For I will not marry a man weighted by the tears and blood of people, whom men point at with their fingers, whom they call an outlaw, a robber, and whom they consider a traitor."

"What, traitor! Do not bring me to madness, lest I do something for which I should be sorry hereafter. May the thunderbolts strike me this minute, may the devils flay me, if I am a traitor,--I, who stood by the country when all hands had dropped!"

"You stand by the country and act like an enemy, for you trample on it. You are an executioner of the people, regarding the laws neither of God nor man. No! though my heart should be rent, I will not marry you; being such a man, I will not!"

"Do not speak to me of refusal, for I shall grow furious. Save me, ye angels! If you will not have me in good-will, then I'll take you without it, though all the rabble from the villages were here, though the Radzivills themselves were here, the very king himself and all the devils with their horns stood in the way, even if I had to sell my soul to the Devil!"

"Do not summon evil spirits, for they will hear you," cried Olenka, stretching forth her hands.

"What do you wish of me?"

"Be honest!"

Both ceased speaking, and silence followed; only the panting of Pan Andrei was heard. The last words of Olenka had penetrated, however, the armor covering his conscience. He felt himself conquered; he knew not what to answer, how to defend himself. Then he began to go with swift steps through the room. She sat there motionless. Above them hung disagreement, dissension, and regret. They were oppressive to each other, and the long silence became every instant more unendurable.

"Farewell!" said Kmita, suddenly.

"Go, and may God give you a different inspiration!" answered Olenka.

"I will go! Bitter was your drink, bitter your bread. I have been treated here to gall and vinegar."

"And do you think you have treated me to sweetness?" answered she, in a voice in which tears were trembling.

"Be well."

"Be well."

Kmita, advancing toward the door, turned suddenly, and springing to her, seized both her hands and said, "By the wounds of Christ! do you wish me to drop from the horse a corpse on the road?"

That moment Olenka burst into tears; he embraced her and held her in his arms, all quivering, repeating through her set teeth, "Whoso believes in God, kill me! kill, do not spare!"

At last he burst out: "Weep not, Olenka; for God's sake, do not weep! In what am I guilty before you? I will do all to please you. I'll send those men away, I'll come to terms in Upita, I will live differently,--for I love you. As God lives, my heart will burst! I will do everything; only do not cry, and love me still."

And so he continued to pacify and pet her; and she, when she had cried to the end, said: "Go now. God will make peace between us. I am not offended, only sore at heart."

The moon had risen high over the white fields when Pan Andrei pushed out on his way to Lyubich, and after him clattered his men, stretching along the broad road like a serpent. They went through Volmontovichi, but by the shortest road, for frost had bound up the swamps, which might therefore be crossed without danger.

The sergeant Soroka approached Pan Andrei. "Captain," inquired he, "where are we to find lodgings in Lyubich?"

"Go away!" answered Kmita.

And he rode on ahead, speaking to no man. In his heart rose regret, at moments anger, but above all, vexation at himself. That was the first night in his life in which he made a reckoning with conscience, and that reckoning weighed him down more than the heaviest armor. Behold, he had come into this region with a damaged reputation, and what had he done to repair it? The first day he had permitted shooting and excess in Lyubich, and thought that he did not belong to it, but he did; then he permitted it every day. Further, his soldiers wronged the townspeople, and he increased those wrongs. Worse, he attacked the Ponyevyej garrison, killed men, sent naked officers on the snow. They will bring an action against him; he will lose it. They will punish him with loss of property, honor, perhaps life. But why can he not, after he has collected an armed party of the rabble, scoff at the law as before? Because he intends to marry, settle in Vodokty, serve not on his own account, but in the contingent; there the law will find him and take him. Besides, even though these deeds should pass unpunished, there is something vile in them, something unworthy of a knight. Maybe this violence can be atoned for; but the memory of it will remain in the hearts of men, in his own conscience, and in the heart of Olenka.

When he remembered that she had not rejected him yet, that when he was going away he read in her eyes forgiveness, she seemed to him as kind as the angels of heaven. And behold the desire was seizing him to go, not to-morrow, but straightway, as fast as the horse could spring, fall at her feet, beg forgetfulness, and kiss those sweet eyes which today had moistened his face with tears. Then he wished to roar with weeping, and felt that he loved that girl as he had never in his life loved any one. "By the Most Holy Lady!" thought he, in his soul, "I will do what she wishes;

I will provide for my comrades bountifully, and send them to the end of the world; for it is true that they urge me to evil."

Then it entered his head that on coming to Lyubich he would find them most surely drunk or with girls; and such rage seized him that he wanted to slash somebody with a sabre, even those soldiers whom he was leading, and cut them up without mercy.

"I'll give it to them!" muttered he, twirling his mustache. "They have not yet seen me as they will see me."

Then from madness he began to prick the horse with his spurs, to pull and drag at the reins till the steed grew wild. Soroka, seeing this, muttered to the soldiers,--

"The captain is mad. God save us from falling under his hand!"

Pan Andrei had become mad in earnest. Round about there was great calm. The moon shone mildly, the heavens were glittering with thousands of stars, not the slightest breeze was moving the limbs on the trees; but in the heart of the knight a tempest was raging. The road to Lyubich seemed to him longer than ever before. A certain hitherto unknown alarm began to play upon him from the gloom of the forest depths, and from the fields flooded with a greenish light of the moon. Finally weariness seized Pan Andrei,--for, to tell the truth, the whole night before he had passed in drinking and frolicking in Upita; but he wished to overcome toil with toil, and rouse himself from unquiet by swift riding; he turned therefore to the soldiers and commanded,--

"Forward!"

He shot ahead like an arrow, and after him the whole party. And in those woods and along those empty fields they flew on like that hellish band of knights of the cross of whom people tell in Jmud,--how at times in the middle of bright moonlight nights they appear and rush through the air, announcing war and uncommon calamities. The clatter flew before them and followed behind, from the horses came steam, and only when at the turn of the road the roofs of Lyubich appeared did they slacken their speed.

The swinging gate stood open. It astonished Kmita that when the yard was crowded with his men and horses no one came out to see or inquire who they were. He expected to find the windows gleaming with lights, to hear the sound of Uhlik's flageolet, of fiddles, or the joyful shouts of conversation. At that time in two windows of the dining-hall quivered an uncertain light; all the rest of the house was dark, quiet, silent. The sergeant Soroka sprang first from his horse to hold the stirrup for the captain.

"Go to sleep," said Kmita; "whoever can find room in the servants' hall, let him sleep there, and others in the stable. Put the horses in the cattle-houses and in the barns, and bring them hay from the shed."

"I hear," answered the sergeant.

Kmita came down from the horse. The door of the entrance was wide open, and the entrance cold.

"Hei! Is there any one here?" cried Kmita.

No one answered.

"Hei there!" repeated he, more loudly.

Silence.

"They are drunk!" muttered Pan Andrei.

And such rage took possession of him that he began to grit his teeth. While riding he was agitated with anger at the thought that he should find drinking and debauchery; now this silence irritated him still more.

He entered the dining-hall. On an enormous table was burning a tallow lamp-pot with a reddish smoking light. The force of the wind which came in from the antechamber deflected the flame so that for a time Pan Andrei could not see anything. Only when the quivering had ceased did he distinguish a row of forms lying just at the wall.

"Have they made themselves dead drunk or what?" muttered he, unquietly.

Then he drew near with impatience to the side of the first figure. He could not see the face, for it was hidden in the shadow; but by the white leather belt and the white sheath of the flageolet he recognized Pan Uhlik, and began to shake him unceremoniously with his foot.

"Get up, such kind of sons! get up!"

But Pan Uhlik lay motionless, with his hands fallen without control at the side of his body, and beyond him were lying others. No one yawned, no one quivered, no one woke, no one muttered. At the same moment Kmita noticed that all were lying on their backs in the same position, and a certain fearful presentiment seized him by the heart. Springing to the table, he took with trembling hand the light and thrust it toward the faces of the prostrate men.

The hair stood on his head, such a dreadful sight met his eyes. Uhlik he was able to recognize only by his white belt, for his face and his head presented one formless, foul, bloody mass, without eyes, without nose or mouth,--only the enormous mustaches were sticking out of the dreadful pool. Kmita pushed the light farther. Next in order lay Zend, with grinning teeth and eyes protruding, in which in glassy fixedness was terror before death. The third in the row, Ranitski, had his eyes closed, and over his whole face were spots, white, bloody, and dark. Kmita took the light farther. Fourth lay Kokosinski,--the dearest to Kmita of all his officers, being his former near neighbor. He seemed to sleep quietly, but in the side of his neck was to be seen a large wound surely given with a thrust. Fifth in the row lay the gigantic Kulvyets-Hippocentaurus, with the vest torn on his bosom and his face slashed many times. Kmita brought the light near each face; and when at last he brought it to the sixth, Rekuts, it seemed that the lids of the unfortunate victim quivered a little from the gleam.

Kmita put the light on the floor and began to shake the wounded man gently. After the eyelids the face began to move, the eyes and mouth opened and closed in turn.

"Rekuts, Rekuts, it is I!" said Kmita.

The eyes of Rekuts opened for a moment; he recognized the face of his friend, and groaned in a low voice, "Yendrus--a priest--"

"Who killed you?" cried Kmita, seizing himself by the hair.

"Bu-try-my-" (The Butryms), answered he, in a voice so low that it was barely audible. Then he stretched himself, grew stiff, his open eyes became fixed, and he died.

Kmita went in silence to the table, put the tallow lamp upon it, sat down in an armchair, and began to pass his hands over his face like a man who waking from sleep does not know yet whether he is awake or still sees dream figures before his eyes. Then he looked again on the bodies lying in the darkness. Cold sweat came out on his forehead, the hair rose on his head, and suddenly he shouted so terribly that the panes rattled in the windows,--

"Come hither, every living man! come hither!"

The soldiers, who had disposed themselves in the servants' hall, heard that cry and fell into the room with a rush. Kmita showed them with his hand the corpses at the wall.

"Murdered! murdered!" repeated he, with hoarse voice.

They ran to look; some came with a taper, and held it before the eyes of the dead men. After the first moment of astonishment came noise and confusion. Those hurried in who had found places in the stables and barns. The whole house was bright with light, swarming with men; and in the midst of all that whirl, shouting, and questioning, the dead lay at the wall unmoved and quiet, indifferent to everything, and, in contradiction to their own nature, calm. The souls had gone out of them, and their bodies could not be raised by the trumpet to battle, or the sound of the goblets to feasting.

Meanwhile in the din of the soldiers shouts of threatening and rage rose higher and higher each instant. Kmita, who till that moment had been as it were unconscious, sprang up suddenly and shouted, "To horse!"

Everything living moved toward the door. Half an hour had not passed when more than one hundred horsemen were rushing with breakneck speed over the broad snowy road, and at the head of them flew Pan Andrei, as if possessed of a demon, bareheaded and with a naked sabre in his hand. In the still night was heard on every side the wild shouts: "Slay! kill!"

The moon had reached just the highest point on its road through the sky, when suddenly its beams began to be mingled and mixed with a rosy light, rising as it were from under the ground; gradually the heavens grew red and still redder as if from the rising dawn, till at last a bloody glare filled the whole neighborhood. One sea of fire raged over the gigantic village of the Butryms; and the wild soldiers of Kmita, in the midst of smoke, burning, and sparks bursting in columns to the sky, cut down the population, terrified and blinded from fright.

The inhabitants of the nearer villages sprang from their sleep. The greater and smaller companies of the Smoky Gostsyeviches and Stakyans, Gashtovts and Domasheviches, collected on the road before their houses, and looking in the direction of the fire, gave alarm from mouth to mouth: "It must be that an enemy has broken in and is burning the Butryms,--that is an unusual fire!"

The report of muskets coming at intervals from the distance confirmed this supposition.

"Let us go to assist them!" cried the bolder; "let us not leave our brothers to perish!"

And when the older ones spoke thus, the younger, who on account of the winter threshing had not gone to Rossyeni, mounted their horses. In Krakin and in Upita they had begun to ring the church bells.

In Vodokty a quiet knocking at the door roused Panna Aleksandra.

"Olenka, get up!" cried Panna Kulvyets.

"Come in, Aunt, what is the matter?"

"They are burning Volmontovichi!"

"In the name of the Father, Son, and Holy Ghost!"

"Shots are heard, there is a battle! God have mercy on us!"

Olenka screamed terribly; then she sprang out of bed and began to throw on her clothes hurriedly. Her body trembled as in a fever. She alone guessed in a moment what manner of enemy had attacked the ill-fated Butryms.

After a while the awakened women of the whole house rushed into the room with crying and sobbing. Olenka threw herself on her knees before an image; they followed her example, and all began to repeat aloud the litany for the dying.

They had scarcely gone through half of it when a violent pounding shook the door of the antechamber. The women sprang to their feet; a cry of alarm was rent from their breasts.

"Do not open! do not open!"

The pounding was heard with redoubled force; it seemed that the door would spring from its hinges. That moment the youth Kostek rushed into the midst of the assembled women.

"Panna!" cried he, "some man is knocking; shall I open or not?"

"Is he alone?"

"Alone."

"Go open."

The youth hurried away. She, taking a light, passed into the dining-room; after her, Panna Kulvyets and all the spinning-women.

She had barely put the light on the table when in the antechamber was heard the rattle of iron bolts, the creak of the opening door; and before the eyes of the women appeared Pan Kmita, terrible, black from smoke, bloody, panting, with madness in his eyes.

"My horse has fallen at the forest," cried he; "they are pursuing me!"

Panna Aleksandra fixed her eyes on him: "Did you burn Volmontovichi?"

"I--I--"

He wanted to say something more, when from the side of the road and the woods came the sound of voices and the tramp of horses approaching with uncommon rapidity.

"The devils are after my soul; let them have it!" cried Kmita, as if in a fever.

Panna Aleksandra that moment turned to the women. "If they ask, say there is no one here; and now go to the servants' hall and come here at daylight!" Then to Kmita: "Go in there," said she, pointing to an adjoining room; and almost by force she pushed him through the open door, which she shut immediately.

Meanwhile armed men filled the front yard; and in the twinkle of an eye the Butryms, Gostsyeviches, Domasheviches, with others, burst into the house. Seeing the lady, they halted in the dining-room; but she, standing with a light in her hand, stopped with her person the passage to doors beyond.

"Men, what has happened? What do you want?" asked she, without blinking an eye before the terrible looks and the ominous gleam of drawn sabres.

"Kmita has burned Volmontovichi!" cried the nobles, in a chorus. "He has slaughtered men, women, children,--Kmita did this."

"We have killed his men," said Yuzva Butrym; "now we are seeking his own head."

"His head, his blood! Cut down the murderer!"

"Pursue him!" cried the lady. "Why do you stand here? Pursue him!"

"Is he not hidden here? We found his horse at the woods."

"He is not here! The house was closed. Look for him in the stables and barns."

"He has gone off to the woods!" cried some noble. "Come, brothers."

"Be silent!" roared with powerful voice Yuzva Butrym. "My lady," said he, "do not conceal him! That is a cursed man!"

Olenka raised both hands above her head: "I join you in cursing him!"

"Amen!" shouted the nobles. "To the buildings, to the woods! We will find him! After the murderer!"

"Come on! come on!"

The clatter of sabres and tramp of feet was heard again. The nobles hurried out through the porch, and mounted with all speed. A part of them searched still for a time in the stables, the cow-houses, and hay-shed; then their voices began to retreat toward the woods.

Panna Aleksandra listened till they had ceased altogether; then she tapped feverishly at the door of the room in which she had hidden Kmita. "There is no one here now, come out."

Pan Andrei pushed himself forth from the room as if drunk. "Olenka!" he began.

She shook her loosened tresses, which then covered her face like a veil. "I wish not to see you or know you. Take a horse and flee hence!"

"Olenka!" groaned Kmita, stretching forth his hands.

"There is blood on your hands, as on Cain's!" screamed she, springing back as if at the sight of a serpent. "Be gone, for the ages!"

CHAPTER VII.

The day rose gray, and lighted a group of ruins in Volmontovichi,--the burned remnants of houses, out-buildings, bodies of people and horses burned or slain with swords. In the ashes amidst dying embers crowds of pale people were seeking for the bodies of the dead or the remains of their property. It was a day of mourning and misfortune for all Lauda. The numerous nobility had obtained, it is true, a victory over Kmita's men, but a grievous and bloody one. Besides the Butryms, who had fallen in greater numbers than the others, there was not a village in which widows were not bewailing husbands, parents sons, or children their fathers. It was the more difficult for the Lauda people to finish the invaders, since the strongest were not at home; only old men or youths of early years took part in the battle. But of Kmita's soldiers not one escaped. Some yielded their lives in Volmontovichi, defending themselves with such rage that they fought after they were wounded; others were caught next day in the woods and killed without mercy. Kmita himself was as if he had dropped into water. The people were lost in surmising what had become of him. Some insisted that he had reached the wilderness of Zyelonka and gone thence to Rogovsk, where the Domasheviches alone might find him. Many too asserted that he had gone over to Hovanski and was bringing the enemy; but these were the fewest, their fears were untimely.

Meanwhile the surviving Butryms marched to Vodokty, and disposed themselves as in a camp. The house was full of women and children. Those who could not find a place there went to Mitruny, which Panna Aleksandra gave up to those whose homes had been burned. There were, besides, in Vodokty for defence about a hundred armed men in parties which relieved one another regularly, thinking that Kmita did not consider the affair ended, but might any day make an attempt on the lady with armed hand. The most important houses in the neighborhood, such as the Schyllings, the Sollohubs, and others, sent their attendant Cossacks and haiduks. Vodokty looked like a place awaiting a siege. And Panna Aleksandra went among the armed men, the nobles, the crowds of women, mournful, pale, suffering, hearing the weeping of people, and the curses of men against Pan Kmita,--which pierced her heart like swords, for she was the mediate cause of all the misfortune. For her it was that that frenzied man had come to the neighborhood, disturbed the peace, and left the memory of blood behind, trampled on laws, killed people, visited villages with fire and sword like an infidel, till it was a wonder that one man could commit so much evil in such a short time, and he a man neither entirely wicked nor entirely corrupt. If there was any one who knew this best, it was Panna Aleksandra, who had become acquainted with him most intimately. There was a precipice between Pan Kmita himself and his deeds. But it was for this reason precisely that so much pain was caused Panna Aleksandra by the thought that that man whom she had loved with the whole first impulse of a young heart might be different, that he possessed qualities to make him the model of a knight, of a cavalier, of a neighbor, worthy to receive the admiration and love of men instead of their contempt, and blessings instead of curses.

At times, therefore, it seemed to the lady that some species of misfortune, some kind of power, great and unclean, impelled him to all those deeds of violence; and then a sorrow really measureless possessed her for that unfortunate man, and unextinguished love rose anew in her heart, nourished by the fresh remembrance of his knightly form, his words, his imploring, his loving.

Meanwhile a hundred complaints were entered against him in the town, a hundred actions threatened, and the starosta, Pan Hlebovich, sent men to seize the criminal. The law was bound to condemn him.

Still, from sentences to their execution the distance was great, for disorder increased every hour in the Commonwealth. A terrible war was hanging over the land, and approaching Jmud with bloody steps. The powerful Radzivill of Birji, who was able alone to support the law with arms, was too much occupied with public affairs and still more immersed in great projects touching his own house, which he wished to elevate above all others in the country, even at the cost of the common weal. Other magnates too were thinking more of themselves than of the State. All the bonds in the strong edifice of the Commonwealth had burst from the time of the Cossack war.

A country populous, rich, filled with a valiant knighthood, had become the prey of neighbors; and straightway arbitrariness and license raised their heads more and more, and insulted the law, so great was the power which they felt behind them. The oppressed could find the best and almost the only defence against the oppressor in their own sabres; therefore all Lauda, while protesting in the courts against Kmita, did not dismount for a long time, ready to resist force with force.

But a month passed, and no tidings of Kmita. People began to breathe with greater freedom. The more powerful nobility withdrew the armed servants whom they had sent to Vodokty as a guard. The lesser nobles were yearning for their labors and occupations at home, and they too dispersed by degrees. But when warlike excitement calmed down, as time passed, an increased desire came to that indigent nobility to overcome the absent man with law and to redress their wrongs before the tribunals. For although decisions could not reach Kmita himself, Lyubich remained a large and handsome estate, a ready reward and a payment for losses endured. Meanwhile Panna Aleksandra restrained with great zeal the desire for lawsuits in the Lauda people. Twice did the elders of Lauda meet at her house for counsel; and she not only took part in these deliberations but presided over them, astonishing all with her woman's wit and keen judgment, so that more than one lawyer might envy her. The elders of Lauda wanted to occupy Lyubich with armed hand and give it to the Butryms, but "the lady" advised against this firmly.

"Do not return violence for violence," said she; "if you do, your case will be injured. Let all the innocence be on your side. He is a powerful man and has connections, he will find too in the courts adherents, and if you give the least pretext you may suffer new wrongs. Let your case be so clear that any court, even if made up of his brothers, could not decide otherwise than in your favor. Tell the Butryms to take neither tools nor cattle, and to leave Lyubich completely in peace. Whatever they need I will give them from Mitruny, where there is more than all the property that was at any time in Volmontovichi. And if Pan Kmita should appear here again, leave him in peace till there is a decision, let them make no attempt on his person. Remember that only while he is alive have you some one from whom to recover for your wrongs."

Thus spoke the wise lady with prudent intent, and they applauded her wisdom, not seeing that delay might benefit also Pan Andrei, and especially in this that it secured his life. Perhaps too Olenka wished to guard that unfortunate life against sudden attack. But the nobility obeyed her, for they were accustomed from very remote times to esteem as gospel every word that came from the mouth of a Billevich. Lyubich remained intact, and had Pan Andrei appeared he might have settled there quietly for a time. He did not appear, but a month and a half later a messenger came to the lady with a letter. He was some strange man, known to no one. The letter was from Kmita, written in the following words:--

"Beloved of my heart, most precious, unrelinquished Olenka! It is natural for all creatures and especially for men, even the lowest, to avenge wrongs done them, and when a man has suffered evil he will pay it back gladly in kind to the one who inflicted it. If I cut down those insolent nobles, God sees that I did so not through cruelty, but because they murdered my officers in defiance of laws human and divine, without regard to their youth and high birth, with a death so pitiless that the like could not be found among Cossacks or Tartars. I will not deny that wrath more than human possessed me; but who will wonder at wrath which had its origin in the blood of one's friends? The spirits of Kokosinski, Ranitski, Uhlik, Rekuts, Kulvyets, and Zend, of sacred memory; slain in the flower of their age and repute, slain without reason, put arms in my hands when I was just thinking.--and I call God to witness,--just thinking of peace and friendship with the nobles of Lauda, wishing to change my life altogether according to your pleasant counsels. While listening to complaints against me, do not forget my defence, and judge justly. I am sorry now for those people in the village. The innocent may have suffered; but a soldier avenging the blood of his brothers cannot distinguish the innocent from the guilty, and respects no one. God grant that nothing has happened to injure me in your eyes. Atonement for other men's sins and faults and my own just wrath is most bitter to me, for since I have lost you I sleep in despair and I wake in despair, without power to forget either you or my love. Let the tribunals pass sentence on me, unhappy man; let the diets confirm the sentences, let them trumpet me forth to infamy, let the ground open under my feet, I will endure everything, suffer everything, only, for God's sake, cast me not out of your heart! I will do all that they ask, give up Lyubich, give up my property in Orsha,--I have captured rubles buried in the woods, let them take those,--if you will promise to keep faith with me as your late grandfather commands from the other world. You have saved my life, save also my soul; let me repair wrongs, let me change my life for the better; for I see that if you will desert me God will desert me, and despair will impel me to still worse deeds."

How many voices of pity rose in the soul of Olenka in defence of Pan Andrei, who can tell! Love flies swiftly, like the seed of a tree borne on by the wind; but when it grows up in the heart like a tree in the ground, you can pluck it out only with the heart. Panna Billevich was of those who love strongly with an honest heart, therefore she covered that letter of Kmita's with tears. But still she could not forget everything, forgive everything after the first word. Kmita's compunction was certainly sincere, but his soul remained wild and his nature untamed; surely it had not changed so much through those events that the future might be thought of without alarm. Not words, but deeds were needed for the future on the part of Pan Andrei. Finally, how could she say to a man who had made the whole neighborhood bloody, whose name no one on either bank of the Lauda mentioned without curses, "Come! in return for the corpses, the burning, the blood, and the tears, I will give you my love and my hand"? Therefore she answered him otherwise:--

"Since I have told you that I do not wish to know you or see you, I remain in that resolve, even though my heart be rent. Wrongs such as you have inflicted on people here are not righted either with property or money, for it is impossible to raise the dead. You have not lost property only, but reputation. Let these nobles whose houses you have burned and whom you have killed forgive you, then I will forgive you; let them receive you, and I will receive you; let them rise up for you first, then I will listen to their intercession. But as this can never be, seek happiness elsewhere; and seek the forgiveness of God before that of man, for you need it more."

Panna Aleksandra poured tears on every word of the letter; then she sealed it with the Billevich seal and took it herself to the messenger.

"Whence art thou?" asked she, measuring with her glance that strange figure, half peasant, half servant.

"From the woods, my lady."

"And where is thy master?"

"That is not permitted me to say. But he is far from here; I rode five days, and wore out my horse."

"Here is a thaler!" said Olenka. "And thy master is well?"

"He is as well, the young hero, as an aurochs."

"And he is not in hunger or poverty?"

"He is a rich lord."

"Go with God."

"I bow to my lady's feet."

"Tell thy master--wait--tell thy master--may God aid him!"

The peasant went away; and again began to pass days, weeks, without tidings of Kmita, but tidings of public affairs came worse and worse. The armies of Moscow under Hovanski spread more and more widely over the Commonwealth. Without counting the lands of the Ukraine, in the Grand Duchy of Lithuania alone, the provinces of Polotsk, Smolensk, Vitebsk, Mstislavsk, Minsk, and Novgorodek were occupied; only a part of Vilna, Brest-Litovsk, Trotsk, and the starostaship of Jmud breathed yet with free breast, but even these expected guests from day to day.

The Commonwealth had descended to the last degree of helplessness, since it was unable to offer resistance to just those forces' which hitherto had been despised and which had always been beaten. It is true that those forces were assisted by the unextinguished and re-arisen rebellion of Hmelnitski, a genuine hundred-headed hydra; but in spite of the rebellion, in spite of the exhaustion of forces in preceding wars, both statesmen and warriors gave assurance that the Grand Duchy alone might be and was in a condition not only to hurl back attack, but to carry its banners victoriously beyond its own borders. Unfortunately internal dissension stood in the way of that strength, paralyzing the efforts even of those citizens who were willing to sacrifice their lives and fortunes.

Meanwhile thousands of fugitives had taken refuge in the lands still unoccupied,--both nobles and common people. Towns, villages, and hamlets in Jmud were filled with men brought by the misfortunes of war to want and despair. The inhabitants of the towns were unable either to give lodgings to all or to give them sufficient food; therefore people died not infrequently of hunger,--namely, those of low degree. Not seldom they took by force what was refused them; hence tumults, battles, and robbery became more and more common.

The winter was excessive in its severity. At last April came, and deep snow was lying not only in the forests but on the fields. When the supplies of the preceding year were exhausted and there were no new ones yet, Famine, the brother of War, began to rage, and extended its rule more and more widely. It was not difficult for the wayfarer to find corpses of men lying in the field, at the roadside, emaciated, gnawed by wolves, which having multiplied beyond example approached the villages and hamlets in whole packs. Their howling was mingled with the cries of people for charity; for in the woods, in the fields, and around the many villages as well, there gleamed in the night-time fires at which needy wretches warmed their chilled limbs; and when any man rode past they rushed after him, begging for a copper coin, for bread, for alms, groaning, cursing, threatening all at the same time. Superstitious dread seized the minds of men. Many said that those wars so disastrous, and those misfortunes till then unexampled, were coupled with the name of the king; they explained readily that the letters "J. C. K." stamped on the coins signified not only "Joannes Casimirus Rex," but also "Initium Calamitatis Regni" (beginning of calamity for the kingdom). And if in the provinces, which were not yet occupied by war, such terror rose with disorder, it is easy to understand what happened in those which were trampled by the fiery foot of war. The whole Commonwealth was distracted, torn by parties, sick and in a fever, like a man before death. New wars were foretold, both foreign and domestic. In fact, motives were not wanting. Various powerful houses in the Commonwealth, seized by the storm of dissension, considered one another as hostile States, and with them entire lands and districts formed hostile camps.

Precisely such was the case in Lithuania, where the fierce quarrel between Yanush Radzivill, the grand hetman, and Gosyevski, full hetman, and also under-treasurer of Lithuania, became almost open war. On the side of the under-treasurer stood the powerful Sapyeha, to whom the greatness of the house of Radzivill had long been as salt in the eye. These partisans loaded the grand hetman with heavy reproaches indeed,--that wishing glory for himself alone, he had destroyed the army at Shklov and delivered the country to plunder; that he desired more than the fortune of the Commonwealth, the right for his house of sitting in the diets of the German Empire; that he even imagined for himself an independent crown, and that he persecuted the Catholics.

It came more than once to battles between the partisans of both sides, as if without the knowledge of their patrons; and the patrons made complaints against one another in Warsaw. Their quarrels were fought out in the diets; at home license was let loose and disobedience established. Such a man as Kmita might be sure of the protection of one of those magnates the moment he stood on his side against his opponent.

Meanwhile the enemy were stopped only here and there by a castle; everywhere else the advance was free and without opposition. Under such circumstances all in the Lauda region had to be on the alert and under arms, especially since there were no hetmans near by, for both hetmans were struggling with the troops of the enemy without being able to effect much, it is true, but at least worrying them with attacks and hindering approach to the provinces still unoccupied. Especially did Pavel Sapyeha show resistance and win glory. Yanush Radzivill, a famous warrior, whose name up to the defeat at Shklov had been a terror to the enemy, gained however a number of important advantages. Gosyevski now fought, now endeavored to restrain the advance of the enemy by negotiations; both leaders assembled troops from winter quarters and whencesoever they could, knowing that with spring war would blaze up afresh. But troops were few, and the treasury empty; the general militia in the provinces already occupied could not assemble, for the enemy prevented them. "It was necessary to think of that before the affair at Shklov," said the partisans of Grosyevski; "now it is too late." And in truth it was too late. The troops of the kingdom could not give aid, for they were all in the Ukraine and had grievous work against Hmelnitski, Sheremetyeff, and Buturlin.

Tidings from the Ukraine of heroic battles, of captured towns, of campaigns without parallel, strengthened failing hearts somewhat, and gave courage for defence. The names of the hetmans of the kingdom thundered with a loud glory, and with them the name of Stefan Charnetski was heard more and more frequently in the mouths of men; but glory could not take the place of troops nor serve as an auxiliary. The hetmans of Lithuania therefore retreated slowly, without ceasing to fight among themselves.

At last Radzivill was in Jmud. With him came momentary peace in Lauda. But the Calvinists, emboldened by the vicinity of their chief, raised their heads in the towns, inflicting wrongs and attacking Catholic churches. As an offset, the leaders of various volunteer bands and parties--it is unknown whose--who under the colors of Radzivill, Grosyevski, and Sapyeha had been ruining the country, vanished in the forests, discharged their ruffians, and let people breathe more freely.

Since it is easy to pass from despair to hope, a better feeling sprang up at once in Lauda. Panna Aleksandra lived quietly in Vodokty. Pan Volodyovski, who dwelt continually in Patsuneli, and just now had begun to return gradually to health, gave out the tidings that the king with newly levied troops would come in the spring, when the war would take another turn. The encouraged nobles began to go out to the fields with their ploughs. The snows too had melted, and on the birch-trees the first buds were opening. Lauda River overflowed widely. A milder sky shone over that region, and a better spirit entered the people.

Meanwhile an event took place which disturbed anew the quiet of Lauda, tore away hands from the plough, and let not the sabres be stained with red rust.

CHAPTER VIII.

Pan Volodyovski--a famous and seasoned soldier, though a young man--was living, as we have said, in Patsuneli with the patriarch of the place, Pakosh Gashtovt, who had the reputation of being the wealthiest noble among all the small brotherhood of Lauda. In fact, he had dowered richly with good silver his three daughters who had married Butryms, for he gave to each one a hundred thalers, besides cattle, and an outfit so handsome that not one noble woman or family had a better. The other three daughters were at home unmarried; and they nursed Volodyovski, whose arm was well at one time and sore at another, when wet weather appeared in the world. All the Lauda people were occupied greatly with that arm, for Lauda men had seen it working at Shklov and Sepyel, and in general they were of the opinion that it would be difficult to find a better in all Lithuania. The young colonel, therefore, was surrounded with exceeding honor in all the neighborhoods. The Gashtovts, the Domasheviches, the Gostsyeviches, the Stakyans, and with them others, sent faithfully to Patsuneli fish, mushrooms, and game for Volodyovski, and hay for his horses, so that the knight and his servants might want for nothing. Whenever he felt worse they vied with one another in going to Ponyevyej for a barber; [10] in a word, all strove to be first in serving him.

Pan Volodyovski was so much at ease that though he might have had more comforts in Kyedani and a noted physician at his call, still he remained in Patsuneli. Old Gashtovt was glad to be his host, and almost blew away the dust from before him, for it increased his importance extremely in Lauda that he had a guest so famous that he might have added to the importance of Radzivill himself.

After the defeat and expulsion of Kmita, the nobility, in love with Volodyovski, searched in their own heads for counsel, and formed the project of marrying him to Panna Aleksandra. "Why seek a husband for her through the world?" said the old men at a special meeting at which they discussed this question. "Since that traitor has so befouled himself with infamous deeds that if he is now alive he should be delivered to the hangman, the lady must cast him out of her heart, for thus was provision made in the will by a special clause. Let Pan Volodyovski marry her. As guardians we can permit that, and she will thus find an honorable cavalier, and we a neighbor and leader."

When this proposition was adopted unanimously, the old men went first to Volodyovski, who, without thinking long, agreed to everything, and then to "the lady," who with still less hesitation opposed it decisively. "My grandfather alone had the right to dispose of Lyubich," said she, "and the property cannot be taken from Pan Kmita until the courts punish him with loss of life; and as to my marrying, do not even mention it. I have too great sorrow on my mind to be able to think of such a thing. I have cast that man out of my heart; but this one, even though the most worthy, bring not hither, for I will not receive him."

There was no answer to such a resolute refusal, and the nobles returned home greatly disturbed. Less disturbed was Pan Volodyovski, and least of all the young daughters of Gashtovt,--Terka, Maryska, and Zonia. They were well-grown, blooming maidens, with hair like flax, eyes like violets, and broad shoulders. In general the Patsuneli girls were famed for beauty; when they went in a flock to church, they were like flowers of the field. Besides, old Gashtovt spared no expense on the education of his daughters. The organist from Mitruny had taught them reading and church hymns, and the eldest, Terka, to play on the lute. Having kind hearts, they nursed Volodyovski sedulously, each striving to surpass the others in watchfulness and care. People said that Maryska was in love with the young knight; but the whole truth was not in that talk, for all three of them, not she alone, were desperately in love with Pan Michael. He loved them too beyond measure, especially Maryska and Zonia, for Terka had the habit of complaining too much of the faithlessness of men.

It happened often in the long winter evenings that old Gashtovt, after drinking his punch, went to bed, and the maidens with Pan Michael sat by the chimney; the charming Terka spinning flax, mild Maryska amusing herself with picking down, and Zonia reeling thread from the spindle into skeins. But when Volodyovski began to tell of the wars or of wonders which he had seen in the great houses of magnates, work ceased, the girls gazed at him as at a rainbow, and one would cry out in astonishment, "Oh! I do not live in the world! Oh, my dears!" and another would say, "I shall not close an eye the whole night!"

Volodyovski, as he returned to health and began at times to use his sword with perfect freedom, was more joyous and told stories more willingly. A certain evening they were sitting as usual, after supper, in front of the chimney, from beneath which the light fell sharply on the entire dark room. They began to chat; the girls wanted stories, and Volodyovski begged Terka to sing something with the lute.

"Sing something yourself," answered she, pushing away the instrument which Volodyovski was handing her; "I have work. Having been in the world, you must have learned many songs."

"True, I have learned some. Let it be so to-day; I will sing first, and you afterward. Your work will not run away. If a woman had asked, you would not have refused; you are always opposed to men."

"For they deserve it."

"And do you disdain me too?"

"Oh, why should I? But sing something."

Volodyovski touched the lute; he assumed a comic air, and began to sing in falsetto,--

"I have come to such places
Where no girl will have me!--"

"Oh, that is untrue for you," interrupted Maryska, blushing as red as a raspberry.

"That's a soldier's song," said Volodyovski, "which we used to sing in winter quarters, wishing some good soul to take pity on us."

"I would be the first to take pity on you."

"Thanks to you. If that is true, then I have no reason to sing longer, and I will give the lute into worthier hands."

Terka did not reject the instrument this time, for she was moved by Volodyovski's song, in which there was more cunning indeed than truth. She struck the strings at once, and with a simpering mien began,--

"For berries of elder go not to the green wood.
Trust not a mad dug, believe not a young man.
Each man in his heart bears rank poison;
If he says that he loves thee, say No."

Volodyovski grew so mirthful that he held his sides from laughter, and cried out: "All the men are traitors? But the military, my benefactress!"

Panna Terka opened her mouth wider and sang with redoubled energy,--

"Far worse than mad dogs are they, far worse, oh, far worse!"

"Do not mind Terka; she is always that way," said Marysia. [11]

"Why not mind," asked Volodyovski, "when she speaks so ill of the whole military order that from shame I know not whither to turn my eyes?"

"You want me to sing, and then make sport of me and laugh at me," said Terka, pouting.

"I do not attack the singing, but the cruel meaning of it for the military," answered the knight. "As to the singing I must confess that in Warsaw I have not heard such remarkable trills. All that would be needed is to dress you in trousers. You might sing at St. Yan's, which is the cathedral church, and in which the king and queen have their box."

"Why dress her in trousers?" asked Zonia, the youngest, made curious by mention of Warsaw, the king, and the queen.

"For in Warsaw women do not sing in the choir, but men and young boys,--the men with voices so deep that no aurochs could bellow like them, and the boys with voices so thin that on a violin no sound could be thinner. I heard them many a time when we came, with our great and lamented voevoda of Rus, to the election of our present gracious lord. It is a real wonder, so that the soul goes out of a man. There is a host of musicians there: Forster, famous for his subtle trills, and Kapula, and Gian Battista, and Elert, a master at the lute, and Marek, and Myelchevski,--beautiful composers. When all these are performing together in the church, it is as if you were listening to choirs of seraphim in the flesh."

"Oh, that is as true as if living!" said Marysia, placing her hands together.

"And the king,--have you seen him often?" asked Zonia.

"I have spoken with him as with you. After the battle of Berestechko he pressed my head. He is a valiant lord, and so kind that whoso has once seen him must love him."

"We love him without having seen him. Has he the crown always on his head?"

"If he were to go around every day in the crown, his head would need to be iron. The crown rests in the church, from which its importance increases; but his Grace the King wears a black cap studded with diamonds from which light flashes through the whole castle."

"They say that the castle of the king is even grander than that at Kyedani?"

"That at Kyedani! The Kyedani castle is a mere plaything in comparison. The king's castle is a tremendous building, all walled in so that you cannot see a stick of wood. Around are two rows of chambers, one more splendid than the other. In them you can see different wars and victories painted with brushes on the wall,--such as the battles of Sigismund III. and Vladislav; a man could not satisfy himself with looking at them, for everything is as if living. The wonder is that they do not move, and that those who are fighting do not shout. But not even the best artist can paint men to shout. Some chambers are all gold; chairs and benches covered with brocade or cloth of gold, tables of marble and alabaster, and the caskets, bottle-cases, clocks showing the hour of day and night, could not be described on an ox-hide. The king and queen walk through those chambers and delight themselves in plenty; in the evening they have a theatre for their still greater amusement--"

"What is a theatre?"

"How can I tell you? It is a place where they play comedies and exhibit Italian dances in a masterly manner. It is a room so large that no church is the equal of it, all with beautiful columns. On one side sit those who wish to see, and on the other the arts are exhibited. Curtains are raised and let down; some are turned with screws to different sides. Darkness and clouds are shown at one moment; at another pleasant light. Above is the sky with the sun or the stars; below you may see at times hell dreadful--"

"Oh, God save us!" cried the girls.

"--with devils. Sometimes the boundless sea; on it ships and sirens. Some persons come down from the skies; others rise out of the earth."

"But I should not like to see hell," cried Zonia, "and it is a wonder to me that people do not run away from such a terrible sight."

"Not only do they not run away, but they applaud from pleasure," said Volodyovski; "for it is all pretended, not real, and those who take farewell do not go away. There is no evil spirit in the affair, only the invention of men. Even bishops come with his Grace the King, and various dignitaries who go with the king afterward and sit down to a feast before sleeping."

"And what do they do in the morning and during the day?"

"That depends on their wishes. When they rise in the morning they take a bath. There is a room in which there is no floor, only a tin tank shining like silver, and in the tank water."

"Water, in a room--have you heard?"

"It is true; and it comes and goes as they wish. It can be warm or altogether cold; for there are pipes with spigots, running here and there. Turn a spigot and the water runs till it is possible to swim in the room as in a lake. No king has such a castle as our gracious lord, that is known, and foreign proverbs tell the same. Also no king reigns over such a worthy people; for though there are various polite nations on earth, still God in his mercy has adorned ours beyond others."

"Our king is happy!" sighed Terka.

"It is sure that he would be happy were it not for unfortunate wars which press down the Commonwealth in return for our discords and sins. All this rests on the shoulders of the king, and besides at the diets they reproach him for our faults. And why is he to blame because people will not obey him? Grievous times have come on the country,--such grievous times as have not been hitherto. Our most despicable enemy now despises us,--us who till recently carried on victorious wars against the Emperor of Turkey. This is the way that God punishes pride. Praise be to Him that my arm works well in its joints,--for it is high time to remember the country and move to the field. 'Tis a sin to be idle in time of such troubles."

"Do not mention going away."

"It is difficult to do otherwise. It is pleasant for me here among you; but the better it is, the worse it is. Let men in the Diet give wise reasons, but a soldier longs for the field. While there is life there is service. After death God, who looks into the heart, will reward best those who serve not for advancement, but through love of the country; and indeed the number of such is decreasing continually, and that is why the black hour has come."

Marysia's eyes began to grow moist; at last they were filled with tears which flowed down her rosy cheeks. "You will go and forget us, and we shall pine away here. Who in this place will defend us from attack?"

"I go, but I shall preserve my gratitude. It is rare to find such honest people as in Patsuneli. Are you always afraid of this Kmita?"

"Of course. Mothers frighten their children with him as with a werewolf."

"He will not come back, and even if he should he will not have with him those wild fellows, who, judging from what people say, were worse than he. It is a pity indeed that such a good soldier stained his reputation and lost his property."

"And the lady."

"And the lady. They say much good in her favor."

"Poor thing! for whole days she just cries and cries."

"H'm!" said Volodyovski; "but is she not crying for Kmita?"

"Who knows?" replied Marysia.

"So much the worse for her, for he will not come back. The hetman sent home a part of the Lauda men, and those forces are here now. We wanted to cut him down at once without the court. He must know that the Lauda men have returned, and he will not show even his nose."

"Likely our men must march again," said Terka, "for they received only leave to come home for a short time."

"Eh!" said Volodyovski, "the hetman let them come, for there is no money in the treasury. It is pure despair! When people are most needed they have to be sent away. But good-night! it is time to sleep, and let none of you dream of Pan Kmita with a fiery sword."

Volodyovski rose from the bench and prepared to leave the room, but had barely made a step toward the closet when suddenly there was a noise in the entrance and a shrill voice began to cry outside the door--

"Hei there! For God's mercy! open quickly, quickly!"

The girls were terribly frightened. Volodyovski sprang for his sabre to the closet, but had not been able to get it when Terka opened the door. An unknown man burst into the room and threw himself at the feet of the knight.

"Rescue, serene Colonel!--The lady is carried away!"

"What lady?"

"In Vodokty."

"Kmita!" cried Volodyovski.

"Kmita!" screamed the girls.

"Kmita!" repeated the messenger.

"Who art thou?" asked Volodyovski.

"The manager in Vodokty."

"We know him," said Terka; "he brought herbs for you."

Meanwhile the drowsy old Gashtovt came forth from behind the stove, and in the door appeared two attendants of Pan Volodyovski whom the uproar had drawn to the room.

"Saddle the horses!" cried Volodyovski. "Let one of you hurry to the Butryms, the other give a horse to me!"

"I have been already at the Butryms," said the manager, "for they are nearer to us; they sent me to your grace."

"When was the lady carried away?" asked Volodyovski.

"Just now--the servants are fighting yet--I rushed for a horse."

Old Gashtovt rubbed his eyes. "What's that? The lady carried off?"

"Yes; Kmita carried her off," answered Volodyovski. "Let us go to the rescue!" Then he turned to the messenger: "Hurry to the Domasheviches; let them come with muskets."

"Now, my kids," cried the old man suddenly to his daughters, "hurry to the village, wake up the nobles, let them take their sabres! Kmita has carried off the lady--is it possible--God forgive him, the murderer, the ruffian! Is it possible?"

"Let us go to rouse them," said Volodyovski; "that will be quicker! Come; the horses are ready, I hear them."

In a moment they mounted, as did also the two attendants, Ogarek and Syruts. All pushed on their way between the cottages of the village, striking the doors and windows, and crying with sky-piercing voices: "To your sabres, to your sabres! The lady of Vodokty is carried away! Kmita is in the neighborhood!"

Hearing these cries, this or that man rushed forth from his cottage, looked to see what was happening, and when he had learned what the matter was, fell to shouting himself, "Kmita is in the neighborhood; the lady is carried away!" And shouting in this fashion, he rushed headlong to the out-buildings to saddle his horse, or to his cottage to feel in the dark for his sabre on the wall. Every moment more voices cried, "Kmita is in the neighborhood!" There was a stir in the village, lights began to shine, the cry of women was heard, the barking of dogs. At last the nobles came out on the road,--some mounted, some on foot. Above the multitude of heads glittered in the night sabres, pikes, darts, and even iron forks.

Volodyovski surveyed the company, sent some of them immediately in different directions, and moved forward himself with the rest.

The mounted men rode in front, those on foot followed, and they marched toward Volmontovichi to join the Butryms. The hour was ten in the evening, and the night clear, though the moon had not risen. Those of the nobles whom the grand hetman had sent recently from the war dropped into ranks at once; the others, namely the infantry, advanced with less regularity, making a clatter with their weapons, talking and yawning aloud, at times cursing that devil of a Kmita who had robbed them of pleasant rest. In this fashion they reached Volmontovichi, at the edge of which an armed band pushed out to meet them.

"Halt! who goes?" called voices from that band.

"The Gashtovts!"

"We are the Butryms. The Domasheviches have come already."

"Who is leading you?" asked Volodyovski.

"Yuzva the Footless at the service of the colonel."

"Have you news?"

"He took her to Lyubich. They went through the swamp to avoid Volmontovichi."

"To Lyubich?" asked Volodyovski, in wonder. "Can he think of defending himself there? Lyubich is not a fortress, is it?"

"It seems he trusts in his strength. There are two hundred with him. No doubt he wants to take the property from Lyubich; they have wagons and a band of led horses. It must be that he did not know of our return from the army, for he acts very boldly."

"That is good for us!" said Volodyovski. "He will not escape this time. How many guns have you?"

"We, the Butryms, have thirty; the Domasheviches twice as many."

"Very good. Let fifty men with muskets go with you to defend the passage in the swamps, quickly; the rest will come with me. Remember the axes."

"According to command."

There was a movement; the little division under Yuzva the Footless went forward at a trot to the swamp. A number of tens of Butryms who had been sent for other nobles now came up.

"Are the Gostsyeviches to be seen?" asked Volodyovski.

"Yes, Colonel. Praise be to God!" cried the newly arrived. "The Gostsyeviches are coming; they can be heard through the woods. You know that they carried her to Lyubich?"

"I know. He will not go far with her."

There was indeed one danger to his insolent venture on which Kmita had not reckoned; he knew not that a considerable force of the nobles had just returned home. He judged that the villages were as empty as at the time of his first stay in Lyubich; while on the present occasion counting the Gostsyeviches, without the Stakyans, who could not come up in season, Volodyovski was able to lead against him about three hundred sabres held by men accustomed to battle and trained.

In fact, more and more nobles joined Volodyovski as he advanced. At last came the Gostsyeviches, who had been expected till that moment. Volodyovski drew up the division, and his heart expanded at sight of the order and ease with which the men stood in ranks. At the first glance it was clear that they were soldiers, not ordinary untrained nobles. Volodyovski rejoiced for another reason; he thought to himself that soon he would lead them to more distant places.

They moved then on a swift march toward Lyubich by the pine-woods through which Kmita had rushed the winter before. It was well after midnight. The moon sailed out at last in the sky, and lighting the woods, the road, and the marching warriors, broke its pale rays on the points of the pikes, and was reflected on the gleaming sabres. The nobles talked in a low voice of the unusual event which had dragged them from their beds.

"Various people have been going around here," said one of the Domasheviches; "we thought they were deserters, but they were surely his spies."

"Of course. Every day strange minstrels used to visit Vodokty as if for alms," said others.

"And what kind of soldiers has Kmita?"

"The servants in Vodokty say they are Cossacks. It is certain that Kmita has made friends with Hovanski or Zolotarenko. Hitherto he was a murderer, now he is an evident traitor."

"How could he bring Cossacks thus far?"

"With such a great band it is not easy to pass. Our first good company would have stopped him on the road."

"Well, they might go through the forests. Besides, are there few lords travelling with domestic Cossacks? Who can tell them from the enemy? If these men are asked they will say that they are domestic Cossacks."

"He will defend himself," said one of the Gostsyeviches, "for he is a brave and resolute man; but our colonel will be a match for him."

"The Butryms too have vowed that even if they have to fall one on the other, he will not leave there alive. They are the most bitter against him."

"But if we kill him, from whom will they recover their losses? Better take him alive and give him to justice."

"What is the use in thinking of courts now when all have lost their heads? Do you know that people say war may come from the Swedes?"

"May God preserve us from that! The Moscow power and Hmelnitski at present; only the Swedes are wanting, and then the last day of the Commonwealth."

At this moment Volodyovski riding in advance turned and said, "Quiet there, gentlemen!"

The nobles grew silent, for Lyubich was in sight. In a quarter of an hour they had come within less than forty rods of the building. All the windows were illuminated; the light shone into the yard, which was full of armed men and horses. Nowhere sentries, no precautions,--it was evident that Kmita trusted too much in his strength. When he had drawn still nearer, Pan Volodyovski with one glance recognized the Cossacks against whom he had warred so much during the life of the great Yeremi, and later under Radzivill.

"If those are strange Cossacks, then that ruffian has passed the limit."

He looked farther; brought his whole party to a halt. There was a terrible bustle in the court. Some Cossacks were giving light with torches; others were running in every direction, coming out of the house and going in again, bringing out things, packing bags into the wagons; others were leading horses from the stable, driving cattle from the stalls. Cries, shouts, commands, crossed one another in every direction. The gleam of torches lighted as it were the moving of a tenant to a new estate on St. John's Eve.

Kryshtof, the oldest among the Domasheviches, pushed up to Volodyovski and said, "They want to pack all Lyubich into wagons."

"They will take away," answered Volodyovski, "neither Lyubich nor their own skins. I do not recognize Kmita, who is an experienced soldier. There is not a single sentry."

"Because he has great force,--it seems to me more than three hundred strong. If we had not returned he might have passed with the wagons through all the villages."

"Is this the only road to the house?" asked Volodyovski.

"The only one, for in the rear are ponds and swamps."

"That is well. Dismount!"

Obedient to this command, the nobles sprang from their saddles. The rear ranks of infantry deployed in a long line, and began to surround the house and the buildings. Volodyovski with the main division advanced directly on the gate.

"Wait the command!" said he, in a low voice. "Fire not before the order."

A few tens of steps only separated the nobles from the gate when they were seen at last from the yard. Men sprang at once to the fence, bent forward, and peering carefully into the darkness, called threateningly, "Hei! Who are there?"

"Halt!" cried Volodyovski; "fire!"

Shots from all the guns which the nobles carried thundered together; but the echo had not come back from the building when the voice of Volodyovski was heard again: "On the run!"

"Kill! slay!" cried the Lauda men, rushing forward like a torrent.

The Cossacks answered with shots, but they had not time to reload. The throng of nobles rushed against the gate, which soon fell before the pressure of armed men. A struggle began to rage in the yard, among the wagons, horses, and bags. The powerful Butryms, the fiercest in hand-to-hand conflict and the most envenomed against Kmita, advanced in line. They went like a herd of stags bursting through a growth of young trees, breaking, trampling, destroying, and cutting wildly. After them rolled the Domasheviches and the Gostsyeviches.

Kmita's Cossacks defended themselves manfully from behind the wagons and packs; they began to fire too from all the windows of the house and from the roof,--but rarely, for the trampled torches were quenched, and it was difficult to distinguish their own from the enemy. After a while the Cossacks were pushed from the yard and the house to the stables; cries for quarter were heard. The nobles had triumphed.

But when they were alone in the yard, fire from the house increased at once. All the windows were bristling with muskets, and a storm of bullets began to fall on the yard. The greater part of the Cossacks had taken refuge in the house.

"To the doors!" cried Volodyovski.

In fact, the discharges from the windows and from the roof could not injure those at the very walls. The position, however, of the besiegers was difficult. They could not think of storming the windows, for fire would greet them straight in the face. Volodyovski therefore commanded to hew down the doors. But that was not easy, for they were bolts rather than doors, made of oak pieces fixed crosswise and fastened with many gigantic nails, on the strong heads of which axes were dented without breaking the doors. The most powerful men pushed then from time to time with their shoulders, but in vain. Behind the doors wore iron bars, and besides they were supported inside by props. But the Butryms hewed with rage. At the doors of the kitchen leading also to the storehouse the Domasheviches and Gashtovts were storming.

After vain efforts of an hour the men at the axes were relieved. Some cross-pieces had fallen, but in place of them appeared gun-barrels. Shots sounded again. Two Butryms fell to the ground with pierced breasts. The others, instead of being put to disorder, hewed still more savagely.

By command of Volodyovski the openings were stopped with bundles of coats. Now in the direction of the road new shouts were heard from the Stakyans, who had come to the aid of their brethren; and following them were armed peasants from Vodokty.

The arrival of these reinforcements had evidently disturbed the besieged, for straightway a voice behind the door called loudly: "Stop there! do not hew! listen! Stop, a hundred devils take you! let us talk."

Volodyovski gave orders to stop the work and asked; "Who is speaking?"

"The banneret of Orsha, Kmita; and with whom am I speaking?"

"Col. Michael Volodyovski."

"With the forehead!" answered the voice from behind the door.

"There is no time for greetings. What is your wish?"

"It would be more proper for me to ask what you want. You do not know me, nor I you; why attack me?"

"Traitor!" cried Volodyovski. "With me are the men of Lauda who have returned from the war, and they have accounts with you for robbery, for blood shed without cause and for the lady whom you have carried away. But do you know what *raptus puellæ* means? You must yield your life."

A moment of silence followed.

"You would not call me traitor a second time," said Kmita, "were it not for the door between us."

"Open it, then! I do not hinder."

"More than one dog from Lauda will cover himself with his legs before it is open. You will not take me alive."

"Then we will drag you out dead, by the hair. All one to us!"

"Listen with care, note what I tell you! If you do not let us go, I have a barrel of powder here, and the match is burning already. I'll blow up the house and all who are in it with myself, so help me God! Come now and take me!"

This time a still longer silence followed. Volodyovski sought an answer in vain. The nobles began to look at one another in fear. There was so much wild energy in the words of Kmita that all believed his threat. The whole victory might be turned into dust by one spark, and Panna Billevich lost forever.

"For God's sake!" muttered one of the Butryms, "he is a madman. He is ready to do what he says."

Suddenly a happy thought came to Volodyovski, as it seemed to him. "There is another way!" cried he. "Meet me, traitor, with a sabre. If you put me down, you will go away in freedom."

For a time there was no answer. The hearts of the Lauda men beat unquietly.

"With a sabre?" asked Kmita, at length. "Can that be?"

"If you are not afraid, it will be."

"The word of a cavalier that I shall go away in freedom?"

"The word--"

"Impossible!" cried a number of voices among the Butryms.

"Quiet, a hundred devils!" roared Volodyovski; "if not, then let him blow you up with himself."

The Butryms were silent; after a while one of them said, "Let it be as you wish."

"Well, what is the matter there?" asked Kmita, derisively. "Do the gray coats agree?"

"Yes, and they will take oath on their swords, if you wish."

"Let them take oath."

"Come together, gentlemen, come together!" cried Volodyovski to the nobles who were standing under the walls and surrounding the whole house.

After a while all collected at the main door, and soon the news that Kmita wanted to blow himself up with powder spread on every side. They were as if petrified with terror. Meanwhile Volodyovski raised his voice and said amid silence like that of the grave,--

"I take you all present here to witness that I have challenged Pan Kmita, the banneret of Orsha, to a duel, and I have promised that if he puts me down he shall go hence in freedom, without obstacle from you; to this you must swear on your sword-hilts, in the name of God and the holy cross--"

"But wait!" cried Kmita,--"in freedom with all my men, and I take the lady with me."

"The lady will remain here," answered Volodyovski, "and the men will go as prisoners to the nobles."

"That cannot be."

"Then blow yourself up with powder! We have already mourned for her; as to the men, ask them what they prefer."

Silence followed.

"Let it be so," said Kmita, after a time. "If I do not take her to-day, I will in a month. You will not hide her under the ground! Take the oath!"

"Take the oath!" repeated Volodyovski.

"We swear by the Most High God and the Holy Cross. Amen!"

"Well, come out, come out!" cried Volodyovski.

"You are in a hurry to the other world?"

"No matter, no matter, only come out quickly."

The iron bars holding the door on the inside began to groan.

Volodyovski pushed back, and with him the nobles, to make room. Soon the door opened, and in it appeared Pan Andrei, tall, straight as a poplar. The dawn was already coming, and the first pale light of day fell on his daring, knightly, and youthful face. He stopped in the door, looked boldly on the crowd of nobles, and said,--

"I have trusted in you. God knows whether I have done well, but let that go. Who here is Pan Volodyovski?"

The little colonel stepped forward. "I am!" answered he.

"Oh! you are not like a giant," said Kmita, with sarcastic reference to Volodyovski's stature, "I expected to find a more considerable figure, though I must confess you are evidently a soldier of experience."

"I cannot say the same of you, for you have neglected sentries. If you are the same at the sabre as at command, I shall not have work."

"Where shall we fight?" asked Kmita, quickly.

"Here,--the yard is as level as a table."

"Agreed! Prepare for death."

"Are you so sure?"

"It is clear that you have never been in Orsha, since you doubt. Not only am I sure, but I am sorry, for I have heard of you as a splendid soldier. Therefore I say for the last time, let me go! We do not know each other; why should we stand the one in the way of the other? Why attack me? The maiden is mine by the will, as well as this property; and God knows I am only seeking my own. It is true that I cut down the nobles in Volmontovichi, but let God decide who committed the first wrong. Whether my officers were men of violence or not, we need not discuss; it is enough that they did no harm to any one here, and they were slaughtered to the last man because they wanted to dance with girls in a public house. Well, let blood answer blood! After that my soldiers were cut to pieces. I swear by the wounds of God that I came to these parts without evil intent, and how was I received? But let wrong balance wrong, I will still add from my own and make losses good in neighbor fashion. I prefer that to another way."

"And what kind of people have you here? Where did you get these assistants?" asked Volodyovski.

"Where I got them I got them. I did not bring them against the country, but to obtain my own rights."

"Is that the kind of man you are? So for private affairs you have joined the enemy. And with what have you paid him for this service, if not with treason? No, brother, I should not hinder you from coming to terms with the nobles, but to call in the enemy is another thing. You will not creep out. Stand up now, stand up, or I shall say that you are a coward, though you give yourself out as a master from Orsha."

"You would have it," said Kmita, taking position.

But Volodyovski did not hurry, and not taking his sabre out yet, he looked around on the sky. Day was already coming in the east. The first golden and azure stripes were extended in a belt of light, but in the yard it was still gloomy enough, and just in front of the house complete darkness reigned.

"The day begins well," said Volodyovski, "but the sun will not rise soon. Perhaps you would wish to have light?"

"It is all one to me."

"Gentlemen!" cried Volodyovski, turning to the nobles, "go for some straw and for torches; it will be clearer for us in this Orsha dance."

The nobles, to whom this humorous tone of the young colonel gave wonderful consolation, rushed quickly to the kitchen. Some of them fell to collecting the torches trampled at the time of the battle, and in a little while nearly fifty red flames were gleaming in the semi-darkness of the early morning.

Volodyovski showed them with his sabre to Kmita. "Look, a regular funeral procession!"

And Kmita answered at once: "They are burying a colonel, so there must be parade."

"You are a dragon!"

Meanwhile the nobles formed in silence a circle around the knights, and raised the burning torches aloft; behind them others took their places, curious and disquieted; in the centre the opponents measured each other with their eyes. A grim silence began; only burned coals fell with a crackle to the ground. Volodyovski was as lively as a goldfinch on a bright morning.

"Begin!" said Kmita.

The first clash raised an echo in the heart of every onlooker. Volodyovski struck as if unwillingly; Kmita warded and struck in his turn; Volodyovski warded. The dry clash grew more rapid. All held breath. Kmita attacked with fury. Volodyovski put his left hand behind his back and stood quietly, making very careless, slight, almost imperceptible movements; it seemed that he wished merely to defend himself, and at the same time spare his opponent. Sometimes he pushed a short step backward, again he advanced; apparently he was studying the skill of Kmita. Kmita was growing heated; Volodyovski was cool as a master testing his pupil, and all the time calmer and calmer. At last, to the great surprise of the nobles, he said,--

"Now let us talk; it will not last long. Ah, ha! is that the Orsha method? 'Tis clear that you must have threshed peas there, for you strike like a man with a flail. Terrible blows! Are they really the best in Orsha? That thrust is in fashion only among tribunal police. This is from Courland, good to chase dogs with. Look to the end of your sabre! Don't bend your hand so, for see what will happen! Raise your sabre!"

Volodyovski pronounced the last words with emphasis; at the same time he described a half-circle, drew the hand and sabre toward him, and before the spectators understood what "raise" meant, Kmita's sabre, like a needle pulled from a thread, flew above Volodyovski's head and fell behind his shoulders; then he said,--

"That is called shelling a sabre."

Kmita stood pale, wild-eyed, staggering, astonished no less than the nobles of Lauda; the little colonel pushed to one side, and repeated again,--

"Take your sabre!"

For a time it seemed as if Kmita would rush at him with naked hands. He was just ready for the spring, when Volodyovski put his hilt to his own breast, presenting the point. Kmita rushed to take his own sabre, and fell with it again on his terrible opponent.

A loud murmur rose from the circle of spectators, and the ring grew closer and closer. Kmita's Cossacks thrust their heads between the shoulders of the nobles, as if they had lived all their lives in the best understanding with them. Involuntarily shouts were wrested from the mouths of the onlookers; at times an outburst of unrestrained, nervous laughter was heard; all acknowledged a master of masters.

Volodyovski amused himself cruelly like a cat with a mouse, and seemed to work more and more carelessly with the sabre. He took his left hand from behind his back and thrust it into his trousers' pocket. Kmita was foaming at the mouth, panting heavily; at last hoarse words came from his throat through his set lips,--

"Finish--spare the shame!"

"Very well!" replied Volodyovski.

A short terrible whistle was heard, then a smothered cry. At the same moment Kmita threw open his arms, his sabre dropped to the ground, and he fell on his face at the feet of the colonel.

"He lives!" said Volodyovski; "he has not fallen on his back!" And doubling the skirt of Kmita's coat, he began to wipe his sabre.

The nobles shouted with one voice, and in those shouts thundered with increasing clearness: "Finish the traitor! finish him! cut him to pieces!"

A number of Butryms ran up with drawn sabres. Suddenly something wonderful happened,--and one would have said that little Volodyovski had grown tall before their eyes: the sabre of the nearest Butrym flew out of his hand after Kmita's, as if a whirlwind had caught it, and Volodyovski shouted with flashing eyes,--

"Stand back, stand back! He is mine now, not yours! Be off!"

All were silent, fearing the anger of that man; and he said: "I want no shambles here! As nobles you should understand knightly customs, and not slaughter the wounded. Enemies do not do that, and how could a man in a duel kill his prostrate opponent?"

"He is a traitor!" muttered one of the Butryms. "It is right to kill such a man."

"If he is a traitor he should be given to the hetman to suffer punishment and serve as an example to others. But as I have said, he is mine now, not yours. If he recovers you will be free to get your rights before a court, and it will be easier to obtain satisfaction from a living than a dead man. Who here knows how to dress wounds?"

"Krysh Domashevich. He has attended to all in Lauda for years."

"Let him dress the man at once, then take him to bed, and I will go to console the ill-fated lady."

So saying, Volodyovski put his sabre into the scabbard. The nobles began to seize and bind Kmita's men, who henceforth were to plough land in the villages. They surrendered without resistance; only a few who had escaped through the rear windows of the house ran toward the ponds, but they fell into the hands of the Stakyans who were stationed there. At the same time the nobles fell to plundering the wagons, in which they found quite a plentiful booty; some of them gave advice to sack the house, but they feared Pan Volodyovski, and perhaps the presence of Panna Billevich restrained the most daring. Their own killed, among whom were three Butryms and two Domasheviches, the nobles put into wagons, so as to bury them according to Christian rites. They ordered the peasants to dig a ditch for Kmita's dead behind the garden.

Volodyovski in seeking the lady burst through the whole house, and found her at last in the treasure-chamber situated in a corner to which a low and narrow door led from the sleeping-room. It was a small chamber, with narrow, strongly barred windows, built in a square and with such mighty walls, that Volodyovski saw at once that even if Kmita had blown up the house with powder that room would have surely remained unharmed. This gave him a better opinion of Kmita. The lady was sitting on a chest not far from the door, with her head drooping, and her face almost hidden by her hair. She did not raise it when she heard the knight coming. She thought beyond doubt that it was Kmita himself or some one of his people. Pan Volodyovski stood in the door, coughed once, a second time, and seeing no result from that, said,--

"My lady, you are free!"

"From under the drooping hair blue eyes looked at the knight, and then a comely face appeared, though pale and as it were not conscious. Volodyovski was hoping for thanks, an outburst of gladness; but the lady sat motionless, distraught, and merely looked at him. Therefore the knight spoke again,--

"Come to yourself, my lady! God has regarded innocence,--you are free, and can return to Vodokty."

This time there was more consciousness in the look of Panna Billevich. She rose from the chest, shook back her hair, and asked, "Who are you?"

"Michael Volodyovski, colonel of dragoons with the voevoda of Vilna."

"Did I hear a battle--shots? Tell me."

"Yes. We came to save you."

She regained her senses completely. "I thank you," said she hurriedly, with a low voice, through which a mortal disquiet was breaking. "But what happened to him?"

"To Kmita? Fear not, my lady! He is lying lifeless in the yard; and without praising myself I did it."

Volodyovski uttered this with a certain boastfulness; but if he expected admiration he deceived himself terribly. She said not a word, but tottered and began to seek support behind with her hands. At last she sat heavily on the same chest from which she had risen a moment before.

The knight sprang to her quickly: "What is the matter, my lady?"

"Nothing, nothing--wait, permit me. Then is Pan Kmita killed?"

"What is Pan Kmita to me?" interrupted Volodyovski; "it is a question here of you."

That moment her strength came back; for she rose again, and looking him straight in the eyes, screamed with anger, impatience, and despair: "By the living God, answer! Is he killed?"

"Pan Kmita is wounded," answered the astonished Volodyovski.

"Is he alive?"

"He is alive."

"It is well! I thank you."

And with step still tottering she moved toward the door. Volodyovski stood for a while moving his mustaches violently and shaking his head; then he muttered to himself, "Does she thank me because Kmita is wounded, or because he is alive?"

He followed Olenka, and found her in the adjoining bed room standing in the middle of it as if turned to stone. Four nobles were bearing in at that moment Pan Kmita; the first two advancing sidewise appeared in the door, and between them hung toward the floor the pale head of Pan Andrei, with closed eyes, and clots of black blood in his hair.

"Slowly," said Krysh Domashevich, walking behind, "slowly across the threshold. Let some one hold his head. Slowly!"

"With what can we hold it when our hands are full?" answered those in front.

At that moment Panna Aleksandra approached them, pale as was Kmita himself, and placed both hands under his lifeless head.

"This is the lady," said Krysh Domashevich.

"It is I. Be careful!" answered she, in a low voice.

Volodyovski looked on, and his mustaches quivered fearfully.

Meanwhile they placed Kmita on the bed. Krysh Domashevich began to wash his head with water; then he fixed a plaster previously prepared to the wound, and said,--

"Now let him lie quietly. Oh, that's an iron head not to burst from such a blow! He may recover, for he is young. But he got it hard."

Then he turned to Olenka: "Let me wash your hands,--here is water. A kind heart is in you that you were not afraid to put blood on yourself for that man."

Speaking thus, he wiped her palms with a cloth; but she grew pale and changed in the eyes.

Volodyovski sprang to her again: "There is nothing here for you, my lady. You have shown Christian charity to an enemy; return home." And he offered her his arm.

She however, did not look at him, but turning to Krysh Domashevich, said, "Pan Kryshtof, conduct me."

Both went out, and Volodyovski followed them. In the yard the nobles began to shout at sight of her, and cry, "Vivat!" But she went forward, pale, staggering, with compressed lips, and with fire in her eyes.

"Long life to our lady! Long life to our colonel!" cried powerful voices.

An hour later Volodyovski returned at the head of the Lauda men toward the villages. The sun had risen already; the early morning in the world was gladsome, a real spring morning. The Lauda men clattered forward in a formless crowd along the highway, discussing the events of the night and praising Volodyovski to the skies; but he rode on thoughtful and silent. Those eyes looking from behind the dishevelled hair did not leave his mind, nor that slender form, imposing though bent by grief and pain.

"It is a marvel what a wonder she is," said he to himself,--"a real princess! I have saved her honor and surely her life, for though the powder would not have blown up the treasure-room she would have died of pure fright. She ought to be grateful. But who can understand a fair head? She looked on me as on some serving-lad, I know not whether from haughtiness or perplexity."

CHAPTER IX.

These thoughts did not let Volodyovski sleep on the night following. For a number of days he was thinking continually of Panna Aleksandra, and saw that she had dropped deeply into his heart. Besides, the Lauda nobles wished to bring about a marriage between them. It is true that she had refused him without hesitation, but at that time she neither knew him nor had seen him. Now it was something quite different. He had wrested her in knightly fashion from the hands of a man of violence, had exposed himself to bullets and sabres, had captured her like a fortress. Whose is she, if not his? Can she refuse him anything, even her hand? Well, shall he not try? Perhaps affection has begun in her from gratitude, since it happens often in the world that the rescued lady gives straightway her hand to her rescuer. If she has not conceived an affection for him as yet, it behooves him all the more to exert himself in the matter.

"But if she remembers and loves the other man still?"

"It cannot be," repeated Volodyovski to himself; "if she had not rejected him, he would not have taken her by force. She showed, it is true, uncommon kindness to him; but it is a woman's work to take pity on the wounded, even if they are enemies. She is young, without guardianship; it is time for her to marry. It is clear that she has no vocation for the cloister, or she would have entered one already. There has been time enough. Men will annoy such a comely lady continually,-- some for her fortune, others for her beauty, and still others for her high blood. Oh, a defence the reality of which she can see with her own eyes will be dear to her. It is time too for thee to settle down, my dear Michael!" said Volodyovski to himself. "Thou art young yet, but the years hurry swiftly. Thou wilt win not fortune in service, but rather more wounds in thy skin, and to thy giddy life will come an end."

Here through the memory of Pan Volodyovski passed a whole line of young ladies after whom he had sighed in his life. Among them were some very beautiful and of high blood, but one more charming and distinguished there was not. Besides, the people of these parts exalted that family and that lady, and from her eyes there looked such honesty that may God give no worse wife to the best man.

Pan Volodyovski felt that a prize was meeting him which might not come a second time, and this the more since he had rendered the lady such uncommon service. "Why delay?" said he to himself. "What better can I wait for? I must try."

Pshaw! but war is at hand. His arm was well. It was a shame for a knight to go courting when his country was stretching forth its hands imploring deliverance. Pan Michael had the heart of an honest soldier; and though he had served almost from boyhood, though he had taken part in nearly all the wars of his time, he knew what he owed his country, and he dreamed not of rest.

Precisely because he had served his country not for gain, reward, or praise, but from his soul, had he in that regard a clean conscience, he felt his worth, and that gave him solace. "Others were frolicking, but I was fighting," thought he. "The Lord God will reward the little soldier, and will help him this time."

But he saw that soon there would be no time for courting; there was need to act promptly, and put everything on the hazard at once,--to make a proposal on the spot, and either marry after short bans or eat a watermelon. [12] "I have eaten more than one; I'll eat another this time," muttered Volodyovski, moving his yellow mustaches. "What harm will it do?"

But there was one side to this sudden decision which did not please him. He put the question to himself if going with a visit so soon after saving the lady he would not be like an importunate creditor who wishes a debt to be paid with usury and as quickly as possible. Perhaps it will not be in knightly fashion? Nonsense! for what can gratitude be asked, if not for service? And if this haste does not please the heart of the lady, if she looks askance at him, why, he can say to her, "Gracious lady, I would have come courting one year, and gazed at you as if I were nearsighted; but I am a soldier, and the trumpets are sounding for battle!"

"So I'll go," said Pan Volodyovski.

But after a while another thought entered his head: if she says, "Go to war, noble soldier, and after the war you will visit me during one year and look at me like a nearsighted man, for I will not give in a moment my soul and my body to one whom I know not!"

Then all will be lost! That it would be lost Pan Volodyovski felt perfectly; for leaving aside the lady whom in the interval some other man might marry, Volodyovski was not sure of his own constancy. Conscience declared that in him love was kindled like straw, but quenched as quickly.

Then all will be lost! And then wander on farther, thou soldier, a vagrant from one camp to another, from battle to battle, with no roof in the world, with no living soul of thy kindred! Search the four corners of earth when the war will be over, not knowing a place for thy heart save the barracks!

At last Volodyovski knew not what to do. It had become in a certain fashion narrow and stifling for him in the Patsuneli house; he took his cap therefore to go out on the road and enjoy the May sun. On the threshold he came upon one of Kmita's men taken prisoner, who in the division of spoils had come to old Pakosh, The Cossack was warming himself in the sun and playing on a bandura.

"What art thou doing here? asked Volodyovski.

"I am playing," answered the Cossack, raising his thin face,

"Whence art thou?" asked Volodyovski, glad to have some interruption to his thoughts.

"From afar, from the Viahla."

"Why not run away like the rest of thy comrades? Oh, such kind of sons! The nobles spared your lives in Lyubich so as to have laborers, and your comrades all ran away as soon as the ropes were removed."

"I will not run away. I'll die here like a dog."

"So it has pleased thee here?"

"He runs away who feels better in the field; it is better for me here. I had my leg shot through, and the old man's daughter here dressed it, and she spoke a kind word. Such a beauty I have not seen before with my eyes. Why should I go away?"

"Which one pleased thee so?"

"Maryska."

"And so thou wilt remain?"

"If I die, they will carry me out; if not, I will remain."

"Dost thou think to earn Pakosh's daughter?"

"I know not."

"He would give death to such a poor fellow before he would his daughter."

"I have gold pieces buried in the woods," said the Cossack,--"two purses."

"From robbery?"

"From robbery."

"Even if thou hadst a pot of gold, thou art a peasant and Pakosh is a noble."

"I am an attendant boyar."

"If thou art an attendant boyar, thou art worse than a peasant, for thou'rt a traitor. How couldst thou serve the enemy?"

"I did not serve the enemy."

"And where did Pan Kmita find thee and thy comrades?"

"On the road. I served with the full hetman; but the squadron went to pieces, for we had nothing to eat. I had no reason to go home, for my house was burned. Others went to rob on the road, and I went with them."

Volodyovski wondered greatly, for hitherto he had thought that Kmita had attacked Olenka with forces obtained from the enemy.

"So Pan Kmita did not get thee from Trubetskoi?"

"Most of the other men had served before with Trubetskoi and Hovanski, but they had run away too and taken to the road."

"Why did you go with Pan Kmita?"

"Because he is a splendid ataman. We were told that when he called on any one to go with him, thalers as it were flowed out of a bag, to that man. That's why we went. Well, God did not give us good luck!"

Volodyovski began to rack his head, and to think that they had blackened Kmita too much; then he looked at the pale attendant boyar and again racked his head.

"And so thou art in love with her?"

"Oi, so much!"

Volodyovski walked away, and while going he thought: "That is a resolute man. He did not break his head; he fell in love and remained. Such men are best. If he is really an attendant boyar, he is of the same rank as the village nobles. When he digs up his gold pieces, perhaps the old man will give him Maryska. And why? Because he did not go to drumming with his fingers, but made up his mind that he would get her. I'll make up my mind too."

Thus meditating, Volodyovski walked along the road in the sunshine. Sometimes he would stop, fix his eyes on the ground or raise them to the sky, then again go farther, till all at once he saw a flock of wild ducks flying through the air. He began to soothsay whether he should go or not. It came out that he was to go.

"I will go; it cannot be otherwise."

When he had said this he turned toward the house; but on the way he went once more to the stable, before which his two servants were playing dice.

"Syruts, is Basior's mane plaited?"

"Plaited, Colonel!"

Volodyovski went into the stable. Basior neighed at him from the manger; the knight approached the horse, patted him on the side, and then began to count the braids on his neck. "Go--not go--go." Again the soothsaying came out favorably.

"Saddle the horse and dress decently," commanded Volodyovski.

Then he went to the house quickly, and began to dress. He put on high cavalry boots, yellow, with gilded spurs, and a new red uniform, besides a rapier with steel scabbard, the hilt ornamented with gold; in addition a half breastplate of bright steel covering only the upper part of the breast near the neck. He had also a lynxskin cap with a beautiful heron feather; but since that was worn only with a Polish dress, he left it in the trunk, put on a Swedish helmet with a vizor, and went out before the porch.

"Where is your grace going?" asked old Pakosh, who was sitting on the railing.

"Where am I going? It is proper for me to go and inquire after the health of your lady; if not, she might think me rude."

"From your grace there is a blaze like fire. Every bulfinch is a fool in comparison! Unless the lady is without eyes, she will fall in love in a minute."

Just then the two youngest daughters of Pakosh hurried up on their way home from the forenoon milking, each with a pail of milk. When they saw Volodyovski they stood as if fixed to the earth from wonder.

"Is it a king or not?" asked Zonia.

"Your grace is like one going to a wedding," added Marysia.

"Maybe there will be a wedding," laughed old Pakosh, "for he is going to see our lady."

Before the old man had stopped speaking the full pail dropped from the hand of Marysia, and a stream of milk flowed along till it reached the feet of Volodyovski.

"Pay attention to what you are holding!" said Pakosh, angrily. "Giddy thing!"

Marysia said nothing; she raised the pail and walked off in silence.

Volodyovski mounted his horse; his two servants followed him, riding abreast, and the three moved on toward Vodokty. The day was beautiful. The May sun played on the breastplate and helmet of the colonel, so that when at a distance he was gleaming among the willows it seemed that another sun was pushing along the road.

"I am curious to know whether I shall come back with a ring or a melon?" said the knight to himself.

"What is your grace saying?" asked Syruts.

"Thou art a blockhead!"

Syruts reined in his horse, and Volodyovski continued: "The whole luck of the matter is that it is not the first time!"

This idea gave him uncommon comfort.

When he arrived at Vodokty, Panna Aleksandra did not recognize him at the first moment, and he had to repeat his name. She greeted him heartily, but ceremoniously and with a certain constraint; but he presented himself befittingly,--for though a soldier, not a courtier, he had still lived long at great houses, had been among people. He bowed to her therefore with great respect, and placing his hand on his heart spoke as follows:--

"I have come to inquire about the health of my lady benefactress, whether some pain has not come from the fright. I ought to have done this the day after, but I did not wish to give annoyance."

"It is very kind of you to keep me in mind after having saved me from such straits. Sit down, for you are a welcome guest."

"My lady," replied Volodyovski, "had I forgotten you I should not have deserved the favor which God sent when he permitted me to give aid to so worthy a person."

"No, I ought to thank first God, and then you."

"Then let us both thank; for I implore nothing else than this,--that he grant me to defend you as often as need comes."

Pan Michael now moved his waxed mustaches, which curled up higher than his nose, for he was satisfied with himself for having gone straight in *medias res* and placed his sentiments, so to speak, on the table. She sat embarrassed and silent, but beautiful as a spring day. A slight flush came on her cheeks, and she covered her eyes with the long lashes from which shadows fell on the pupils.

"That confusion is a good sign," thought Volodyovski; and coughing he proceeded: "You know, I suppose, that I led the Lauda men after your grandfather?"

"I know," answered Olenka. "My late grandfather was unable to make the last campaign, but he was wonderfully glad when he heard whom the voevoda of Vilna had appointed to the command, and said that he knew you by reputation as a splendid soldier."

"Did he say that?"

"I myself heard how he praised you to the skies, and how the Lauda men did the same after the campaign."

"I am a simple soldier, not worthy of being exalted to the skies, nor above other men. Still I rejoice that I am not quite a stranger, for you do not think now that an unknown and uncertain guest has fallen with the last rain from the clouds. Many people are wandering about who call themselves persons of high family and say they are in office, and God knows who they are; perhaps often they are not even nobles."

Pan Volodyovski gave the conversation this turn with the intent to speak of himself and of what manner of man he was. Olenka answered at once,--

"No one would think that of you, for there are nobles of the same name in Lithuania."

"But they have the seal Ossorya, while I am a Korchak Volodyovski and we take our origin from Hungary from a certain noble, Atylla, who while pursued by his enemies made a vow to the Most Holy Lady that he would turn from Paganism to the Catholic faith if he should escape with his life. He kept this vow after he had crossed three rivers in safety,--the same rivers that we bear on our shield."

"Then your family is not from those parts?"

"No, my lady, I am from the Ukraine of the Russian Volodyovskis, and to this time I own villages there which the enemy have occupied; but I serve in the army from youth, thinking less of land than of the harm inflicted on our country by strangers. I have served from the earliest years with the voevoda of Rus, our not sufficiently lamented Prince Yeremi, with whom I have been in all his wars. I was at Mahnovka and at Konstantinoff; I endured the hunger of Zbaraj, and after Berestechko our gracious lord the king pressed my head. God is my witness that I have not come here to praise myself, but desire that you might know, my lady, that I am no hanger-on, whose work is in shouting and who spares his own blood, but that my life has been passed in honorable service in which some little fame was won, and my conscience stained in nothing, so God be my aid! And to this worthy people can give testimony."

"Would that all were like you!" sighed Olenka.

"Surely you have now in mind that man of violence who dared to raise his godless hand against you."

Panna Aleksandra fixed her eyes on the floor, and said not a word.

"He has received pay for his deeds," continued Volodyovski, "though it is said that he will recover, still he will not escape punishment. All honorable people condemn him, and even too much; for they say that he had relations with the enemy so as to obtain reinforcements,-- which is untrue, for those men with whom he attacked you did not come from the enemy, but were collected on the highway."

"How do you know that?" asked the lady, raising her blue eyes to Volodyovski.

"From the Cossacks themselves. He is a wonderful man, that Kmita; for when I accused him of treason before the duel he made no denial, though I accused him unjustly. It is clear that there is a devilish pride in him."

"And have you said everywhere that he is not a traitor?"

"I have not, for I did not know that he was not a traitor; but now I will say so. It is wrong to cast such a calumny even on our own greatest enemy."

Panna Aleksandra's eyes rested a second time on the little knight with an expression of sympathy and gratitude. "You are so honorable a man that your equal is rare."

Volodyovski fell to twitching his mustaches time after time with contentment. "To business, Michael dear!" said he, mentally. Then aloud to the lady: "I will say more: I blame Pan Kmita's method, but I do not wonder that he tried to obtain you, my lady, in whose service Venus herself might act as a maid. Despair urged him on to an evil deed, and will surely urge him a second time, should opportunity offer. How will you remain alone, with such beauty and without protection? There are more men like Kmita in the world; you will rouse more such ardors, and will expose your honor to fresh perils. God sent me favor that I was able to free you, but now the trumpets of Gradivus call me. Who will watch over you? My gracious lady, they accuse soldiers of fickleness, but unjustly. Neither is my heart of rock, and it cannot remain indifferent to so many excellent charms."

Here Volodyovski fell on both knees before Olenka. "My gracious lady," said he, while kneeling, "I inherited the command after your grandfather; let me inherit the granddaughter too. Give me guardianship over you; let me enjoy the bliss of mutual affection. Take me as a perpetual protection, and you will be at rest and free from care, for though I go to the war my name itself will defend you."

The lady sprang from the chair and heard Pan Volodyovski with astonishment; but he still spoke on:--

"I am a poor soldier, but a noble, and a man of honor. I swear to you that on my shield and on my conscience not the slightest stain can be found. I am at fault perhaps in this haste; but understand too that I am called by the country, which will not yield even for you. Will you not comfort me,--will you not give me solace, will you not say a kind word?"

"You ask the impossible. As God lives, that cannot be!" answered Olenka, with fright.

"It depends on your will."

"For that reason I say no to you promptly." Here she frowned. "Worthy sir, I am indebted to you much, I do not deny it. Ask what you like, I am ready to give everything except my hand."

Pan Volodyovski rose. "Then you do not wish me, my lady? Is that true?"

"I cannot."

"And that is your last word?"

"The last and irrevocable word."

"Perhaps the haste only has displeased you. Give me some hope."

"I cannot, I cannot."

"Then there is no success for me here, as elsewhere there was none. My worthy lady, offer not pay for services, I have not come for that; and if I ask your hand it is not as pay, but from your own good-will. Were you to say that you give it because you must, I would not take it. Where there is no freedom there is no happiness. You have disdained me. God grant that a worse do not meet you. I go from this house as I entered, save this that I shall not come here again. I am accounted here as nobody. Well, let it be so. Be happy even with that very Kmita, for perhaps you are angry because I placed a sabre between you. If he seems better to you, then in truth you are not for me."

Olenka seized her temples with her hands, and repeated a number of times: "O God! O God! O God!"

But that pain of hers made no impression on Volodyovski, who, when he had bowed, went out angry and wrathful; then he mounted at once and rode off.

"A foot of mine shall never stand there again!" said he, aloud.

His attendant Syruts riding behind pushed up at once. "What does your grace say?"

"Blockhead!" answered Volodyovski.

"You told me that when we were coming hither."

Silence followed; then Volodyovski began to mutter again: "Ah, I was entertained there with ingratitude, paid for affection with contempt. It will come to me surely to serve in the cavalry till death; that is fated. Such a devil of a lot fell to me,--every move a refusal! There is no justice on earth. What did she find against me?"

Here Pan Michael frowned, and began to work mightily with his brain; all at once he slapped his leg with his hand. "I know now," shouted he; "she loves that fellow yet,--it cannot be otherwise."

But this idea did not clear his face. "So much the worse for me," thought he, after a while; "for if she loves him yet, she will not stop loving him. He has already done his worst. He may go to war, win glory, repair his reputation. And it is not right to hinder him; he should rather be aided, for that is a service to the country. He is a good soldier, 'tis true. But how did he fascinate her so? Who can tell? Some have such fortune that if one of them looks on a woman she is ready to follow him into fire. If a man only knew how this is done or could get some captive spirit, perhaps he might effect something. Merit has no weight with a fair head. Pan Zagloba said wisely that a fox and a woman are the most treacherous creatures alive. But I grieve that all is lost. Oh, she is a terribly beautiful woman, and honorable and virtuous, as they say; ambitious as the devil,--that's evident. Who knows that she will marry him though she loves him, for he has offended and disappointed her sorely. He might have won her in peace, but he chose to be lawless. She is willing to resign everything,--marriage and children. It is grievous for me, but maybe it is worse for her, poor thing!"

Here Volodyovski fell into a fit of tenderness over the fate of Olenka, and began to rack his brain and smack his lips. At last he said,--

"May God aid her! I have no ill feeling against her! It is not the first refusal for me, but for her it is the first suffering. The poor woman can scarcely recover now from sorrows. I have put out her eyes with this Kmita, and besides have given her gall to drink. It was not right to do that, and I must repair the wrong. I wish bullets had struck me, for I have acted rudely. I will write a letter asking forgiveness, and then help her in what way I can."

Further thoughts concerning Pan Kmita were interrupted by the attendant Syruts, who riding forward again said: "Pardon, but over there on the hill is Pan Kharlamp riding with some one else."

"Where?"

"Over there!"

"It is true that two horsemen are visible, but Pan Kharlamp remained with the prince voevoda of Vilna. How dost thou know him so far away?"

"By his cream-colored horse. The whole array knows that horse anywhere."

"As true as I live, there is a cream-colored horse in view, but it may be some other man's horse."

"When I recognize the gait, it is surely Pan Kharlamp."

They spurred on; the other horsemen did the same, and soon Volodyovski saw that Pan Kharlamp was in fact approaching.

Pan Kharlamp was the lieutenant of a light-horse squadron in the Lithuanian quota. Pan Volodyovski's acquaintance of long standing, an old soldier and a good one. Once he and the little knight had quarrelled fiercely, but afterward while serving together and campaigning they acquired a love for each other. Volodyovski sprang forward quickly, and opening his arms cried,--

"How do you prosper, O Great-nose? Whence do you come?"

The officer--who in truth deserved the nickname of Great-nose, for he had a mighty nose--fell into the embraces of the colonel, and greeted him joyously; then after he had recovered his breath, he said, "I have come to you with a commission and money."

"But from whom?"

"From the prince voevoda of Vilna, our hetman. He sends you a commission to begin a levy at once, and another commission to Pan Kmita, who must be in this neighborhood."

"To Pan Kmita also? How shall we both make a levy in one neighborhood?"

"He is to go to Troki, and you to remain in these parts."

"How did you know where to look for me?"

"The hetman himself inquired carefully till the people from this place who have remained near him told where to find you. I came with sure information. You are in great and continual favor there. I have heard the prince himself say that he had not hoped to inherit anything from Prince Yeremi, but still he did inherit the greatest of knights."

"May God grant him to inherit the military success of Yeremi! It is a great honor for me to conduct a levy. I will set about it at once. There is no lack of warlike people here, if there was only something with which to give them an outfit. Have you brought much money?"

"You will count it at Patsuneli."

"So you have been there already? But be careful; for there are shapely girls in Patsuneli, like poppies in a garden."

"Ah, that is why stopping there pleased you! But wait, I have a private letter from the hetman to you."

"Then give it."

Kharlamp drew forth a letter with the small seal of the Radzivills. Volodyovski opened it and began to read:--

Worthy Colonel Pan Volodyovski,--Knowing your sincere wish to serve the country, I send you a commission to make a levy, and not as is usually done, but with great haste, for *periculum in mora* (there is danger in delay). If you wish to give us joy, then let the squadron be mustered and ready for the campaign by the end of July, or the middle of August at the latest. We are anxious to know how you can find good horses, especially since we send money sparingly, for more we could not hammer from the under-treasurer, who after his old fashion is unfriendly to us. Give one half of this money to Pan Kmita, for whom Pan Kharlamp has also a commission. We hope that he will serve us zealously. But tidings have come to our ears of his violence in Upita, therefore it is better for you to take the letter directed to him from Kharlamp, and discover yourself whether to deliver it to him or not. Should you consider the accusations against him too great, and creating infamy, then do not give it, for we are afraid lest our enemies--such as the under-treasurer, and the voevoda of Vityebsk--might raise outcries against us because we commit such functions to unworthy persons.

But if you give the letter after having found that there is nothing important, let Pan Kmita endeavor to wipe away his faults by the greatest exertion in service, and in no case to appear in the courts, for he belongs to our hetman's jurisdiction,--we and no one else will judge him. Pay attention to our charge at once, in view of the confidence which we have in your judgment and faithful service.

Yanush Radzivill,

Prince in Birji and Dubinki, Voevoda of Vilna.

"The hetman is terribly anxious about horses for you," said Kharlamp, when the little knight had finished reading.

"It will surely be difficult in the matter of horses," answered Volodyovski. "A great number of the small nobility here will rally at the first summons, but they have only wretched little Jmud ponies, not very capable of service. For a good campaign it would be needful to give them all fresh horses."

"Those are good horses; I know them of old, wonderfully enduring and active."

"Bah!" responded Volodyovski, "but small, and the men here are large. If they should form in line on such horses, you would think them a squadron mounted on dogs. There is where the rub is. I will work with zeal, for I am in haste myself. Leave Kmita's commission with me, as the hetman commands; I will give it to him. It has come just in season."

"But why?"

"For he has acted here in Tartar fashion and taken a lady captive. There are as many lawsuits and questions hanging over him as he has hairs on his head. It is not a week since I had a sabre-duel with him."

"Ai!" cried Kharlamp. "If you had a sabre-duel with him, he is in bed at this moment."

"But he is better already. In a week or two he will be well. What is to be heard *de publicis*?"

"Evil in the old fashion. The under-treasurer, Pan Gosyevski, the full hetman, is ever quarrelling with the prince; and as the hetmans do not agree, affairs do not move in harmony. Still we have improved a little, and I think that if we had concord we might manage the enemy. God will permit us yet to ride on their necks to their own land. Gosyevski is to blame for all."

"But others say it is specially the grand hetman, Prince Radzivill."

"They are traitors. The voevoda of Vityebsk talks that way, for he and the under-treasurer are cronies this long time."

"The voevoda of Vityebsk is a worthy citizen."

"Are you on the side of Sapyeha against the Radzivills?"

"I am on the side of the country, on whose side all should be. In this is the evil,--that even soldiers are divided into parties, instead of fighting. That Sapyeha is a worthy citizen, I would say in the presence of the prince himself, even though I serve under him."

"Good people have striven to bring about harmony, but with no result," said Kharlamp. "There is a terrible movement of messengers from the king to our prince. They say that something is hatching. We expected with the visit of the king a call of the general militia; it has not come! They say that it may be necessary in some places."

"In the Ukraine, for instance."

"I know. But once Lieutenant Brohvich told what he heard with his own ears. Tyzenhauz came from the king to our hetman, and when they had shut themselves in they talked a long time about something which Brohvich could not overhear; but when they came out, with his own ears he heard the hetman say, 'From this a new war may come.' We racked our heads greatly to find what this could mean."

"Surely he was mistaken. With whom could there be a new war? The emperor is more friendly to us now than to our enemies, since it is proper for him to take the side of a civilized people. With the Swedes the truce is not yet at an end, and will not be for six years; the Tartars are helping us in the Ukraine, which they would not do without the will of Turkey."

"Well, we could not get at anything."

"For there was nothing. But, praise God, I have fresh work; I began to yearn for war."

"Do you wish to carry the commission yourself to Kmita?"

"I do, because, as I have told you, the hetman has so ordered. It is proper for me to visit Kmita now according to knightly custom, and having the commission I shall have a still better chance to talk with him. Whether I give the commission is another thing; I think that I shall, for it is left to my discretion."

"That suits me; I am in such haste for the road. I have a third commission to Pan Stankyevich. Next I am commanded to go to Kyedani, to remove the cannon which are there; then to inspect Birji and see if everything is ready for defence."

"And to Birji too?"

"Yes."

"That is a wonder to me. The enemy have won no new victories, and it is far for them to go to Birji on the boundary of Courland. And since, as I see, new squadrons are being formed, there will be men to defend even those parts which have fallen under the power of the enemy. The Courlanders do not think of war with us. They are good soldiers, but few; and Radzivill might put the breath out of them with one hand."

"I wonder too," answered Kharlamp, "all the more that haste is enjoined on me, and instructions given that if I find anything out of order I am to inform quickly Prince Boguslav Radzivill, who is to send Peterson the engineer."

"What can this mean? I hope 'tis no question of domestic war. May God preserve us from that! But when Prince Boguslav touches an affair the devil will come of the amusement."

"Say nothing against him; he is a valiant man."

"I say nothing against his valor, but there is more of the German or Frenchman in him than the Pole. And of the Commonwealth he never thinks; his only thought is how to raise the house of Radzivill to the highest point and lower all others. He is the man who rouses pride in the voevoda of Vilna, our hetman, who of himself has no lack of it; and those quarrels with Sapyeha and Gosyevski are the tree and the fruit of Prince Boguslav's planting."

"I see that you are a great statesman. You should marry, Michael dear, as soon as possible, so that such wisdom is not lost."

Volodyovski looked very attentively at his comrade. "Marry,--why is that?"

"Maybe you are going courting, for I see that you are dressed as on parade."

"Give us peace!"

"Oh, own up!"

"Let each man eat his own melons, not inquire about those of other men. You too have eaten more than one. It is just the time now to think of marriage when we have a levy on our hands!"

"Will you be ready in July?"

"At the end of July, even if I have to dig horses out of the ground. Thank God that this task has come, or melancholy would have devoured me."

So tidings from the hetman and the prospect of heavy work gave great consolation to Pan Michael; and before he reached Patsuneli, he had scarcely a thought of the rebuff which had met him an hour before. News of the commission flew quickly through the whole village. The nobles came straightway to inquire if the news was true; and when Volodyovski confirmed it, his words made a great impression. The readiness was universal, though some were troubled because they would have to march at the end of July before harvest. Volodyovski sent messengers to other neighborhoods,--to Upita, and to the most considerable noble houses. In the evening a number of Butryms, Stakyans, and Domasheviches came.

They began to incite one another, show greater readiness, threaten the enemy, and promise victory to themselves. The Butryms alone were silent; but that was not taken ill, for it was known that they would rise as one man. Next day it was as noisy in all the villages as in bee-hives. People talked no more of Pan Kmita and Panna Aleksandra, but of the future campaign. Volodyovski also forgave Olenka sincerely the refusal, comforting himself meanwhile in his heart that that was not the last one, as the love was not the last. At the same time he pondered somewhat on what he had to do with the letter to Kmita.

CHAPTER X.

A time of serious labor began now for Volodyovski,--of letter-writing and journeying. The week following he transferred his head-quarters to Upita, where he began the levy. The nobles flocked to him willingly, both great and small, for he had a wide reputation. But especially came the Lauda men, for whom horses had to be provided. Volodyovski hurried around as if in boiling water; but since he was active and spared no pains, everything went on successfully enough. Meanwhile he visited in Lyubich Pan Kmita, who had advanced considerably toward health; and though he had not risen yet from his bed, it was known that he would recover.

Kmita recognized the knight at once, and turned a little pale at sight of him. Even his hand moved involuntarily toward the sabre above his head; but he checked himself when he saw a smile on the face of his guest, put forth his thin hand, and said,--

"I thank you for the visit. This is courtesy worthy of such a cavalier."

"I have come to inquire if you cherish ill feeling against me," said Pan Michael.

"I have no ill feeling; for no common man overcame me, but a swordsman of the first degree. Hardly have I escaped."

"And how is your health?"

"It is surely a wonder to you that I have come out alive. I confess myself that it is no small exploit." Here Kmita laughed. "Well, the affair is not lost. You may finish me at your pleasure."

"I have not come with such intent--"

"You must be the devil," interrupted Kmita, "or must have a captive spirit. God knows I am far from self-praise at this moment, for I am returning from the other world; but before meeting you I thought, 'If I am not the best sabre in the Commonwealth, I am the second.' But I could not have warded off the first blow if you had not wished it. Tell me where did you learn so much?"

"I had some little innate capacity, and my father taught me from boyhood. He said many a time, 'God has given you insignificant stature; if men do not fear you, they will laugh at you.' Later on, while serving with the voevoda of Rus, I finished my course. With him were a few men who could stand boldly before me."

"But could there be such?"

"There could, for there were. There was Pan Podbipienta, a Lithuanian of high birth, who fell at Zbaraj,--the Lord light his soul!--a man of such strength that there were no means to stop him, for he could cut through opponent and weapons. Then there was Skshetuski, my heartfelt friend and confidant, of whom you must have heard."

"Of course! He came out of Zbaraj, and burst through the Cossacks. So you are of such a brace, and a man of Zbaraj! With the forehead! with the forehead! Wait a moment; I have heard of you at the castle of Radzivill, voevoda of Vilna. Your name is Michael?"

"Exactly; I am Michael. My first name is Yerzi; but since Saint Michael leads the whole host of heaven, and has gamed so many victories over the banners of hell, I prefer him as a patron."

"It is sure that Yerzi is not equal to Michael. Then you are that same Volodyovski of whom it is said that he cut up Bogun?"

"I am he."

"Well, to receive a slash on the head from such a man is not a misfortune. If God would grant us to be friends! You called me a traitor, 'tis true, but you were mistaken." When he said this, Kmita frowned as if his wound caused him pain again.

"I confess my mistake," answered Volodyovski. "I do not learn that from you; your men told me. And know that if I had not learned it I should not have come here."

"Tongues have cut me and cut me," said Kmita, with bitterness. "Let come what may, I confess more than one mark is against me; but in this neighborhood men have received me ungraciously."

"You injured yourself most by burning Volmontovichi, and by the last seizure."

"Now they are crushing me with lawsuits. I am summoned to courts. They will not give a sick man time to recover. I burned Volmontovichi, 'tis true, and cut down some people; but let God judge me if I did that from caprice. The same night, before the burning I made a vow to live with all men in peace, to attract to myself these homespuns around here, to satisfy the basswood barks in Upita, for there I really played the tyrant. I returned to my house, and what did I find? I found my comrades cut up like cattle, lying at the wall. When I learned that the Butryms had done this, the devil entered me, and I took stern vengeance. Would you believe why they were cut up, why they were slaughtered? I learned myself later from one of the Butryms, whom I found in the woods. Behold, it was for this,--that they wanted to dance with the women of the nobles in a public house! Who would not have taken vengeance?"

"My worthy sir," answered Volodyovski, "it is true that they acted severely with your comrades; but was it the nobles who killed them? No; their previous reputation killed them,--that which they brought with them; for if orderly soldiers had wished to dance, surely they would not have slain them."

"Poor fellows!" said Kmita, following his own thoughts, "while I was lying here now in a fever, they came in every evening through that door from the room outside. I saw them around this bed as if living, blue, hacked up, and groaning continually, 'Yendrus! give money to have a Mass for our souls; we are in torments!' Then I tell you the hair stood on my head, for the smell of sulphur from them was in the room. I gave money for a Mass. Oh, may it help them!"

A moment of silence then followed.

"As to the carrying off," continued Kmita, "no one could have told you about that; for in truth she saved my life when the nobles were hunting me, but afterward she ordered me to depart and not show myself before her eyes. What was there left for me after that?"

"Still it was a Tartar method."

"You know not what love is, and to what despair it may bring a man when he loses that which he prizes most dearly."

"I know not what love is?" cried Volodyovski, with excitement. "From the time that I began to carry a sabre I was in love. It is true that the object changed, for I was never rewarded with a return. Were it not for that, there could have been no Troilus more faithful than I."

"What kind of love can that be when the object is changing?" said Kmita.

"I will tell you something else which I saw with my own eyes. In the first period of the Hmelnitski affair, Bogun, the same who next to Hmelnitski has now the highest respect of the Cossacks, carried off Princess Kurtsevich, a maiden loved by Skshetuski above all things. That was a love! The whole army was weeping in view of Skshetuski's despair; for his beard at some years beyond twenty grew gray, and can you guess what he did?"

"I have no means of knowing."

"Well, because the country was in need, in humiliation, because the terrible Hmelnitski was triumphing, he did not go to seek the girl. He offered his suffering to God, and fought under Prince Yeremi in all the battles, including Zbaraj, and covered himself with such glory that to-day all repeat his name with respect. Compare his action with your own and see the difference."

Kmita was silent, gnawed his mustache. Volodyovski continued,--

"Then God rewarded and gave him the maiden. They married immediately after Zbaraj, and now have three children, though he has not ceased to serve. But you by making disturbance have given aid to the enemy and almost lost your own life, not to mention that a few days ago you might have lost the lady forever."

"How is that?" asked Kmita, sitting up in the bed; "what happened to her?"

"Nothing; but there was found a man who asked for her hand and wanted to marry her."

Kmita grew very pale; his hollow eyes began to shoot flames. He wanted to rise, even struggled for a moment; then cried, "Who was this devil's son? By the living God, tell me!"

"I," said Pan Volodyovski.

"You,--you?" asked Kmita, with astonishment, "Is it possible?"

"It is."

"Traitor! that will not go with you! But she--what--tell me everything. Did she accept?"

"She refused me on the spot, without thinking."

A moment of silence followed. Kmita breathed heavily, and fixed his eyes on Volodyovski, who said,--

"Why call me traitor? Am I your brother or your best man? Have I broken faith with you? I conquered you in battle, and could have done what I liked."

"In old fashion one of us would seal this with his blood,--if not with a sabre, with a gun. I would shoot you; then let the devils take me."

"Then you would have shot me, for if she had not refused I should not have accepted a second duel. What had I to fight for? Do you know why she refused me?"

"Why?" repeated Kmita, like an echo.

"Because she loves you."

That was more than the exhausted strength of the sick man could bear. His head fell on the pillows, a copious sweat came out on his forehead, and he lay there in silence.

"I am terribly weak," said he, after a while. "How do you know that she loves me?"

"Because I have eyes and see, because I have reason and observe; just after I had received the refusal my head became clear. To begin with, when after the duel I came to tell her that she was free, for I had slain you, she was dazed, and instead of showing gratitude she ignored me entirely; second, when the Domasheviches were bringing you in, she carried your head like a mother; and third, because when I visited her, she received me as if some one were giving me a slap in the face. If these explanations are not sufficient, it is because your reason is shaken and your mind impaired."

"If that is true," said Kmita, with a feeble voice, "many plasters are put on my wounds; better balsam than your words there could not be."

"But a traitor applies this balsam."

"Oh, forgive me! Such happiness cannot find place in my mind, that she has a wish for me still."

"I said that she loves you; I did not say that she has a wish for you,--that is altogether different."

"If she has no wish for me, I will break my head against the wall; I cannot help it."

"You might if you had a sincere desire of effacing your faults. There is war now; you may go, you may render important services to our dear country, you may win glory with bravery, and mend your reputation. Who is without fault? Who has no sin on his conscience? Every one has. But the road to penance and correction is open to all. You sinned through violence, then avoid it henceforth; you offended against the country by raising disturbance in time of war, save the country now; you committed wrongs against men, make reparation for them. This is a better and a surer way for you than breaking your head."

Kmita looked attentively at Volodyovski; then said, "You speak like a sincere friend of mine."

"I am not your friend, but in truth I am not your enemy; and I am sorry for that lady, though she refused me and I said a sharp word to her in parting. I shall not hang myself by reason of the refusal; it is not the first for me, and I am not accustomed to treasure up offences. If I persuade you to the right road, that will be to the country a service on my part, for you are a good and experienced soldier."

"Is there time for me to return to this road? How many summonses are waiting for me? I shall have to go from the bed to the court--unless I flee hence, and I do not wish to do that. How many summonses, and every case a sure sentence of condemnation!"

"Look, here is a remedy!" said Volodyovski, taking out the commission.

"A commission!" cried Kmita; "for whom?"

"For you! You need not appear at any court, for you are in the hetman's jurisdiction. Hear what the prince voevoda writes me."

Volodyovski read to Kmita the private letter of Radzivill, drew breath, moved his mustaches, and said, "Here, as you see, it depends on me either to give you the commission or to retain it."

Uncertainty, alarm, and hope were reflected on Kmita's face. "What will you do?" asked he, in a low voice.

"T will give the commission," said Volodyovski.

Kmita said nothing at first; he dropped his head on the pillow, and looked some time at the ceiling. Suddenly his eyes began to grow moist; and tears, unknown guests in those eyes, were hanging on the lashes.

"May I be torn with horses," said he at last, "may I be pulled out of my skin, if I have seen a more honorable man! If through me you have received a refusal,--if Olenka, as you say, loves me,--another would have taken vengeance all the more, would have pushed me down deeper; but you give your hand and draw me forth as it were from the grave."

"Because I will not sacrifice to personal interests the country, to which you may render notable service. But I say that if you had obtained those Cossacks from Trubetskoi or Hovanski, I should have kept the commission. It is your whole fortune that you did not do that."

"It is for others to take an example from you," said Kmita. "Give me your hand. God permit me to repay you with some good, for you have bound me in life and in death."

"Well, we will speak of that later. Now listen! There is no need of appearing before any court, but go to work. If you will render service to the Commonwealth, these nobles will forgive you, for they are very sensitive to the honor of the State. You may blot out your offences yet, win reputation, walk in glory as in sunlight, and I know of one lady who will give you a lifelong reward."

"Hei!" cried Kmita, in ecstasy, "why should I rot here in bed when the enemy is trampling the country? Hei! is there any one there? Come, boy, give me my boots; come hither! May the thunderbolts strike me in this bed if I stay here longer in uselessness!"

Volodyovski smiled with satisfaction and said, "Your spirit is stronger than your body, for the body is not able to serve you yet."

When he had said this he began to take farewell; but Kmita would not let him go, thanked him, and wished to treat him with wine. In fact, it was well toward evening when the little knight left Lyubich and directed his course to Vodokty.

"I will reward her in the best fashion for her sharp word," said he to himself, "when I tell her that Kmita will rise, not only from his bed, but from evil fame. He is not ruined yet, only very passionate. I shall comfort her wonderfully too, and I think she will meet me better this time than when I offered myself to her."

Here our honest Van Michael sighed and muttered: "Could it be known that there is one in the world predestined to me?"

In the midst of such meditations he came to Vodokty. The tow-headed man of Jmud ran out to the gate, but made no hurry to open; he only said,--

"The heiress is not at home."

"Has she gone away?"

"She has gone away."

"Whither?"

"Who knows?"

"When will she come back?"

"Who knows?"

"Speak in human fashion. Did she not say when she would return?"

"Maybe she will not return at all, for she went away with wagons and bags. From that I think she has gone far for a long time."

"Is that true?" muttered Pan Michael. "See what I have done!"

CHAPTER XI.

Usually when the warm rays of the sun begin to break through the wintry veil of clouds, and when the first buds appear on the trees and the green fleece spreads over the damp fields, a better hope enters the hearts of men. But the spring of 1655 brought not the usual comfort to the afflicted inhabitants of the Commonwealth. The entire eastern boundary, from the north to the wilderness on the south, was bound as it were by a border of flame; and the spring torrents could not quench the conflagration, but that border grew wider continually and occupied broader regions. And besides there appeared in the sky signs of evil omen, announcing still greater defeats and misfortunes. Time after time from the clouds which swept over the heavens were formed as it were lofty towers like the flanks of fortresses, which afterward rolled down with a crash. Thunderbolts struck the earth while it was still covered with snow, pine-woods became yellow, and the limbs of trees crossed one another in strange sickly figures; wild beasts and birds fell down and died from unknown diseases. Finally, strange spots were seen on the sun, having the form of a hand holding an apple, of a heart pierced through, and a cross. The minds of men were disturbed more and more; monks were lost in calculating what these signs might mean. A wonderful kind of disquiet seized all hearts.

New and sudden wars were foretold, God knows from what source. An ominous report began to circulate from mouth to mouth in villages and towns that a tempest was coming from the side of the Swedes. Apparently nothing seemed to confirm this report, for the truce concluded with Sweden had six years yet to run; and still people spoke of the danger of war, even at the Diet, which Yan Kazimir the king had called on May 19 in Warsaw.

Anxious eyes were turned more and more to Great Poland, on which the storm would come first. Leshchynski, the voevoda of Lenchytsk, and Narushevich, chief secretary of Lithuania, went on an embassy to Sweden; but their departure, instead of quieting the alarmed, increased still more the disquiet.

"That embassy smells of war," wrote Yanush Radzivill.

"If a storm were not threatening from that direction, why were they sent?" asked others.

Kanazyl, the first ambassador, had barely returned from Stockholm; but it was to be seen clearly that he had done nothing, since immediately after him important senators were sent.

However people of more judgment did not believe yet in the possibility of war. "The Commonwealth," said they, "has given no cause, and the truce endures in full validity. How could oaths be broken, the most sacred agreements violated, and a harmless neighbor attacked in robber fashion? Besides, Sweden remembers the wounds inflicted by the Polish sabre at Kirchholm and Putsk; and Gustavus Adolphus, who in western Europe found not his equal, yielded a number of times to Pan Konyetspolski. The Swedes will not expose such great military glory won in the world to uncertain hazard before an opponent against whom they have never been able to stand in the field. It is true that the Commonwealth is exhausted and weakened by war; but Prussia and Great Poland, which in the last wars did not suffer at all, will of themselves be able to drive that hungry people beyond the sea to their barren rocks. There will be no war."

To this alarmists answered again that even before the Diet at Warsaw counsel was taken by advice of the king at the provincial diet in Grodno concerning the defence of the boundary of Great Poland, and taxes and soldiers assigned, which would not have been done unless danger was near.

And so minds were wavering between fear and hope; a grievous uncertainty weighed down the spirits of people, when suddenly an end was put to it by the proclamation of Boguslav Leshchynski, commander in Great Poland, summoning the general militia of the provinces of Poznan and Kalisk for the defence of the boundaries against the impending Swedish storm.

Every doubt vanished. The shout, "War!" was heard throughout Great Poland and all the lands of the Commonwealth.

That was not only a war, but a new war. Hmelnitski, reinforced by Buturlin, was raging in the south and the east; Hovanski and Trubetskoi on the north and east; the Swede was approaching from the west! The fiery border had become a fiery wheel.

The country was like a besieged camp; and in the camp evil was happening. One traitor, Radzeyovski, had fled from it, and was in the tent of the invaders. He was guiding them to ready spoil, he was pointing out the weak sides; it was his work to tempt the garrisons. And in addition there was no lack of ill will and envy,--no lack of magnates quarrelling among themselves or angry with the king by reason of offices refused, and ready at any moment to sacrifice the cause of the nation to their own private profit; there was no lack of dissidents wishing to celebrate their own triumph even on the grave of the fatherland; and a still greater number was there of the disorderly, the heedless, the slothful, and of those who were in love with themselves, their own ease and well being.

Still Great Poland, a country wealthy and hitherto untouched by war, did not spare at least money for defence. Towns and villages of nobles furnished as many infantry as were assigned to them; and before the nobles moved in their own persons to the camp many-colored regiments of land infantry had moved thither under the leadership of captains appointed by the provincial diet from among men experienced in the art of war.

Tan Stanislav Dembinski led the land troops of Poznan, Pan Vladyslav Vlostovski those of Kostsian, and Pan Golts, a famous soldier and engineer, those of Valets. The peasants of Kalisk were commanded by Pan Stanislav Skshetuski, from a stock of valiant warriors, a cousin of the famous Yan from Zbaraj. Pan Katsper Jyhlinski led the millers and bailiffs of Konin. From Pyzdri marched Pan Stanislav Yarachevski, who had spent his youth in foreign wars; from Ktsyna, Pan Pyotr Skorashevski, and from Naklo, Pan Kosletski. But in military experience no one was equal to Pan Vladyslav Skorashevski, whose voice was listened to even by the commander in Great Poland himself and the voevodas.

In three places--at Pila, Uistsie, Vyelunie--had the captains fixed the lines on the Notets, waiting for the arrival of the nobles summoned to the general militia. The infantry dug trenches from morning till evening, looking continually toward the rear to see if the wished for cavalry were coming.

The first dignitary who came was Pan Andrei Grudzinski, voevoda of Kalisk. He lodged in the house of the mayor, with a numerous retinue of servants arrayed in white and blue colors. He expected that the nobles of Kalisk would gather round him straightway; but when no one appeared he sent for Captain Stanislav Skshetuski, who was occupied in digging trenches at the river.

"Where are my men?" asked he, after the first greetings of the captain, whom he had known from childhood.

"What men?" asked Pan Stanislav.

"The general militia of Kalisk."

A smile of pain mingled with contempt appeared on the swarthy face of the soldier.

"Serene great mighty voevoda," said he, "this is the time for shearing sheep, and in Dantzig they will not pay for badly washed wool. Every noble is now at a pond washing or weighing, thinking correctly that the Swedes will not run away."

"How is that?" asked the troubled voevoda; "is there no one here yet?"

"Not a living soul, except the land infantry. And, besides, the harvest is near. A good manager will not leave home at such a season."

"What do you tell me?"

"But the Swedes will not run away, they will only come nearer," repeated the captain.

The pock-pitted face of the voevoda grew suddenly purple. "What are the Swedes to me? But this will be a shame for me in the presence of the other lords if I am here alone like a finger."

Pan Stanislav laughed again: "Your grace will permit me to remark," said he, "that the Swedes are the main thing here, and shame afterward.

Besides, there will be no shame; for not only the nobles of Kalisk, but all other nobles, are absent."

"They have run mad!" exclaimed Grudzinski.

"No; but they are sure of this,--if they will not go to the Swedes, the Swedes will not fail to come to them."

"Wait!" said the voevoda. And clapping his hands for an attendant, he gave command to bring ink, pen, and paper; then he sat down and began to write. In half an our he had covered the paper; he struck it with his hand, and said,--

"I will send another call for them to be here at the latest *pro die 27 praesentis* (on the 27th of the present month), and I think that surely they will wish at this last date *non deesse patriæ* (not to fail the country). And now tell me have you any news of the enemy?"

"We have. Wittemberg is mustering his troops on the fields at Dama."

"Are there many?"

"Some say seventeen thousand, others more."

"H'm! then there will not be so many of ours. What is your opinion? Shall we be able to oppose them?"

"If the nobles do not appear, there is nothing to talk about."

"They will come; why should they not come? It is a known fact that the general militia always delay. But shall we be able to succeed with the aid of the nobles?"

"No," replied Pan Stanislav, coolly. "Serene great mighty voevoda, we have no soldiers."

"How no soldiers?"

"Your grace knows as well as I that all the regular troops are in the Ukraine. Not even two squadrons were sent here, though at this moment God alone knows which storm is greater."

"But the infantry, and the general militia?"

"Of twenty peasants scarcely one has seen war; of ten, one knows how to hold a gun. After the first war they will be good soldiers, but they are not soldiers now. And as to the general militia let your grace ask any man who knows even a little about war whether the general militia can stand before regulars, and besides such soldiers as the Swedes, veterans of the whole Lutheran war, and accustomed to victory."

"Do you exalt the Swedes, then, so highly above your own?"

"I do not exalt them above my own; for if there were fifteen thousand such men here as were at Zbaraj, quarter soldiers and cavalry, I should have no fear. But with such as we have God knows whether we can do anything worth mention."

The voevoda placed his hands on his knees, and looked quickly into the eyes of Pan Stanislav, as if wishing to read some hidden thought in them. "What have we come here for, then? Do you not think it better to yield?"

Pan Stanislav spat in answer, and said: "If such a thought as that has risen in my head, let your grace give command to impale me on a stake. To the question do I believe in victory I answer, as a soldier, that I do not. But why we have come here,--that is another question, to which as a citizen I will answer. To offer the enemy the first resistance, so that by detaining them we shall enable the rest of the country to make ready and march, to restrain the invasion with our bodies until we fall one on the other."

"Your intention is praiseworthy," answered the voevoda, coldly; "but it is easier for you soldiers to talk about death than for us, on whom will fall all the responsibility for so much noble blood shed in vain."

"What is noble blood for unless to be shed?"

"That is true, of course. We are ready to die, for that is the easiest thing of all. But duty commands us, the men whom providence has made leaders, not to seek our own glory merely, but also to look for results. War is as good as begun, it is true; but still Carolus Gustavus is a relative of our king, and must remember this fact. Therefore it is necessary to try negotiations, for sometimes more can be effected by speech than by arms."

"That does not pertain to me," said Pan Stanislav, dryly.

Evidently the same thought occurred to the voevoda at that moment, for he nodded and dismissed the captain.

Pan Stanislav, however, was only half right in what he said concerning the delay of the nobles summoned to the general militia. It was true that before sheep-shearing was over few came to the camp between Pila and Uistsie; but toward the 27th of June,--that is, the date mentioned in the second summons--they began to assemble in numbers considerable enough.

Every day clouds of dust, rising by reason of the dry and settled weather, announced the approach of fresh reinforcements one after another. And the nobles travelled noisily on horses, on wheels, and with crowds of servants, with provisions, with wagons, and abundance on them of every kind of thing, and so loaded with weapons that many a man carried arms of every description for three lances, muskets, pistols, sabres, double-handed swords and hussar hammers, out of use even in that time, for smashing armor. Old soldiers recognized at once by these weapons men unaccustomed to war and devoid of experience.

Of all the nobles inhabiting the Commonwealth just those of Great Poland were the least warlike. Tartars, Turks, and Cossacks had never trampled those regions which from the time of the Knights of the Cross had almost forgotten how war looked in the country. Whenever a noble of Great Poland felt the desire for war he joined the armies of the kingdom, and fought there as well as the best; but those who preferred to stay at home became real householders, in love with wealth and with ease,--real agriculturists, filling with their wool and especially with their wheat the markets of Prussian towns. But now when the Swedish storm swept them away from their peaceful pursuits, they thought it impossible to pile up too many arms, provide too great supplies, or take too many servants to protect the persons and goods of the master.

They were marvellous soldiers, whom the captains could not easily bring to obedience. For example, one would present himself with a lance nineteen feet long, with a breastplate on his breast, but with a straw hat on his head "for coolness;" another in time of drill would complain of the heat; a third would yawn, eat, or drink; a fourth would call his attendant; and all who were in the ranks thought it nothing out of the way to talk so loudly that no man could hear the command of an officer. And it was difficult to introduce discipline, for it offended the brotherhood terribly, as being opposed to the dignity of a citizen. It is true that "articles" were proclaimed, but no one would obey them.

An iron ball on the feet of this army was the innumerable legion of wagons, of reserve and draft horses, of cattle intended for food, and especially of the multitude of servants guarding the tents, utensils, millet, grits, hash, and causing on the least occasion quarrels and disturbance.

Against such an army as this was advancing from the side of Stettin and the plains on the Oder, Arwid Wittemberg, an old leader, whose youth had been passed in the thirty years' war; he came at the head of seventeen thousand veterans bound together by iron discipline.

On one side stood the disordered Polish camp, resembling a crowd at a country fair, vociferous, full of disputes, discussions about the commands of leaders, and of dissatisfaction; composed of worthy villagers turned into prospective infantry, and nobles taken straight from sheep-shearing. From the other side marched terrible, silent quadrangles, which at one beck of their leaders turned, with the precision of machines, into lines and half-circles, unfolding into wedges and triangles as regularly as a sword moves in the hands of a fencer, bristling with musket-barrels and darts: genuine men of war, cool, calm; real masters who had attained perfection in their art. Who among men of experience could doubt the outcome of the meeting and on whose side the victory must fall?

The nobles, however, were assembling in greater and greater numbers; and still earlier the dignitaries of Great Poland and other provinces began to meet, bringing bodies of attendant troops and servants. Soon after the arrival of Pan Grudzinski at Pila came Pan Kryshtof Opalinski, the powerful voevoda of Poznan. Three hundred haiduks in red and yellow uniforms and armed with muskets went before the carriage of the voevoda; a crowd of attendant nobles surrounded his worthy person; following them in order of battle came a division of horsemen with uniforms similar to those of the haiduks; the voevoda himself was in a carriage attended by a jester, Staha Ostrojka, whose duty it was to cheer his gloomy master on the road.

The entrance of such a great dignitary gave courage and consolation to all; for those who looked on the almost kingly majesty of the voevoda, on that lordly face in which under the lofty vaulting of the forehead there gleamed eyes wise and severe, and on the senatorial dignity of his whole posture, could hardly believe that any evil fate could come to such power.

To those accustomed to give honor to office and to person it seemed that even the Swedes themselves would not dare to raise a sacrilegious hand against such a magnate. Even those whose hearts were beating in their breasts with alarm felt safer at once under his wing. He was greeted therefore joyfully and warmly; shouts thundered along the street through which the retinue pushed slowly toward the house of the mayor, and all heads inclined before the voevoda, who was as visible as on the palm of the hand through the windows of the gilded carriage. To these bows Ostrojka answered, as well as the voevoda, with the same importance and gravity as if they had been given exclusively to him.

Barely had the dust settled after the passage of Opalinski when couriers rushed in with the announcement that his cousin was coming, the voevoda of Podlyasye, Pyotr Opalinski, with his brother-in-law Yakob Rozdrajevski, the voevoda of Inovratslav. These brought each a hundred and fifty armed men, besides nobles and servants. Then not a day passed without the arrival of dignitaries such as Sendzivoi Charnkovski, the brother-in-law of Krishtof Opalinski, and himself castellan of Kalisk; Maksymilian Myaskovski, the castellan of Kryvinsk; and Pavel Gembitski, the lord of Myendzyrechka. The town was so filled with people that houses failed for the lodging even of nobles. The neighboring meadows were many-colored with the tents of the general militia. One might say that all the various colored birds had flown to Pila from the entire Commonwealth. Red, green, blue, azure, white were gleaming on the various coats and garments; for leaving aside the general militia, in which each noble wore a dress different from his neighbor, leaving aside the servants of the magnates, even the infantry of each district were dressed in their own colors.

Shop-keepers came too, who, unable to find places in the market-square, built a row of booths by the side of the town, on these they sold military supplies, from clothing to arms and food. Field-kitchens were steaming day and night, bearing away in the steam the odor of hash, roast meat, millet; in some liquors were sold. Nobles swarmed in front of the booths, armed not only with swords but with spoons, eating, drinking, and discussing, now the enemy not yet to be seen, and now the incoming dignitaries, on whom nicknames were not spared.

Among the groups of nobles walked Ostrojka, in a dress made of party-colored rags, carrying a sceptre ornamented with bells, and with the mien of a simple rogue. Wherever he showed himself men came around in a circle, and he poured oil on the fire, helped them to backbite the dignitaries, and gave riddles over which the nobles held their sides from laughter, the more firmly the more biting the riddles.

On a certain midday the voevoda of Poznan himself came to the bazaar, speaking courteously with this one and that, or blaming the king somewhat because in the face of the approaching enemy he had not sent a single squadron of soldiers.

"They are not thinking of us, worthy gentlemen," said he, "and leave us without assistance. They say in Warsaw that even now there are too few troops in the Ukraine, and that the hetmans are not able to make head against Hmelnitski. Ah, it is difficult! It is pleasanter to see the Ukraine than Great Poland. We are in disfavor, worthy gentlemen, in disfavor! They have delivered us here as it were to be slaughtered."

"And who is to blame?" asked Pan Shlihtyng, the judge of Vskov.

"Who is to blame for all the misfortunes of the Commonwealth," asked the voevoda,--"who, unless we brother nobles who shield it with our breasts?"

The nobles, hearing this, were greatly flattered that the "Count in Bnino and Opalenitsa" put himself on an equality with them, and recognized himself in brotherhood; hence Pan Koshutski answered,--

"Serene great mighty voevoda, if there were more such counsellors as your grace near his Majesty, of a certainty we should not be delivered to slaughter here; but probably those give counsel who bow lower."

"I thank you, brothers, for the good word. The fault is his who listens to evil counsellors. Our liberties are as salt in the eye to those people. The more nobles fall, the easier will it be to introduce *absolutum dominium* (absolute rule)."

"Must we die, then, that our children may groan in slavery?"

The voevoda said nothing, and the nobles began to look at one another and wonder.

"Is that true then?" cried many. "Is that the reason why they sent us here under the knife? And we believe! This is not the first day that they are talking about *absolutum dominium*. But if it comes to that, we shall be able to think of our own heads."

"And of our children."

"And of our fortunes, which the enemy will destroy *igne et ferro* (with fire and sword)."

The voevoda was silent. In a marvellous manner did this leader add to the courage of his soldiers.

"The king is to blame for all!" was shouted more and more frequently.

"But do you remember, gentlemen, the history of Yan Olbracht?" asked the voevoda.

"The nobles perished for King Olbracht. Treason, brothers!"

"The king is a traitor!" cried some bold voices.

The voevoda was silent.

Now Ostrojka, standing by the side of the voevoda, struck himself a number of times on the legs, and crowed like a cock with such shrillness that all eyes were turned to him. Then he shouted, "Gracious lords! brothers, dear hearts! listen to my riddle."

With the genuine fickleness of March weather, the stormy militia changed in one moment to curiosity and desire to hear some new stroke of wit from the jester.

"We hear! we hear!" cried a number of voices.

The jester began to wink like a monkey and to recite in a squeaking voice,--

"After his brother he solace! himself with a crown and a wife,
But let pilory go down to the grave with his brother.
He drove out the vice-chancellor; hence now has the fame
Of being vice-chancellor to--the vice-chancellor's wife."

"The king! the king! As alive! Yan Kazimir!" they began to cry from every side; and laughter, mighty as thunder, was heard in the crowd.

"May the bullets strike him, what a masterly explanation!" cried the nobles.

The voevoda laughed with the others, and when it had grown somewhat calm he said, with increased dignity: "And for this affair we must pay now with our blood and our heads. See what it has come to! Here, jester, is a ducat for thy good verse."

"Kryshtofek! Krysh dearest!" said Ostrojka, "why attack others because they keep jesters, when thou not only keepest me, but payest separately for riddles? Give me another ducat and I'll tell thee another riddle."

"Just as good?"

"As good, only longer. Give me the ducat first."

"Here it is!"

The jester slapped his sides with his hands, as a cock with his wings, crowed again, and cried out, "Gracious gentlemen, listen! Who is this?"

"He complains of self-seeking, stands forth as a Cato;
Instead of a sabre he took a goose's tail-feather
He wanted the legacy of a traitor, and not getting that
He lashed the whole Commonwealth with a biting rhyme.

"God grant him love for the sabre! less woe would it bring.
Of his satire the Swedes have no fear.
But he has barely tasted the hardships of war
When following a traitor he is ready to betray his king."

All present guessed that riddle as well as the first. Two or three laughs, smothered at the same instant, were heard in the assembly; then a deep silence fell.

The voevoda grew purple, and he was the more confused in that all eyes were fixed on him at that moment. But the jester looked on one noble and then on another; at last he said, "None of you gentlemen can guess who that is?"

When silence was the only answer, he turned with the most insolent mien to the voevoda: "And thou, dost thou too not know of what rascal the speech is? Dost thou not know? Then pay me a ducat."

"Here!" said the voevoda.

"God reward thee. But tell me, Krysh, hast thou not perchance tried to get the vice-chancellorship after Radzeyovski?"

"No time for jests," replied Opalinski; and removing his cap to all present: "With the forehead, gentlemen! I must go to the council of war."

"To the family council thou didst wish to say, Krysh," added Ostrojka; "for there all thy relatives will hold council how to be off." Then he turned to the nobles and imitating the voevoda in his bows, he added, "And to you, gentlemen, that's the play."

Both withdrew; but they had barely gone a few steps when an immense outburst of laughter struck the ears of the voevoda, and thundered long before it was drowned in the general noise of the camp.

The council of war was held in fact, and the voevoda of Poznan presided. That was a strange council! Those very dignitaries took part in it who knew nothing of war; for the magnates of Great Poland did not and could not follow the example of those "kinglets" of Lithuania or the Ukraine who lived in continual fire like salamanders.

In Lithuania or the Ukraine whoever was a voevoda or a chancellor was a leader whose armor pressed out on his body red stripes which never left it, whose youth was spent in the steppes or the forests on the eastern border, in ambushes, battles, struggles, pursuits, in camp or in tabors. In Great Poland at this time dignitaries were in office who, though they had marched in times of necessity with the general militia, had never held positions of command in time of war. Profound peace had put to sleep the military courage of the descendants of those warriors, before whom in former days the iron legions of the Knights of the Cross were unable to stand, and turned them into civilians, scholars, and writers. Now the stern school of Sweden was teaching them what they had forgotten.

The dignitaries assembled in council looked at one another with uncertain eyes, and each feared to speak first, waiting for what "Agamemnon," voevoda of Poznan, would say.

But "Agamemnon" himself knew simply nothing, and began his speech again with complaints of the ingratitude and sloth of the king, of the frivolity with which all Great Poland and they were delivered to the sword. But how eloquent was he; what a majestic figure did he present, worthy in truth of a Roman senator! He held his head erect while speaking; his dark eyes shot lightnings, his mouth thunderbolts; his iron-gray beard trembled with excitement when he described the future misfortunes of the land.

"For in what does the fatherland suffer," said he, "if not in its sons? and we here suffer, first of all. Through our private lands, through our private fortunes won by the services and blood of our ancestors, will advance the feet of those enemies who now like a storm are approaching from the sea. And why do we suffer? For what will they take our herds, trample our harvests, burn our villages built by our labor? Have we wronged Radzeyovski, who, condemned unjustly, hunted like a criminal, had to seek the protection of strangers? No! Do we insist that that empty title 'King of Sweden,' which has cost so much blood already, should remain with the signature of our Yan Kazimir? No! Two wars are blazing on two boundaries; was it needful to call forth a third? Who was to blame, may God, may the country judge him! We wash our hands, for we are innocent of the blood which will be shed."

And thus the voevoda thundered on further; but when it came to the question in hand he was not able to give the desired advice.

They sent then for the captains leading the land infantry, and specially for Vladyslav Skorashevski, who was not only a famous and incomparable knight, but an old, practised soldier, knowing war as he did the Lord's Prayer. In fact, genuine leaders listened frequently to his advice; all the more eagerly was it sought for now.

Pan Skorashevski advised then to establish three camps,--at Pila, Vyelunie, and Uistsie,--so near one another that in time of attack they might give mutual aid, and besides this to cover with trenches the whole extent of the river-bank occupied by a half-circle of camps which were to command the passage.

"When we know," said Skorashevski, "the place where the enemy will attempt the crossing, we shall unite from all three camps and give him proper resistance. But I with the permission of your great mighty lordships, will go with a small party to Chaplinko. That is a lost position, and in time I shall withdraw from it; but there I shall first get knowledge of the enemy, and then will inform your great mighty lordships."

All accepted this counsel, and men began to move around somewhat more briskly in the camp. At last the nobles assembled to the number of fifteen thousand. The land infantry dug trenches over an extent of six miles. Uistsie, the chief position, was occupied by the voevoda of Poznan and his men. A part of the knights remained in Vyelunie, a part in Pila, and Vladyslav Skorashevski went to Chaplinko to observe the enemy.

July began; all the days were clear and hot. The sun burned on the plains so violently that the nobles hid in the woods between the trees, under the shade of which some of them gave orders to set up their tents. There also they had noisy and boisterous feasts; and still more of an uproar was made by the servants, especially at the time of washing and watering the horses which, to the number of several thousand at once, were driven thrice each day to the Notets and Berda, quarrelling and fighting for the best approach to the bank. But in the beginning there was a good spirit in the camp; only the voevoda of Poznan himself acted rather to weaken it.

If Wittemberg had come in the first days of July, it is likely that he would have met a mighty resistance, which in proportion as the men warmed to battle might have been turned into an invincible rage, of which there were often examples. For still there flowed knightly blood in the veins of these people, though they had grown unaccustomed to war.

Who knows if another Yeremi Vishnyevetski might not have changed Uistsie into another Zbaraj, and described in those trenches a new illustrious career of knighthood? Unfortunately the voevoda of Poznan was a man who could only write; he knew nothing of war.

Wittemberg, a leader knowing not merely war but men, did not hasten, perhaps on purpose. Experience of long years had taught him that a newly enrolled soldier is most dangerous in the first moments of enthusiasm, and that often not bravery is lacking to him, but soldierly endurance, which practice alone can develop. More than once have new soldiers struck like a storm on the oldest regiments, and passed over their corpses. They are iron which while it is hot quivers, lives, scatters sparks, burns, destroys, but which when it grows cold is a mere lifeless lump.

In fact, when a week had passed, a second, and the third had come, long inactivity began to weigh upon the general militia. The heat became greater each day. The nobles would not go to drill, and gave as excuse that their horses tormented by flies would not stand in line, and as to marshy places they could not live from mosquitoes. Servants raised greater and greater quarrels about shady places, concerning which it came to sabres among their masters. This or that one coming home in the evening from the water rode off to one side from the camp not to return.

Evil example from above was also not wanting. Pan Skorashevski had given notice from Chaplinko that the Swedes were not distant, when at the military council Zygmunt Grudzinski got leave to go home; on this leave his uncle Andrei Grudzinski, voevoda of Kalisk, had greatly insisted. "I have to lay down my head and my life here," said he; "let my nephew inherit after me my memory and glory, so that my services may not be lost." Then he grew tender over the youth and innocence of his nephew, praising the liberality with which he had furnished one hundred very choice soldiers; and the military council granted the prayer of the uncle.

On the morning of July 16, Zygmunt with a few servants left the camp openly for home, on the eve almost of a siege and a battle. Crowds of nobles conducted him amid jeering cries to a distance beyond the camp. Ostrojka led the party, and shouted from afar after the departing,--

"Worthy Pan Zygmunt, I give thee a shield, and as third name Deest!" [13]

"Vivat Deest-Grudzinski!"

"But weep not for thy uncle," continued Ostrojka. "He despises the Swedes as much as thou; and let them only show themselves, he will surely turn his back on them."

The blood of the young magnate rushed to his face, but he pretended not to hear the insults. He put spurs to his horse, however, and pushed aside the crowds, so as to be away from the camp and his persecutors as soon as possible, who at last, without consideration for the birth and dignity of the departing, began to throw clods of earth at him and to cry,--

"Here is a gruda, Grudzinski! [14] You hare, you coward!"

They made such an uproar that the voevoda of Poznan hastened up with a number of captains to quiet them, and explain that Grudzinski had taken leave only for a week on very urgent affairs.

Still the evil example had its effect; and that same day there were several hundred nobles who did not wish to be worse than Grudzinski, though they slipped away with less aid and more quietly. Stanislav Skshetuski, a captain from Kalisk and cousin of the famous Yan of Zbaraj, tore the hair on his head; for his land infantry, following the example of "officers," began to desert from the camp. A new council of war was held in which crowds of nobles refused absolutely to take part. A stormy night followed, full of shouts and quarrels. They suspected one another of the intention to desert. Cries of "Either all or none!" flew from mouth to mouth.

Every moment reports were given out that the voevodas were departing, and such an uproar prevailed that the voevodas had to show themselves several times to the excited multitude. A number of thousands of men were on their horses before daybreak. But the voevoda of Poznan rode between the ranks with uncovered head like a Roman senator, and repeated from moment to moment the great words,--

"Worthy gentlemen, I am with you to live and die."

He was received in some places with vivats; in others shouts of derision were thundering. The moment he had pacified the crowd he returned to the council, tired, hoarse, carried away by the grandeur of his own words, and convinced that he had rendered inestimable service to his country that night. But at the council he had fewer words in his mouth, twisted his beard, and pulled his foretop from despair, repeating,--

"Give counsel if you can; I wash my hands of the future, for it is impossible to make a defence with such soldiers."

"Serene great mighty voevoda," answered Stanislav Skshetuski, "the enemy will drive away that turbulence and uproar. Only let the cannon play, only let it come to defence, to a siege, these very nobles in defence of their own lives must serve on the ramparts and not be disorderly in camp. So it has happened more than once."

"With what can we defend ourselves? We have no cannon, nothing but saluting pieces good to fire off in time of a feast."

"At Zbaraj Hmelnitski had seventy cannon, and Prince Yeremi only a few eight-pounders and mortars."

"But he had an army, not militia,--his own squadrons famed in the world, not country nobles fresh from sheep-shearing."

"Send for Pan Skorashevski," said the castellan of Poznan. "Make him commander of the camp. He is at peace with the nobles, and will be able to keep them in order."

"Send for Skorashevski. Why should he be in Drahim or Chaplinko?" repeated Yendrei Grudzinski, the voevoda of Kalisk.

"Yes, that is the best counsel!" cried other voices.

A courier was despatched for Skorashevski. No other decisions were taken at the council; but they talked much, and complained of the king, the queen, the lack of troops, and negligence.

The following morning brought neither relief nor calm spirits. The disorder had become still greater. Some gave out reports that the dissidents, namely the Calvinists, were favorable to the Swedes, and ready on the first occasion to go over to the enemy. What was more, this news was not contradicted by Pan Shlihtyng nor by Edmund and Yatsck Kurnatovski, also Calvinists, but sincerely devoted to the country. Besides they gave final proof that the dissidents formed a separate circle and consulted with one another under the lead of a noted disturber and cruel man. Pan Rei, who serving in Germany during his youth as a volunteer on the Lutheran side, was a great friend of the Swedes. Scarcely had this suspicion gone out among the nobles when several thousand sabres were gleaming, and a real tempest rose in the camp.

"Let us punish the traitors, punish the serpents, ready to bite the bosom of their mother!" cried the nobles.

"Give them this way!"

"Cut them to pieces! Treason is most infectious, worthy gentlemen. Tear out the cockle or we shall all perish!"

The voevodas and captains had to pacify them again, but this time it was more difficult than the day before. Besides, they were themselves convinced that Rei was ready to betray his country in the most open manner; for he was a man completely foreignized, and except his language had nothing Polish in him. It was decided therefore to send him out of the camp, which at once pacified somewhat the angry multitude. Still shouts continued to burst forth for a long time,--

"Give them here! Treason, treason!"

Wonderful conditions of mind reigned finally in the camp. Some fell in courage and were sunk in grief; others walked in silence, with uncertain steps, along the ramparts, casting timid and gloomy glances along the plains over which the enemy had to approach, or communicated in whispers worse and worse news. Others were possessed of a sort of desperate, mad joy and readiness for death. In consequence of this readiness they arranged feasts and drinking-bouts so as to pass the last days of life in rejoicing. Some thought of saving their souls, and spent the nights in prayer. But in that whole throng of men no one thought of victory, as if it were altogether beyond reach. Still the enemy had not superior forces; they had more cannon, better trained troops, and a leader who understood war.

And while in this wise on one side the Polish camp was seething, shouting, and feasting, rising up with a roar, dropping down to quiet, like a sea lashed by a whirlwind, while the general militia were holding diets as in time of electing a king, on the other side, along the broad green meadows of the Oder, pushed forward in calmness the legions of Sweden.

In front marched a brigade of the royal guard, led by Benedykt Horn, a terrible soldier, whose name was repeated in Germany with fear. The soldiers were chosen men, large, wearing lofty helmets with rims covering their ears, in yellow leather doublets, armed with rapiers and muskets; cool and constant in battle, ready at every beck of the leader.

Karl Schedding, a German, led the West Gothland brigade, formed of two regiments of infantry and one of heavy cavalry, dressed in armor without shoulder-pieces. Half of the infantry had muskets; the others spears. At the beginning of a battle the musketeers stood in front, but in case of attack by cavalry they stood behind the spearmen, who, placing each the butt of his spear in the ground, held the point against the onrushing horses. At a battle in the time of Sigismund III. one squadron of hussars cut to pieces with their sabres and with hoofs this same West Gothland brigade, in which at present Germans served mainly.

The two Smaland brigades were led by Irwin, surnamed Handless, for he had lost his right hand on a time while defending his flag; but to make up for this loss he had in his left such strength that with one blow he could hew off the head of a horse. He was a gloomy warrior, loving battles and bloodshed alone, stern to himself and to soldiers. While other captains trained themselves in continual wars into followers of a craft, and loved war for its own sake, he remained the same fanatic, and while slaying men he sang psalms to the Lord.

The brigade of Westrmanland marched under Drakenborg; and that of Helsingor, formed of sharpshooters famed through the world, under Gustav Oxenstiern, a relative of the renowned chancellor,--a young soldier who roused great hopes. Fersen commanded the East Gothland brigade; the Nerik and Werland brigades were directed by Wittemberg himself, who at the same time was supreme chief of the whole army.

Seventy-two cannon pounded out furrows in the moist meadows; of soldiers there were seventeen thousand, the fierce plunderers of all Germany, and in battle they were so accurate, especially the infantry, that the French royal guard could hardly compare with them. After the regiments followed the wagons and tents. The regiments marched in line, ready each moment for battle. A forest of lances was bristling above the mass of heads, helmets, and hats; and in the midst of that forest flowed on toward the frontier of Poland the great blue banners with white crosses in the centre. With each day the distance decreased between the two armies.

At last on July 27, in the forest at the village of Heinrichsdorf, the Swedish legions beheld for the first time the boundary pillar of Poland. At sight of this the whole army gave forth a mighty shout; trumpets and drums thundered, and all the flags were unfurled. Wittemberg rode to the front attended by a brilliant staff, and all the regiments passed before him, presenting arms,--the cavalry with drawn rapiers, the cannon with lighted matches. The time was midday; the weather glorious. The forest breeze brought the odor of resin.

The gray road, covered with the rays of the sun,--the road over which the Swedish regiments had passed,--bending out of the

Heinrichsdorf forest, was lost on the horizon. When the troops marching by it had finally passed the forest, their glances discovered a gladsome land, smiling, shining with yellow fields of every kind of grain, dotted in places with oak groves, in places green from meadows. Here and there out of groups of trees, behind oak groves and far away rose bits of smoke to the sky; on the grass herds were seen grazing. Where on the meadows the water gleamed widely spread, walked storks at their leisure.

A certain calm and sweetness was spread everywhere over that land flowing with milk and honey, and it seemed to open its arms ever wider and wider before the army, as if it greeted not invaders but guests coming with God.

At this sight a new shout was wrested from the bosoms of all the soldiers, especially the Swedes by blood, who were accustomed to the bare, poor, wild nature of their native land. The hearts of a plundering and needy people rose with desire to gather those treasures and riches which appeared before their eyes. Enthusiasm seized the ranks.

But the soldiers, tempered in the fire of the Thirty Years' War, expected that this would not come to them easily; for that grainland was inhabited by a numerous and a knightly people, who knew how to defend it. The memory was still living in Sweden of the terrible defeat of Kirchholm, where three thousand cavalry under Hodkyevich ground into dust eighteen thousand of the best troops of Sweden. In the cottages of West Gothland, Smaland, or Delakarlia they told tales of those winged knights, as of giants from a saga. Fresher still was the memory of the struggles in the time of Gustavus Adolphus, for the warriors were not yet extinct who had taken part in them. But that eagle of Scandinavia, ere he had flown twice through all Germany, broke his talons on the legions of Konyetspolski.

Therefore with the gladness there was joined in the hearts of the Swedes a certain fear, of which the supreme chief, Wittemberg himself, was not free. He looked on the passing regiments of infantry and cavalry with the eye with which a shepherd looks on his flock; then he turned to the rear man, who wore a hat with a feather, and a light-colored wig falling to his shoulders.

"Your grace assures me," said he, "that with these forces it is possible to break the army occupying Uistsie?"

The man with the light wig smiled and answered: "Your grace may rely completely on my words, for which I am ready to pledge my head. If at Uistsie there were regular troops and some one of the hetmans, I first would give counsel not to hasten, but to wait till his royal Grace should come with the whole army; but against the general militia and those gentlemen of Great Poland our forces will be more than sufficient."

"But have not reinforcements come to them?"

"Reinforcements have not come for two reasons,--first, because all the regular troops, of which there are not many, are occupied in Lithuania and the Ukraine; second, because in Warsaw neither the King Yan Kazimir, the chancellor, nor the senate will believe to this moment that his royal Grace Karl Gustav has really begun war in spite of the truce, and notwithstanding the last embassies and his readiness to compromise. They are confident that peace will be made at the last hour,--ha, ha!"

Here the rear man removed his hat, wiped the sweat from his red face, and added: "Trubetskoi and Dolgoruki in Lithuania, Hmelnitski in the Ukraine, and we entering Great Poland,--behold what the government of Yan Kazimir has led to."

Wittemberg gazed on him with a look of astonishment, and asked, "But, your grace, do you rejoice at the thought?"

"I rejoice at the thought, for my wrong and my innocence will be avenged; and besides I see, as on the palm of my hand, that the sabre of your grace and my counsels will place that new and most beautiful crown in the world on the head of Karl Gustav."

Wittemberg turned his glance to the distance, embraced with it the oak-groves, the meadows, the grain-fields, and after a while said: "True, it is a beautiful country and fertile. Your grace may be sure that after the war the king will give the chancellorship to no one else but you."

The man in the rear removed his cap a second time. "And I, for my part, wish to have no other lord," added he, raising his eyes to heaven.

The heavens were clear and fair; no thunderbolt fell and crashed to the dust the traitor who delivered his country, groaning under two wars already and exhausted, to the power of the enemy on that boundary.

The man conversing with Wittemberg was Hieronim Kailzeyovski, late under-chancellor of the Crown, now sold to Sweden in hostility to his country.

They stood a time in silence. Meanwhile the last two brigades, those of Nerik and Wermland, passed the boundary; after them others began to draw in the cannon; the trumpets still played unceasingly; the roar and rattle of drums outsounded the tramp of the soldiers, and filled the forest with ominous echoes. At last the staff moved also. Radzeyovski rode at the side of Wittemberg.

"Oxenstiern is not to be seen," said Wittemberg. "I am afraid that something may have happened to him. I do not know whether it was wise to send him as a trumpeter with letters to Uistsie."

"It was wise," answered Radzeyovski, "for he will look at the camp, will see the leaders, and learn what they think there; and this any kind of camp-follower could not do."

"But if they recognize him?"

"Rei alone knows him, and he is ours. Besides, even if they should recognize him, they will do him no harm, but will give him supplies for the road and reward him. I know the Poles, and I know they are ready for anything, merely to show themselves polite people before strangers. Our whole effort is to win the praise of strangers. Your grace may be at rest concerning Oxenstiern, for a hair will not fall from his head. He has not come because it is too soon for his return."

"And does your grace think our letters will have any effect?"

Radzeyovski laughed. "If your grace permits, I will foretell what will happen. The voevoda of Poznan is a polished and learned man, therefore he will answer us very courteously and very graciously; but because he loves to pass for a Roman, his answer will be terribly Roman. He will say, to begin with, that he would rather shed the last drop of his blood than surrender, that death is better than dishonor, and the love which he bears his country directs him to fall for her on the boundary."

Radzeyovski laughed still louder. The stern face of Wittemberg brightened also.

"Your grace does not think that he will be ready to act as he writes?" asked Wittemberg.

"He?" answered Radzeyovski. "It is true that he nourishes a love for his country, but with ink; and that is not over-strong food. His love is in fact more scant than that of his jester who helps him to put rhymes together. I am certain that after that Roman answer will come good wishes for health, success, offers of service, and at last a request to spare his property and that of his relatives, for which again he with all his relatives will be thankful."

"And what at last will be the result of our letters?"

"The courage of the other side will weaken to the last degree, senators will begin to negotiate with us, and we shall occupy all Great Poland after perhaps a few shots in the air."

"Would that your grace be a true prophet!"

"I am certain that it will be as I say, for I know these people. I have friends and adherents in the whole country, and I know how to begin. And that I shall neglect nothing is made sure by the wrong which I endure from Van Kazimir, and my love for Karl Gustav. People with us are more tender at present about their own fortunes than the integrity of the Commonwealth. All those lands upon which we shall now march are the estates of the Opalinskis, the Charnkovskis, the Grudzinskis; and because they are at Uistsie in person they will be milder in negotiating. As to the nobles, if only their freedom of disputing at the diets is guaranteed, they will follow the voevodas."

"By knowledge of the country and the people your grace renders the king unexampled service, which cannot remain without an equally noteworthy reward. Therefore from what you say I conclude that I may look on this land as ours."

"You may, your grace, you may, you may," repeated Radzeyovski hurriedly, a number of times.

"Therefore I occupy it in the name of his Royal Grace Karl Gustav," answered Wittemberg, solemnly.

While the Swedish troops were thus beginning beyond Heinrichsdorf to walk on the land of Great Poland, and even earlier, for it was on July 18, a Swedish trumpeter arrived at the Polish camp with letters from Radzeyovski and Wittemberg to the voevodas.

Vladyslav Skorashevski himself conducted the trumpeter to the voevoda of Poznan, and the nobles of the general militia gazed with curiosity on the "first Swede," wondering at his valiant bearing, his manly face, his blond mustaches, the ends combed upward in a broad brush, and his really lordlike mien. Crowds followed him to the voevoda; acquaintances called to one another, pointing him out with their fingers, laughed somewhat at his boots with enormous round legs, and at the long straight rapier, which they called a spit, hanging from a belt richly worked with silver. The Swede also cast curious glances from under his broad hat, as if wishing to examine the camp and estimate the forces, and then looked repeatedly at the crowd of nobles whose oriental costumes were apparently novel to him. At last he was brought to the voevoda, around whom were grouped all the dignitaries in the camp.

The letters were read immediately, and a council held. The voevoda committed the trumpeter to his attendants to be entertained in soldier fashion; the nobles took him from the attendants, and wondering at the man as a curiosity, began to drink for life and death with him.

Pan Skorashevski looked at the Swede with equal scrutiny; but because he suspected him to be some officer in disguise, he went in fact to convey that idea in the evening to the voevoda. The latter, however, said it was all one, and did not permit his arrest.

"Though he were Wittemberg himself, he has come hither as an envoy and should go away unmolested. In addition I command you to give him ten ducats for the road."

The trumpeter meanwhile was talking in broken German with those nobles who, through intercourse with Prussian towns, understood that language. He told them of victories won by Wittemberg in various lands, of the forces marching against Uistsie, and especially of the cannon of a range hitherto unknown and which could not be resisted. The nobles were troubled at this, and no small number of exaggerated accounts began to circulate through the camp.

That night scarcely any one slept in Uistsie. About midnight those men came in who had stood hitherto in separate camps, at Pila and Vyelunie. The dignitaries deliberated over their answer to the letters till daylight, and the nobles passed the time in stories about the power of the Swedes.

With a certain feverish curiosity they asked the trumpeter about the leaders of the army, the weapons, the method of fighting; and every answer of his was given from mouth to mouth. The nearness of the Swedish legions lent unusual interest to all the details, which were not of a character to give consolation.

About daylight Stanislav Skshetuski came with tidings that the Swedes had arrived at Valch, one day's march from the Polish camp. There rose at once a terrible hubbub; most of the horses with the servants were at pasture on the meadows. They were sent for then with all haste. Districts mounted and formed squadrons. The moment before battle was for the untrained soldier the most terrible; therefore before the captains were able to introduce any kind of system there reigned for a long time desperate disorder.

Neither commands nor trumpets could be heard; nothing but voices crying on every side: "Yan! Pyotr! Onufri! This way! I wish thou wert killed! Bring the horses! Where are my men? Yan! Pyotr!" If at that moment one cannon-shot had been heard, the disorder might easily have been turned to a panic.

Gradually, however, the districts were ranged in order. The inborn capacity of the nobles for war made up for the want of experience, and about midday the camp presented an appearance imposing enough. The infantry stood on the ramparts looking like flowers in their many-colored coats, smoke was borne away from the lighted matches, and outside the ramparts under cover of the guns the meadows and plain were swarming with the district squadrons of cavalry standing in line on sturdy horses, whose neighing roused an echo in the neighboring forests and filled all hearts with military ardor.

Meanwhile the voevoda of Poznan sent away the trumpeter with an answer to the letter reading more or less as Radzeyovski had foretold, therefore both courteous and Roman; then he determined to send a party to the northern bank of the Notets to seize an informant from the enemy.

Pyotr Opalinski, voevoda of Podlyasye, a cousin of the voevoda Poznan, was to go in person with a party together with his own dragoons, a hundred and fifty of whom he had brought to Uistsie; and besides this it was given to Captains Skorashevski and Skshetuski to call out volunteers from the nobles of the general militia, so that they might also look in the eyes of the enemy.

Both rode before the ranks, delighting the eye by manner and posture,--Pan Stanislav black as a beetle, like all the Skshetuskis, with a manly face, stern and adorned with a long sloping scar which remained from a sword-blow, with raven black beard blown aside by the wind; Pan Vladyslav portly, with long blond mustaches, open under lip, and eyes with red lids, mild and honest, reminding one less of Mars,--but none the less a genuine soldier spirit, as glad to be in fire as a salamander,--a knight knowing war as his ten fingers, and of incomparable daring. Both, riding before the ranks extended in a long line, repeated from moment to moment,--

"Now, gracious gentlemen, who is the volunteer against the Swedes? Who wants to smell powder? Well, gracious gentlemen, volunteer!"

And so they continued for a good while without result, for no man pushed forward from the ranks. One looked at another. There were those who desired to go and had no fear of the Swedes, but indecision restrained them. More than one nudged his neighbor and said, "Go you, and then I'll go." The captains were growing impatient, till all at once, when they had ridden up to the district of Gnyezno, a certain man dressed in many colors sprang forth on a hoop, not from the line but from behind the line, and cried,--

"Gracious gentlemen of the militia, I'll be the volunteer and ye will be jesters!"

"Ostrojka! Ostrojka!" cried the nobles.

"I am just as good a noble as any of you!" answered the jester.

"Tfu! to a hundred devils!" cried Pan Rosinski; under-judge, "a truce to jesting! I will go."

"And I! and I!" cried numerous voices.

"Once my mother bore me, once for me is death!"

"As good as thou will be found!"

"Freedom to each. Let no man here exalt himself above others."

And as no one had come forth before, so now nobles began to rush out from every district, spurring forward their horses, disputing with one another and fighting to advance. In the twinkle of an eye there were five hundred horsemen, and still they were riding forth from the ranks. Pan Skorashevski began to laugh with his honest, open laugh.

"Enough, worthy gentlemen, enough! We cannot all go."

Then the two captains put the men in order and marched.

The voevoda of Podlyasye joined the horsemen as they were riding out of camp. They were seen as on the palm of the hand crossing the Notets; after that they glittered some time on the windings of the road, then vanished from sight.

At the expiration of half an hour the voevoda of Poznan ordered the troops to their tents, for he saw that it was impossible to keep them in the ranks when the enemy were still a day's march distant. Numerous pickets were thrown out, however; it was not permitted to drive horses to pasture, and the order was given that at the first low sound of the trumpet through the mouthpiece all were to mount and be ready.

Expectation and uncertainty had come to an end, quarrels and disputes were finished at once, for the nearness of the enemy had raised their courage as Pan Skshetuski had predicted. The first successful battle might raise it indeed very high; and in the evening an event took place which seemed of happy omen.

The sun was just setting,--lighting with enormous glitter, dazzling the eyes, the Notets, and the pine-woods beyond,--when on the other side of the river was seen first a cloud of dust, and then men moving in the cloud. All that was living went out on the ramparts to see what manner of guests these were. At that moment a dragoon of the guards rushed in from the squadron of Pan Grudzinski with intelligence that the horsemen were returning.

"The horsemen are returning with success! The Swedes have not eaten them!" was repeated from mouth to mouth.

Meanwhile they in bright rolls of dust approached nearer and nearer, coming slowly; then they crossed the Notets.

The nobles with their hands over their eyes gazed at them; for the glitter became each moment greater, and the whole air was filled with gold and purple light.

"Hei! the party is somewhat larger than when it went out," said Shlihtyng.

"They must be bringing prisoners, as God is dear to me!" cried a noble, apparently without confidence and not believing his eyes.

"They are bringing prisoners! They are bringing prisoners!"

They had now come so near that their faces could be recognized. In front rode Skorashevski, nodding his head as usual and talking joyously with Skshetuski; after them the strong detachment of horse surrounded a few tens of infantry wearing round hats. They were really Swedish prisoners.

At this sight the nobles could not contain themselves; and ran forward with shouts: "Vivat Skorashevski! Vivat Skshetuski!"

A dense crowd surrounded the party at once. Some looked at the prisoners; some asked, "How was the affair?" others threatened the Swedes.

"Ah-hu! Well now, good for you, ye dogs! Ye wanted to war with the Poles? Ye have the Poles now!"

"Give them here! Sabre them, make mince-meat of them!"

"Ha, broad-breeches! ye have tried the Polish sabres?"

"Gracious gentlemen, don't shout like little boys, for the prisoners will think that this is your first war," said Skorashevski; "it is a common thing to take prisoners in time of war."

The volunteers who belonged to the party looked with pride on the nobles who overwhelmed them with questions: "How was it? Did they surrender easily? Had you to sweat over them? Do they fight well?"

"They are good fellows," said Rosinski, "they defended themselves well; but they are not iron,--a sabre cuts them."

"So they couldn't resist you, could they?"

"They could not resist the impetus."

"Gracious gentlemen, do you hear what is said,--they could not resist the impetus. Well, what does that mean? Impetus is the main thing."

"Remember if only there is impetus!--that is the best method against the Swedes."

If at that moment those nobles had been commanded to rush at the enemy, surely impetus would not have been lacking; but it was well into the night when the sound of a trumpet was heard before the forepost. A trumpeter arrived with a letter from Wittemberg summoning the nobles to surrender. The crowds hearing of this wanted to cut the messenger to pieces; but the voevodas took the letter into consideration, though the substance of it was insolent.

The Swedish general announced that Karl Gustav sent his troops to his relative Yan Kazimir, as reinforcements against the Cossacks, that therefore the people of Great Poland should yield without resistance. Pan Grudzinski on reading this letter could not restrain his indignation, and struck the table with his fist; but the voevoda of Poznan quieted him at once with the question,--

"Do you believe in victory? How many days can we defend ourselves? Do you wish to take the responsibility for so much noble blood which may be shed to-morrow?"

After a long deliberation it was decided not to answer, and to wait for what would happen. They did not wait long. On Saturday, July 24, the pickets announced that the whole Swedish army had appeared before Pila. There was as much bustle in camp as in a beehive on the eve of swarming.

The nobles mounted their horses; the voevodas hurried along the ranks, giving contradictory commands till Vladyslav Skorashevski took everything in hand; and when he had established order he rode out at the head of a few hundred volunteers to try skirmishing beyond the river and accustom the men to look at the enemy.

The cavalry went with him willingly enough, for skirmishing consisted generally of struggles carried on by small groups or singly, and such struggles the nobles trained to sword exercise did not fear at all.

They went out therefore beyond the river, and stood before the enemy, who approached nearer and nearer, and blackened with a long line the horizon, as if a grove had grown freshly from the ground. Regiments of cavalry and infantry deployed, occupying more and more space.

The nobles expected that skirmishers on horseback might rush against them at any moment. So far they were not to be seen; but on the low hills a few hundred yards distant small groups halted, in which were to be seen men and horses, and they began to turn around on the place. Seeing this, Skorashevski commanded without delay, "To the left! to the rear!"

But the voice of command had not yet ceased to sound when on the hills long white curls of smoke bloomed forth, and as it were birds of some kind flew past with a whistle among the nobles; then a report shook the air, and at the same moment were heard cries and groans of a few wounded.

"Halt!" cried Skorashevski.

The birds flew past a second and a third time; again groans accompanied the whistle. The nobles did not listen to the command of the chief, but retreated at increased speed, shouting, and calling for the aid of heaven. Then the division scattered, in the twinkle of an eye, over the plain, and rushed on a gallop to the camp. Skorashevski was cursing, but that did no good.

Wittemberg, having dispersed the skirmishers so easily pushed on farther, till at last he stood in front of Uistsie, straight before the trenches defended by the nobles of Kalish. The Polish guns began to play, but at first no answer was made from the Swedish side. The smoke fell away quietly in the clear air in long streaks stretching between the armies, and in the spaces between them the nobles saw the Swedish regiments, infantry and cavalry, deploying with terrible coolness as if certain of victory.

On the hills the cannon were fixed, trenches raised; in a word, the enemy came into order without paying the least attention to the balls which, without reaching them, merely scattered sand and earth on the men working in the trenches.

Pan Skshetuski led out once more two squadrons of the men of Kalish, wishing by a bold attack to confuse the Swedes. But they did not go willingly; the division fell at once into a disorderly crowd, for when the most daring urged their horses forward the most cowardly held theirs back on purpose. Two regiments of cavalry sent by Wittemberg drove the nobles from the field after a short struggle, and pursued them to the camp. Now dusk came, and put an end to the bloodless strife.

There was firing from cannon till night, when firing ceased; but such a tumult rose in the Polish camp that it was heard on the other bank of the Notets. It rose first for the reason that a few hundred of the general militia tried to slip away in the darkness. Others, seeing this, began to threaten and detain them. Sabres were drawn. The words "Either all or none" flew again from mouth to mouth. At every moment it seemed most likely that all would go. Great dissatisfaction burst out against the leaders: "They sent us with naked breasts against cannon," cried the militia.

They were enraged in like degree against Wittemberg, because without regard to the customs of war he had not sent skirmishers against skirmishers, but had ordered to fire on them unexpectedly from cannon. "Every one will do for himself what is best," said they; "but it is the custom of a swinish people not to meet face to face." Others were in open despair. "They will smoke us out of this place like badgers out of a hole," said they. "The camp is badly planned, the trenches are badly made, the place is not fitted for defence." From time to time voices were heard: "Save yourselves, brothers!" Still others cried: "Treason! treason!"

That was a terrible night: confusion and relaxation increased every moment; no one listened to commands. The voevodas lost their heads, and did not even try to restore order; and the imbecility of the general militia appeared as clearly as on the palm of the hand. Wittemberg might have taken the camp by assault on that night with the greatest ease.

Dawn came. The day broke pale, cloudy, and lighted a chaotic gathering of people fallen in courage, lamenting, and the greater number drunk, more ready for shame than for battle. To complete the misfortune, the Swedes had crossed the Notets at Dzyembovo and surrounded the Polish camp.

At that side there were scarcely any trenches, and there was nothing from behind which they could defend themselves. They should have raised breastworks without delay. Skorashevski and Skshetuski had implored to have this done, but no one would listen to anything.

The leaders and the nobles had one word on their lips, "Negotiate!" Men were sent out to parley. In answer there came from the Swedish camp a brilliant party, at the head of which rode Radzeyovski and General Wirtz, both with green branches.

They rode to the house in which the voevoda of Poznan was living; but on the way Radzeyovski stopped amid the crowd of nobles, bowed with the branch, with his hat, laughed, greeted his acquaintants, and said in a piercing voice,--

"Gracious gentlemen, dearest brothers, be not alarmed! Not as enemies do we come. On you it depends whether a drop of blood more will be shed. If you wish instead of a tyrant who is encroaching on your liberties, who is planning for absolute power, who has brought the country to final destruction,--if you wish, I repeat, a good ruler, a noble one, a warrior of such boundless glory that at bare mention of his name all the enemies of the Commonwealth will flee,--give yourselves under the protection of the most serene Karl Gustav. Gracious gentlemen, dearest brothers, behold, I bring to you the guarantee of all your liberties, of your freedom, of your religion. On yourselves your salvation depends. Gracious gentlemen, the most serene Swedish king undertakes to quell the Cossack rebellion, to finish the war in Lithuania; and only he can do that. Take pity on the unfortunate country if you have no pity on yourselves."

Here the voice of the traitor quivered as if stopped by tears. The nobles listened with astonishment; here and there scattered voices cried, "Vivat Radzeyovski, our vice-chancellor!" He rode farther, and again bowed to new throngs, and again was heard his trumpet-like voice: "Gracious gentlemen, dearest brothers!" And at last he and Wirtz with the whole retinue vanished in the house of the voevoda of Poznan.

The nobles crowded so closely before the house that it would have been possible to ride on their heads, for they felt and understood that there in that house men were deciding the question not only of them but of the whole country. The servants of the voevodas, in scarlet colors, came out and began to invite the more important personages to the council. They entered quickly, and after them burst in a few of the smaller; but the rest remained at the door, they pressed to the windows, put their ears even to the walls.

A deep silence reigned in the throng. Those standing nearest the windows heard from time to time the sound of shrill voices from within the chamber, as it were the echo of quarrels, disputes, and fights. Hour followed hour, and no end to the council.

Suddenly the doors wore thrown open with a crash, and out burst Vladyslav Skorashevski. Those present pushed back in astonishment. That man, usually so calm and mild, of whom it was said that wounds might be healed under his hand, had that moment a terrible face. His eyes were red, his look wild, his clothing torn open on his breast; both hands were grasping his hair, and he rushed out like a thunderbolt among the nobles, and cried with a piercing voice,--

"Treason! murder! shame! We are Sweden now, and Poland no longer!"

He began to roar with an awful voice, with a spasmodic cry, and to tear his hair like a man who is losing his reason. A silence of the grave reigned all around. A certain fearful foreboding seized all hearts.

Skorashevski sprang away quickly, began to run among the nobles and cry with a voice of the greatest despair: "To arms, to arms, whoso believes in God! To arms, to arms!"

Then certain murmurs began to fly through the throngs,--certain momentary whispers, sudden and broken, like the first beatings of the wind before a storm. Hearts hesitated, minds hesitated, and in that universal distraction of feelings the tragic voice was calling continually, "To arms, to arms!"

Soon two other voices joined his,--those of Pyotr Skorashevski and Stanislav Shshetuski. After them ran up Klodzinski, the gallant captain of the district of Pozpan. An increasing circle of nobles began to surround them. A threatening murmur was heard round about; flames ran over the faces and shot out of the eyes; sabres rattled. Vladyslav Skorashevski mastered the first transport, and began to speak, pointing to the house in which the council was being held,--

"Do you hear, gracious gentlemen? They are selling the country there like Judases, and disgracing it. Do you know that we belong to Poland no longer? It was not enough for them to give into the hands of the enemy all of you,--camp, army, cannon. Would they were killed! They have affirmed with their own signatures and in your names that we abjure our ties with the country, that we abjure our king; that the whole land--towns, towers, and we all--shall belong forever to Sweden. That an army surrenders happens, but who has the right to renounce his country and his king? Who has the right to tear away a province, to join strangers, to go over to another people, to renounce his own blood? Gracious gentlemen, this is disgrace, treason, murder, parricide! Save the fatherland, brothers! In God's name, whoever is a noble, whoever has virtue, let him save our mother. Let us give our lives, let us shed our blood! We do not want to be Swedes; we do not, we do not! Would that he had never been born who will spare his blood now! Let us rescue our mother!"

"Treason!" cried several hundred voices, "treason! Let us cut them to pieces."

"Join us, whoever has virtue!" cried Skshetuski.

"Against the Swedes till death!" added Klodzinski.

And they went along farther in the camp, shouting: "Join us! Assemble! There is treason!" and after them moved now several hundred nobles with drawn sabres.

But an immense majority remained in their places; and of those who followed some, seeing that they were not many, began to look around and stand still.

Now the door of the council-house was thrown open, and in it appeared the voevoda of Poznan, Pan Opalinski, having on his right side General Wirtz, and on the left Radzeyovski. After them came Andrei Grudzinski, voevoda of Kalisk; Myaskovski, castellan of Kryvinsk; Gembitski, castellan of Myendzyrechka, and Andrei Slupski.

Pan Opalinski had in his hand a parchment with seals appended; he held his head erect, but his face was pale and his look uncertain, though evidently he was trying to be joyful. He took in with his glance the crowds, and in the midst of a deathlike silence began to speak with a piercing though somewhat hoarse voice,--

"Gracious gentlemen, this day we have put ourselves under the protection of the most serene King of Sweden. Vivat Carolus Gustavus Rex!"

Silence gave answer to the voevoda; suddenly some loud voice thundered, "Veto!"

The voevoda turned his eyes in the direction of the voice and said: "This is not a provincial diet, therefore a veto is not in place. And whoever wishes to veto let him go against the Swedish cannon turned upon us, which in one hour could make of this camp a pile of ruins."

Then he was silent, and after a while inquired, "Who said Veto?"

No one answered.

The voevoda again raised his voice, and began still more emphatically: "All the liberties of the nobles and the clergy will be maintained; taxes will not be increased, and will be collected in the same manner as hitherto; no man will suffer wrongs or robbery. The armies of his royal Majesty have not the right to quarter on the property of nobles nor to other exactions, unless to such as the quota of the Polish squadrons enjoy."

Here he was silent, and heard an anxious murmur of the nobles, as if they wished to understand his meaning; then he beckoned with his hand.

"Besides this, we have the word and promise of General Wirtz, given in the name of his royal Majesty, that if the whole country will follow our saving example, the Swedish armies will move promptly into Lithuania and the Ukraine, and will not cease to war until all the lands and all the fortresses of the Commonwealth are won back. Vivat Carolus Gustavus Rex!"

"Vivat Carolus Gustavus Rex!" cried hundreds of voices. "Vivat Carolus Gustavus Rex!" thundered still more loudly in the whole camp.

Here, before the eyes of all, the voevoda of Poznan turned to Radzeyovski and embraced him heartily; then he embraced Wirtz; then all began to embrace one another. The nobles followed the example of the dignitaries, and joy became universal. They gave vivats so loud that the echoes thundered throughout the whole region. But the voevoda of Poznan begged yet the beloved brotherhood for a moment of quiet, and said in a tone of cordiality,--

"Gracious gentlemen! General Wittemberg invites us today to a feast in his camp, so that at the goblets a brotherly alliance may be concluded with a manful people."

"Vivat Wittemberg! vivat! vivat! vivat!"

"And after that, gracious gentlemen," added the voevoda, "let us go to our homes, and with the assistance of God let us begin the harvest with the thought that on this day we have saved the fatherland."

"Coming ages will render us justice," said Radzeyovski.

"Amen!" finished the voevoda of Poznan.

Meanwhile he saw that the eyes of many nobles were gazing at and scanning something above his head. He turned and saw his own jester, who, holding with one hand to the frame above the door, was writing with a coal on the wall of the council-house over the door: "Mene Tekel-Peres." [15]

In the world the heavens were covered with clouds, and a tempest was coming.

CHAPTER XII.

In the district of Lukovo, on the edge of Podlyasye, stood the village of Bujets, owned by the Skshetuskis. In a garden between the mansion and a pond an old man was sitting on a bench; and at his feet were two little boys,--one five, the other four years old,--dark and sunburned as gypsies, but rosy and healthy. The old man, still fresh, seemed as sturdy as an aurochs. Age had not bent his broad shoulders; from his eyes--or rather from his eye, for he had one covered with a cataract--beamed health and good-humor; he had a white beard, but a look of strength and a ruddy face, ornamented on the forehead with a broad scar, through which his skull-bone was visible.

The little boys, holding the straps of his boot-leg, were pulling in opposite directions; but he was gazing at the pond, which gleamed with the rays of the sun,--at the pond, in which fish were springing up frequently, breaking the smooth surface of the water.

"The fish are dancing," muttered he to himself. "Never fear, ye will dance still better when the floodgate is open, or when the cook is scratching you with a knife." Then he turned to the little boys: "Get away from my boot-leg, for when I catch one of your ears, I'll pull it off. Just like mad horse-flies! Go and roll balls there on the grass and let me alone! I do not wonder at Longinek, for he is young; but Yaremka ought to have sense by this time. Ah, torments! I'll take one of you and throw him into the pond."

But it was clear that the old man was in terrible subjection to the boys, for neither had the least fear of his threats; on the contrary, Yaremka, the elder, began to pull the boot-leg still harder, bracing his feet and repeating,--

"Oh, Grandfather, be Bogun and steal away Longinek."

"Be off, thou beetle, I say, thou rogue, thou cheese-roll!"

"Oh, Grandfather, be Bogun!"

"I'll give thee Bogun; wait till I call thy mother!"

Yaremka looked toward the door leading from the house to the garden, but finding it closed, and seeing no sign of his mother, he repeated the third time, pouting, "Grandfather, be Bogun!"

"Ah, they will kill me, the rogues; it cannot be otherwise. Well, I'll be Bogun, but only once. Oh, it is a punishment of God! Mind ye do not plague me again!"

When he had said this, the old man groaned a little, raised himself from the bench, then suddenly grabbed little Longinek, and giving out loud shouts, began to carry him off in the direction of the pond.

Longinek, however, had a valiant defender in his brother, who on such occasions did not call himself Yaremka, but Pan Michael Volodyovski, captain of dragoons.

Pan Michael, then, armed with a basswood club, which took the place of a sabre in this sudden emergency, ran swiftly after the bulky Bogun, soon caught up with him, and began to beat him on the legs without mercy.

Longinek, playing the rôle of his mamma, made an uproar, Bogun made an uproar, Yaremka-Volodyovski made an uproar; but valor at last overcame even Bogun, who, dropping his victim, began to make his way back to the linden-tree. At last he reached the bench, fell upon it, panting terribly and repeating,--

"Ah, ye little stumps! It will be a wonder if I do not suffocate."

But the end of his torment had not come yet, for a moment later Yaremka stood before him with a ruddy face, floating hair, and distended nostrils, like a brisk young falcon, and began to repeat with greater energy,--

"Grandfather, be Bogun!"

After much teasing and a solemn promise given to the two boys that this would surely be the last time, the story was repeated in all its details; then they sat three in a row on the bench and Yaremka began,--

"Oh, Grandfather, tell who was the bravest."

"Thou, thou!" said the old man.

"And shall I grow up to be a knight?"

"Surely thou wilt, for there is good soldier blood in thee. God grant thee to be like thy father; for if brave thou wilt not tease so much-- understand me?"

"Tell how many men has Papa killed?"

"It's little if I have told thee a hundred times! Easier for thee to count the leaves on this linden-tree than all the enemies which thy father and I have destroyed. If I had as many hairs on my head as I myself have put down, the barbers in Lukovsk would make fortunes just in shaving my temples. I am a rogue if I li--"

Here Pan Zagloba--for it was he--saw that it did not become him to adjure or swear before little boys, though in the absence of other listeners he loved to tell even the children of his former triumphs; he grew silent this time especially because the fish had begun to spring up in the pond with redoubled activity.

"We must tell the gardener," said he, "to set the net for the night; a great many fine fish are crowding right up to the bank."

Now that door of the house which led into the garden opened, and in it appeared a woman beautiful as the midday sun, tall, firm, black-haired, with bloom on her brunette face, and eyes like velvet. A third boy, three years old, dark as an agate ball, hung to her skirt. She, shading her eyes with her hand, looked in the direction of the linden-tree. This was Pani Helena Skshetuski, of the princely house of Bulyga-Kurtsevich.

Seeing Pan Zagloba with Yaremka and Longinek under the tree, she went forward a few steps toward the ditch, full of water, and called: "Come here, boys! Surely you are plaguing Grandfather?"

"How plague me! They have acted nicely all the time," said the old man.

The boys ran to their mother; but she asked Zagloba, "What will Father drink to-day,--dembniak or mead?"

"We had pork for dinner; mead will be best."

"I'll send it this minute; but Father must not fall asleep in the air, for fever is sure to come."

"It is warm to-day, and there is no wind. But where is Yan, Daughter?"

"He has gone to the barns."

Pani Skshetuski called Zagloba father, and he called her daughter, though they were in no way related. Her family dwelt beyond the Dnieper, in the former domains of Vishnyevetski; and as to him God alone knew his origin, for he told various tales about it himself. But Zagloba had rendered famous services to Pani Skshetuski when she was still a maiden, and he had rescued her from terrible dangers; therefore she and her husband treated him as a father, and in the whole region about he was honored beyond measure by all, as well for his inventive mind as for the uncommon bravery of which he had given many proofs in various wars, especially in those against the Cossacks. His name was known in the whole Commonwealth. The king himself was enamored of his stories and wit; and in general he was more spoken of than even Pan Skshetuski, though the latter in his time had burst through besieged Zbaraj and all the Cossack armies.

Soon after Pani Skshetuski had gone into the house a boy brought a decanter and glass to the linden-tree. Zagloba poured out some mead, then closed his eyes and began to try it diligently.

"The Lord God knew why he created bees," said he, with a nasal mutter. And he fell to drinking slowly, drawing deep breaths at the same time, while gazing at the pond and beyond the pond, away to the dark and blue pine-woods stretching as far as the eye could reach on the other side. The time was past one in the afternoon, and the heavens were cloudless. The blossoms of the linden were falling noiselessly to the earth, and on the tree among the leaves were buzzing a whole choir of bees, which soon began to settle on the edge of the glass and gather the sweet fluid on their shaggy legs.

Above the great pond, from the far-off reeds obscured by the haze of distance, rose from time to time flocks of ducks, teal, or wild geese, and moved away swiftly in the blue ether like black crosses; sometimes a row of cranes looked dark high in the air, and gave out a shrill cry. With these exceptions all around was quiet, calm, sunny, and gladsome, as is usual in the first days of August, when the grain has ripened, and the sun is scattering as it were gold upon the earth.

The eyes of the old man were raised now to the sky, following the flocks of birds, and now they were lost in the distance, growing more and more drowsy, as the mead in the decanter decreased; his lids became heavier and heavier,--the bees buzzed their song in various tones as if on purpose for his after-dinner slumber.

"True, true, the Lord God has given beautiful weather for the harvest," muttered Zagloba. "The hay is well gathered in, the harvest will be finished in a breath. Yes, yes--"

Here he closed his eyes, then opened them again for a moment, muttered once more, "The boys have tormented me," and fell asleep in earnest.

He slept rather long, but after a certain time he was roused by a light breath of cooler air, together with the conversation and steps of two men drawing near the tree rapidly. One of them was Yan Skshetuski, the hero of Zbaraj, who about a month before had returned from the hetmans in the Ukraine to cure a stubborn fever; Pan Zagloba did not know the other, though in stature and form and even in features he resembled Yan greatly.

"I present to you, dear father," said Yan, "my cousin Pan Stanislav Skshetuski, the captain of Kalish."

"You are so much like Yan," answered Zagloba, blinking and shaking the remnants of sleep from his eyelids, "that had I met you anywhere I should have said at once, 'Skshetuski!' Hei, what a guest in the house!"

"It is dear to me to make your acquaintance, my benefactor," answered Stanislav, "the more since the name is well known to me, for the knighthood of the whole Commonwealth repeat it with respect and mention it as an example."

"Without praising myself, I did what I could, while I felt strength in my bones. And even now one would like to taste of war, for *consuetudo altera natura* (habit is a second nature). But why, gentlemen, are you so anxious, so that Yan's face is pale?"

"Stanislav has brought dreadful news," answered Yan. "The Swedes have entered Great Poland, and occupied it entirely."

Zagloba sprang from the bench as if forty years had dropped from him, opened wide his eyes, and began involuntarily to feel at his side, as if he were looking for a sabre.

"How is that?" asked he, "how is that? Have they occupied all of it?"

"Yes, for the voevoda of Poznan and others at Uistsie have given it into the hands of the enemy," answered Stanislav.

"For God's sake! What do I hear? Have they surrendered?"

"Not only have they surrendered, but they have signed a compact renouncing the King and the Commonwealth. Henceforth Sweden, not Poland, is to be there."

"By the mercy of God, by the wounds of the Crucified! Is the world coming to an end? What do I hear! Yesterday Yan and I were speaking of this danger from Sweden, for news had come that they were marching; but we were both confident that it would end in nothing, or at most in the renunciation of the title of King of Sweden by our lord, Yan Kazimir."

"But it has begun with the loss of a province, and will end with God knows what."

"Stop, for the blood will boil over in me! How was it? And you were at Uistsie and saw all this with your own eyes? That was simply treason the most villanous, unheard of in history."

"I was there and looked on, and whether it was treason you will decide when you hear all. We were at Uistsie, the general militia and the land infantry, fifteen thousand men in all, and we formed our lines on the Notets *ab incursione hostili* (against hostile invasion). True the army was small, and as an experienced soldier you know best whether the place of regular troops can be filled by general militia, especially that of Great Poland, where the nobles have grown notably unused to war. Still, if a leader had been found, they might have shown opposition to the enemy in old fashion, and at least detained them till the Commonwealth could find reinforcements. But hardly had Wittemberg shown himself when negotiations were begun before a drop of blood had been shed. Then Radzeyovski came up, and with his persuasions brought about what I have said,--that is, misfortune and disgrace, the like of which has not been hitherto."

"How was that? Did no one resist, did no one protest? Did no one hurl treason in the eyes of those scoundrels? Did all agree to betray the country and the king?"

"Virtue is perishing, and with it the Commonwealth, for nearly all agreed. I, the two Skorashevskis, Pan Tsisvitski, and Pan Klodzinski did what we could to rouse a spirit of resistance among the nobles. Pan Vladyslav Skorashevski went almost frantic. We flew through the camp from the men of one district to those of another, and God knows there was no beseeching that we did not use. But what good was it when the majority chose to go in bonds to the banquet which Wittemberg promised, rather than with sabres to battle? Seeing that the best went in every direction,--some to their homes, others to Warsaw,--the Skorashevskis went to Warsaw, and will bring the first news to the king; but I, having neither wife nor children, came here to my cousin, with the idea that we might go together against the enemy. It was fortunate that I found you at home."

"Then you are directly from Uistsie?"

"Directly. I rested on the road only as much as my horses needed, and as it was I drove one of them to death. The Swedes must be in Poznan at present, and thence they will quickly spread over the whole country."

Here all grew silent. Yan sat with his palms on his knees, his eyes fixed on the ground, and he was thinking gloomily. Pan Stanislav sighed; and Zagloba, not having recovered, looked with a staring glance, now on one, now on the other.

"Those are evil signs," said Yan at last, gloomily. "Formerly for ten victories there came one defeat, and we astonished the world with our valor. Now not only defeats come, but treason,--not merely of single persons, but of whole provinces. May God pity the country!"

"For God's sake," said Zagloba, "I have seen much in the world. I can hear, I can reason, but still belief fails me."

"What do you think of doing, Yan?" asked Stanislav.

"It is certain that I shall not stay at home, though fever is shaking me yet. It will be necessary to place my wife and children somewhere in safety. Pan Stabrovski, my relative, is huntsman of the king in the wilderness of Byalovyej, and lives in Byalovyej. Even if the whole Commonwealth should fall into the power of the enemy, they would not touch that region. To-morrow I will take my wife and children straight there."

"And that will not be a needless precaution," said Stanislav; "for though 'tis far from Great Poland to this place, who knows whether the flame may not soon seize these regions also?"

"The nobles must be notified," said Yan, "to assemble and think of defence, for here no one has heard anything yet." Here he turned to Zagloba: "And, Father, will you go with us, or do you wish to accompany Helena to the wilderness?"

"I?" answered Zagloba, "will I go? If my feet had taken root in the earth, I might not go; but even then I should ask some one to dig me out. I want to try Swedish flesh again, as a wolf does mutton. Ha! the rascals, trunk-breeches, long-stockings! The fleas make raids on their calves, their legs are itching, and they can't sit at home, but crawl into foreign lands. I know them, the sons of such a kind, for when I was under Konyetspolski I worked against them; and, gentlemen, if you want to know who took Gustavus Adolphus captive, ask the late Konyetspolski. I'll say no more! I know them, but they know me too. It must be that the rogues have heard that Zagloba has grown old. Isn't that true? Wait! you'll see him yet! O Lord! O Lord, all-Powerful! why hast thou unfenced this unfortunate Commonwealth, so that all the neighboring swine are running into it now, and they have rooted up three of the best provinces? What is the condition? Ba! but who is to blame, if not traitors? The plague did not know whom to take; it took honest men, but left the traitors. O Lord, send thy pest once more on the voevoda of Poznan and on him of Kalish, but especially on Radzeyovski and his whole family. But if 'tis thy will to favor hell with more inhabitants, send thither all those who signed the pact at Uistsie. Has Zagloba grown old? has he grown old? You will find out! Yan, let us consider quickly what to do, for I want to be on horseback."

"Of course we must know whither to go. It is difficult to reach the hetmans in the Ukraine, for the enemy has cut them off from the Commonwealth and the road is open only to the Crimea. It is lucky that the Tartars are on our side this time. According to my head it will be necessary for us to go to Warsaw to the king, to defend our dear lord."

"If there is time," remarked Stanislav. "The king must collect squadrons there in haste, and will march on the enemy before we can come, and perhaps the engagement is already taking place."

"And that may be."

"Let us go then to Warsaw, if we can go quickly," said Zagloba. "Listen, gentlemen! It is true that our names are terrible to the enemy, but still three of us cannot do much, therefore I should give this advice: Let us summon the nobles to volunteer; they will come in such numbers that we may lead even a small squadron to the king. We shall persuade them easily, for they must go anyhow when the call comes for the general militia,--it will be all one to them--and we shall tell them that whoever volunteers before the call will do an act dear to the king. With greater power we can do more, and they will receive us (in Warsaw) with open arms."

"Wonder not at my words," said Pan Stanislav, "but from what I have seen I feel such a dislike to the general militia that I choose to go alone rather than with a crowd of men who know nothing of war."

"You have no acquaintance with the nobles of this place. Here a man cannot be found who has not served in the army; all have experience and are good soldiers."

"That may be."

"How could it be otherwise? But wait! Yan knows that when once I begin to work with my head I have no lack of resources. For that reason I lived in great intimacy with the voevoda of Rus, Prince Yeremi. Let Yan tell how many times that greatest of warriors followed my advice, and thereby was each time victorious."

"But tell us, Father, what you wish to say, for time is precious."

"What I wish to say? This is it: not he defends the country and the king who holds to the king's skirts, but he who beats the enemy; and he beats the enemy best who serves under a great warrior. Why go on uncertainties to Warsaw, when the king himself may have gone to Cracow, to Lvoff or Lithuania? My advice is to put ourselves at once under the banners of the grand hetman of Lithuania, Prince Yanush Radzivill. He is an honest man and a soldier. Though they accuse him of pride, he of a certainty will not surrender to Swedes. He at least is a chief and a hetman of the right kind. It will be close there, 'tis true, for he is working against two enemies; but as a recompense we shall see Pan Michael Volodyovski, who is serving in the Lithuanian quota, and again we shall be together as in old times. If I do not counsel well, then let the first Swede take me captive by the sword-strap."

"Who knows, who knows?" answered Yan, with animation. "Maybe that will be the best course."

"And besides we shall take Halshka[16] with the children, for we must go right through the wilderness."

"And we shall serve among soldiers, not among militia," added Stanislav.

"And we shall fight, not debate, nor eat chickens and cheese in the villages."

"I see that not only in war, but in council you can hold the first place," said Stanislav.

"Well, are you satisfied?"

"In truth, in truth," said Yan, "that is the best advice. We shall be with Michael as before; you will know, Stanislav, the greatest soldier in the Commonwealth, my true friend, my brother. We will go now to Halshka, and tell her so that she too may be ready for the road."

"Does she know of the war already?" asked Zagloba.

"She knows, she knows, for in her presence Stanislav told about it first. She is in tears, poor woman! But if I say to her that it is necessary to go, she will say straightway. Go!"

"I would start in the morning," cried Zagloba.

"We will start in the morning and before daybreak," said Yan. "You must be terribly tired after the road, Stanislav, but you will rest before morning as best you can. I will send horses this evening with trusty men to Byala, to Lostsi, to Drohichyn and Byelsk, so as to have relays everywhere. And just beyond Byelsk is the wilderness. Wagons will start to-day also with supplies. It is too bad to so into the world from the dear corner, but 'tis God's will! This is my comfort: I am safe as to my wife and children, for the wilderness is the best fortress in the world. Come to the house, gentlemen; it is time for me to prepare for the journey."

They went in. Pan Stanislav, greatly road-weary, had barely taken food and drink when he went to sleep straightway; but Pan Yan and

Zagloba were busied in preparations. And as there was great order in Pan Yan's household the wagons and men started that evening for an all-night journey, and next morning at daybreak the carriage followed in which sat Helena with the children and an old maid, a companion. Pan Stanislav and Pan Yan with five attendants rode on horseback near the carriage. The whole party pushed forward briskly, for fresh horses were awaiting them.

Travelling in this manner and without resting even at night, they reached Byelsk on the fifth day, and on the sixth they sank in the wilderness from the side of Hainovshyna.

They were surrounded at once by the gloom of the gigantic pine-forest, which at that period occupied a number of tens of square leagues, joining on one side with an unbroken line the wilderness of Zyelonka and Rogovsk, and on the other the forests of Prussia.

No invader had ever trampled with a hoof those dark depths in which a man who knew them not might go astray and wander till he dropped from exhaustion or fell a prey to ravenous beasts. In the night were heard the bellowing of the aurochs, the growling of bears, with the howling of wolves and the hoarse screams of panthers. Uncertain roads led through thickets or clean-trunked trees, along fallen timber, swamps, and terrible stagnant lakes to the scattered villages of guards, pitch-burners, and hunters, who in many cases did not leave the wilderness all their lives. To Byalovyej itself a broader way led, continued by the Suha road, over which the kings went to hunt. By that road also the Skshetuskis came from the direction of Byelsk and Hainovshyna.

Pan Stabrovski, chief-hunter of the king, was an old hermit and bachelor, who like an aurochs stayed always in the wilderness. He received the visitors with open arms, and almost smothered the children with kisses. He lived with beaters-in, never seeing the face of a noble unless when the king went to hunt. He had the management of all hunting matters and all the pitch-making of the wilderness. He was greatly disturbed by news of the war, of which he heard first from Pan Yan.

Often did it happen in the Commonwealth that war broke out or the king died and no news came to the wilderness; the chief-hunter alone brought news when he returned from the treasurer of Lithuania, to whom he was obliged to render account of his management of the wilderness each year.

"It will be dreary here, dreary," said Stabrovski to Helena, "but safe as nowhere else in the world. No enemy will break through these walls, and even if he should try the beaters-in would shoot down all his men. It would be easier to conquer the whole Commonwealth--which may God not permit!--than the wilderness. I have been living here twenty years, and even I do not know it all, for there are places where it is impossible to go, where only wild beasts live and perhaps evil spirits have their dwelling, from whom men are preserved by the sound of church-bells. But we live according to God's law, for in the village there is a chapel to which a priest from Byelsk comes once a year. You will be here as if in heaven, if tedium does not weary you. As a recompense there is no lack of firewood."

Pan Yan was glad in his whole soul that he had found for his wife such a refuge; but Pan Stabrovski tried in vain to delay him awhile and entertain him.

Halting only one night, the cavaliers resumed at daybreak their journey across the wilderness. They were led through the forest labyrinths by guides whom the hunter sent with them.

CHAPTER XIII.

When Pan Skshetuski with his cousin Stanislav and Zagloba, after a toilsome journey from the wilderness, came at last to Upita, Pan Volodyovski went almost wild from delight, especially since he had long had no news of them; he thought that Yan was with a squadron of the king which he commanded under the hetmans in the Ukraine.

Pan Michael took them in turn by the shoulders, and after he had pressed them once he pressed them again and rubbed his hands. When they told him of their wish to serve under Radzivill, he rejoiced still more at the thought that they would not separate soon.

"Praise God that we shall be together, old comrades of Zbaraj!" said he. "A man has greater desire for war when he feels friends near him."

"That was my idea," said Zagloba; "for they wanted to fly to the king. But I said, 'Why not remember old times with Pan Michael? If God will give us such fortune as he did with Cossacks and the Tartars, we shall soon have more than one Swede on our conscience.'"

"God inspired you with that thought," said Pan Michael.

"But it is a wonder to me," added Yan, "how you know already of the war. Stanislav came to me with the last breath of his horse, and we in that same fashion rode hither, thinking that we should be first to announce the misfortune."

"The tidings must have come through the Jews," said Zagloba; "for they are first to know everything, and there is such communication between them that if one sneezes in Great Poland in the morning, others will call to him in the evening from Lithuania and the Ukraine, 'To thy health!'"

"I know not how it was, but we heard of it two days ago," said Pan Michael, "and there is a fearful panic here. The first day we did not credit the news greatly, but on the second no one denied it. I will say more; before the war came, you would have said that the birds were singing about it in the air, for suddenly and without cause all began to speak of war. Our prince voevoda must also have looked for it and have known something before others, for he was rushing about like a fly in hot water, and during these last hours he has hastened to Kyedani. Levies were made at his order two months ago. I assembled men, as did also Stankyevich and a certain Kmita, the banneret of Orsha, who, as I hear, has already sent a squadron to Kyedani. Kmita was ready before the rest of us."

"Michael, do you know Prince Radzivill well?" asked Yan.

"Why should I not know him, when I have passed the whole present war [17] under his command?"

"What do you know of his plans? Is he an honest man?"

"He is a finished warrior; who knows if after the death of Prince Yeremi he is not the greatest in the Commonwealth? He was defeated in the last battle, it is true; but against eighteen thousand he had six thousand men. The treasurer and the voevoda of Vityebsk blame him terribly for this, saying that with small forces he rushed against such a disproportionate power to avoid sharing victory with them. God knows how it was! But he stood up manfully and did not spare his own life. And I who saw it all, say only this, that if we had had troops and money enough, not a foot of the enemy would have left the country. So I think that he will begin at the Swedes more sharply, and will not wait for them here, but march on Livonia."

"Why do you think that?"

"For two reasons,--first, because he will wish to improve his reputation, shattered a little after the battle of Tsybihova; and second, because he loves war."

"That is true," said Zagloba. "I know him, for we were at school together and I worked out his tasks for him. He was always in love with war, and therefore liked to keep company with me rather than others, for I too preferred a horse and a lance to Latin."

"It is certain that he is not like the voevoda of Poznan; he is surely a different kind of man altogether," said Pan Stanislav.

Volodyovski inquired about everything that had taken place at Uistsie, and tore his hair as he listened to the story. At last, when Pan Stanislav had finished, he said,--

"You are right! Our Radzivill is incapable of such deeds. He is as proud as the devil, and it seems to him that in the whole world there is not a greater family than the Radzivills. He will not endure opposition, that is true; and at the treasurer, Pan Gosyevski, an honest man, he is angry because the latter will not dance when Radzivill plays. He is displeased also with his Grace the king, because he did not give him the grand baton of Lithuania soon enough. All true, as well as this,--that he prefers to live in the dishonorable error of Calvinism rather than turn to the true faith, that he persecutes Catholics where he can, that he founds societies of heretics. But as recompense for this, I will swear that he would rather shed the last drop of his proud blood than sign a surrender like that at Uistsie. We shall have war to wade in; for not a scribe, but a warrior, will lead us."

"That's my play," said Zagloba, "I want nothing more. Pan Opalinski is a scribe, and he showed soon what he was good for. They are the meanest of men! Let but one of them pull a quill out of a goose's tail and he thinks straightway that he has swallowed all wisdom. He will say to others, 'Son of a such kind,' and when it comes to the sabre you cannot find him. When I was young myself, I put rhymes together to captivate the hearts of fair heads, and I might have made a goat's horn of Pan Kohanovski with his silly verses, but later on the soldier nature got the upper hand."

"I will add, too," continued Volodyovski, "that the nobles will soon move hither. A crowd of people will come, if only money is not lacking, for that is most important."

"In God's name I want no general militia!" shouted Pan Stanislav. "Yan and Pan Zagloba know my sentiments already, and to you I say now that I would rather be a camp-servant in a regular squadron than hetman over the entire general militia."

"The people here are brave," answered Volodyovski, "and very skilful. I have an example from my own levy. I could not receive all who came, and among those whom I accepted there is not a man who has not served before. I will show you this squadron, gentlemen, and if you had not learned from me you would not know that they are not old soldiers. Every one is tempered and hammered in fire, like an old horseshoe, and stands in order like a Roman legionary. It will not be so easy for the Swedes with them, as with the men of Great Poland at Uistsie."

"I have hope that God will change everything," said Pan Yan. "They say that the Swedes are good soldiers, but still they have never been able to stand before our regular troops. We have beaten them always,--that is a matter of trial; we have beaten them even when they were led by the greatest warrior they have ever had."

"In truth I am very curious to know what they can do," answered Volodyovski; "and were it not that two other wars are now weighing on the country, I should not be angry a whit about the Swedes. We have tried the Turks, the Tartars, the Cossacks, and God knows whom we have not tried; it is well now to try the Swedes. The only trouble in the kingdom is that all the troops are occupied with the hetmans in the Ukraine. But I see already what will happen here. Prince Radzivill will leave the existing war to the treasurer and full hetman Pan Gosyevski, and will go himself at the Swedes in earnest. It will be heavy work, it is true. But we have hope that God will assist us."

"Let us go, then, without delay to Kyedani," said Pan Stanislav.

"I received an order to have the squadron ready and to appear in Kyedani myself in three days," answered Pan Michael. "But I must show you, gentlemen this last order, for it is clear from it that the prince is thinking of the Swedes."

When he had said this, Volodyovski unlocked a box standing on a bench under the window, took out a paper folded once, and opening it began to read:--

Colonel Volodyovski:

Gracious Sir,--We have read with great delight your report that the squadron is ready and can move to the campaign at any moment. Keep it ready and alert, for such difficult times are coming as have not been yet; therefore come yourself as quickly as possible to Kyedani, where we shall await you with impatience. If any reports come to you, believe them not till you have heard everything from our lips. We act as God himself and our conscience command, without reference to what malice and the ill will of man may invent against us. But at the same time we console ourselves with this,--that times are coming in which it will be shown definitely who is a true and real friend of the house of Radzivill and who even *in rebus adversis* is willing to serve it. Kmita, Nyevyarovski, and Stankyevich have brought their squadrons here already; let yours remain in Upita, for it may be needed there, and it may have to march to Podlyasye under command of my cousin Prince Boguslav, who has considerable bodies of our troops under his command there. Of all this you will learn in detail from our lips; meanwhile we confide to your loyalty the careful execution of orders, and await you in Kyedani.

Yanush Radzivill,

Prince in Birji and Dubinki, voevoda of Vilna,
grand hetman of Lithuania.

"Yes, a new war is evident from this letter," said Zagloba.

"And the prince's statement that he will act as God commands him, means that he will fight the Swedes," added Stanislav.

"Still it is a wonder to me," said Pan Yan, "that he writes about loyalty to the house of Radzivill, and not to the country, which means more than the Radzivills, and demands prompter rescue."

"That is their lordly manner," answered Volodyovski; "though that did not please me either at first, for I too serve the country and not the Radzivills."

"When did you receive this letter?" asked Pan Yan.

"This morning, and I wanted to start this afternoon. You will rest to-night after the journey; to-morrow I shall surely return, and then we will move with the squadron wherever they command."

"Perhaps to Podlyasye?" said Zagloba.

"To Prince Boguslav," added Pan Stanislav.

"Prince Boguslav is now in Kyedani," said Volodyovski. "He is a strange person, and do you look at him carefully. He is a great warrior and a still greater knight, but he is not a Pole to the value of a copper. He wears a foreign dress, and talks German or French altogether; you might think he was cracking nuts, might listen to him a whole hour, and not understand a thing."

"Prince Boguslav at Berestechko bore himself well," said Zagloba, "and brought a good number of German infantry."

"Those who know him more intimately do not praise him very highly," continued Volodyovski, "for he loves only the Germans and French. It cannot be otherwise, since he was born of a German mother, the daughter of the elector of Brandenburg, with whom his late father not only received no dowry, but, since those small princes (the electors) as may be seen have poor housekeeping, he had to pay something. But with the Radzivills it is important to have a vote in the German Empire, of which they are princes, and therefore they make alliances with the Germans. Pan Sakovich, an old client of Prince Boguslav, who made him starosta of Oshmiani, told me about this. He and Pan Nyevyarovski, a colonel, were abroad with Prince Boguslav in various foreign lands, and acted always as seconds in his duels."

"How many has he fought?" asked Zagloba.

"As many as he has hairs on his head! He cut up various princes greatly and foreign counts, French and German, for they say that he is very fiery, brave, and daring, and calls a man out for the least word."

Pan Stanislav was roused from his thoughtfulness and said: "I too have heard of this Prince Boguslav, for it is not far from us to the elector, with whom he lives continually. I have still in mind how my father said that when Prince Boguslav's father married the elector's daughter, people complained that such a great house as that of the Radzivills made an alliance with strangers. But perhaps it happened for the best; the elector as a relative of the Radzivills ought to be very friendly now to the Commonwealth, and on him much depends at present. What you say about their poor housekeeping is not true. It is certain, however, that if any one were to sell all the possessions of the Radzivills, he could buy with the price of them the elector and his whole principality; but the present kurfürst, Friedrich Wilhelm, has saved no small amount of money, and has twenty thousand very good troops with whom he might boldly meet the Swedes,--which as a vassal of the Commonwealth he ought to do if he has God in his heart, and remembers all the kindness which the Commonwealth has shown his house."

"Will he do that?" asked Pan Yan.

"It would be black ingratitude and faith-breaking on his part if he did otherwise," answered Pan Stanislav.

"It is hard to count on the gratitude of strangers, and especially of heretics," said Zagloba. "I remember this kurfürst of yours when he was still a stripling. He was always sullen; one would have said that he was listening to what the devil was whispering in his ear. When I was in Prussia with the late Konyetspolski, I told the kurfürst that to his eyes,-

-for he is a Lutheran, the same as the King of Sweden. God grant that they make no alliance against the Commonwealth!"

"Do you know, Michael," said Pan Yan, suddenly, "I will not rest here; I will go with you to Kyedani. It is better at this season to travel in the night, for it is hot in the daytime, and I am eager to escape from uncertainty. There is resting-time ahead, for surely the prince will not march to-morrow."

"Especially as he has given orders to keep the squadron in Upita," answered Pan Michael.

"You speak well!" cried Zagloba; "I will go too."

"Then we will all go together," said Pan Stanislav.

"We shall be in Kyedani in the morning," said Pan Michael, "and on the road we can sleep sweetly in our saddles."

Two hours later, after they had eaten and drunk somewhat, the knights started on their journey, and before sundown reached Krakin.

On the road Pan Michael told them about the neighborhood, and the famous nobles of Lauda, of Kmita, and of all that had happened during a certain time. He confessed also his love for Panna Billevich, unrequited as usual.

"It is well that war is near," said he, "otherwise I should have suffered greatly, when I think at times that such is my misfortune, and that probably I shall die in the single state."

"No harm will come to you from that," said Zagloba, "for it is an honorable state and pleasing to God. I have resolved to remain in it to the end of my life. Sometimes I regret that there will be no one to leave my fame and name to; for though I love Yan's children as if they were my own, still the Skshetuskis are not the Zaglobas."

"Ah, evil man! You have made this choice with a feeling like that of the wolf when he vowed not to kill sheep after all his teeth were gone."

"But that is not true," said Zagloba. "It is not so long, Michael, since you and I were in Warsaw at the election. At whom were all the women looking if not at me? Do you not remember how you used to complain that not one of them was looking at you? But if you have such a desire for the married state, then be not troubled; your turn will come too. This seeking is of no use; you will find just when you are not seeking. This is a time of war, and many good cavaliers perish every year. Only let this Swedish war continue, the girls will be alone, and we shall find them in market by the dozen."

"Perhaps I shall perish too," said Pan Michael "I have had enough of this battering through the world. Never shall I be able to tell you, gentlemen, what a worthy and beautiful lady Panna Billevich is. And if it were a man who had loved and petted her in the tenderest way--No! the devils had to bring this Kmita. It must be that he gave her something, it cannot be otherwise; for if he had not, surely she would not have let me go. There, look! Just beyond the hills Vodokty is visible; but there is no one in the house. She has gone God knows whither. The bear has his den, the pig his nest, but I have only this crowbait and this saddle on which I sit."

"I see that she has pierced you like a thorn," said Zagloba.

"True, so that when I think of myself or when riding by I see Vodokty, I grieve still. I wanted to strike out the wedge with a wedge, [18] and went to Pan Schilling, who has a very comely daughter. Once I saw her on the road at a distance, and she took my fancy greatly. I went to his house, and what shall I say, gentlemen? I did not find the father at home, but the daughter Panna Kahna thought that I was not Pan Volodyovski, but only Pan Volodyovski's attendant. I took the affront so to heart that I have never shown myself there again."

Zagloba began to laugh. "God help you, Michael! The whole matter is this,--you must find a wife of such stature as you are yourself. But where did that little rogue go to who was in attendance on Princess Vishnyevetski, and whom the late Pan Podbipienta--God light his soul!--was to marry? She was just your size, a regular peach-stone, though her eyes did shine terribly."

"That was Anusia Borzabogati," said Pan Yan. "We were all in love with her in our time,--Michael too. God knows whore she is now!"

"I might seek her out and comfort her," said Pan Michael. "When you mention her it grows warm around my heart. She was a most respectable girl. Ah, those old days of Lubni were pleasant, but never will they return. They will not, for never will there be such a chief as our Prince Yeremi. A man knew that every battle would be followed by victory. Radzivill was a great warrior, but not such, and men do not serve him with such heart, for he has not that fatherly love for soldiers, and does not admit them to confidence, having something about him of the monarch, though the Vishnyevetskis were not inferior to the Radzivills."

"No matter," said Pan Yan. "The salvation of the country is in his hands now, and because he is ready to give his life for it, God bless him!"

Thus conversed the old friends, riding along in the night. They called up old questions at one time; at another they spoke of the grievous days of the present, in which three wars at once had rolled on the Commonwealth. Later they repeated "Our Father" and the litany; and when they had finished, sleep wearied them, and they began to doze and nod on the saddles.

The night was clear and warm; the stars twinkled by thousands in the sky. Dragging on at a walk, they slept sweetly till, when day began to break. Pan Michael woke.

"Gentlemen, open your eyes; Kyedani is in sight!" cried he.

"What, where?" asked Zagloba. "Kyedani, where?"

"Off there! The towers are visible."

"A respectable sort of place," said Pan Stanislav.

"Very considerable," answered Volodyovski; "and of this you will be able to convince yourselves better in the daytime."

"But is this the inheritance of the prince?"

"Yes. Formerly it belonged to the Kishkis, from whom the father of the present prince received it as dowry with Panna Anna Kishki, daughter of the voevoda of Vityebsk. In all Jmud there is not such a well-ordered place, for the Radzivills do not admit Jews, save by permission to each one. The meads here are celebrated."

Zagloba opened his eyes.

"But do people of some politeness live here? What is that immensely great building on the eminence?"

"That is the castle just built during the rule of Yanush."

"Is it fortified?"

"No, but it is a lordly residence. It is not fortified, for no enemy has ever entered these regions since the time of the Knights of the Cross. That pointed steeple in the middle of the town belongs to the parish church built by the Knights of the Cross in pagan times; later it was given to the Calvinists, but the priest Kobylinski won it back for the Catholics through a lawsuit with Prince Krishtof."

"Praise be to God for that!"

Thus conversing they arrived near the first cottages of the suburbs. Meanwhile it grew brighter and brighter in the world, and the sun began to rise. The knights looked with curiosity at the new place, and Pan Volodyovski continued to speak,--

"This is Jew street, in which dwell those of the Jews who have permission to be here. Following this street, one comes to the market. Oho! people are up already, and beginning to come out of the houses. See, a crowd of horses before the forges, and attendants not in the Radzivill colors! There must be some meeting in Kyedani. It is always full of nobles and high personages here, and sometimes they come from foreign countries, for this is the capital for heretics from all Jmud, who under the protection of the Radzivills carry on their sorcery and superstitious practices. That is the market-square. See what a clock is on the town-house! There is no better one to this day in Dantzig. And that which looks like a church with four towers is a Helvetic (Calvinistic) meeting-house, in which every Sunday they blaspheme God; and farther on the Lutheran church. You think that the townspeople are Poles or Lithuanians,--not at all. Real Germans and Scots, but more Scots. The Scots are splendid infantry, and cut terribly with battle-axes. The prince has also one Scottish regiment of volunteers of Kyedani. Ei, how many wagons with packs on the market-square! Surely there is some meeting. There are no inns in the town; acquaintances stop with acquaintances, and nobles go to the castle, in which there are rooms tens of ells long, intended for guests only. There they entertain, at the prince's expense, every one honorably, even if for a year; there are people who stay there all their lives."

"It is a wonder to me that lightning has not burned that Calvinistic meeting-house," said Zagloba.

"But do you not know that that has happened? In the centre between the four towers was a cap-shaped cupola; on a time such a lightning-flash struck this cupola that nothing remained of it. In the vault underneath lies the father of Prince Boguslav, Yanush,--he who joined the mutiny against Sigismund III. His own haiduk laid open his skull, so that he died in vain, as he had lived in sin."

"But what is that broad building which looks like a walled tent?" asked Pan Yan.

"That is the paper-mill founded by the prince; and at the side of it is a printing-office, in which heretical books are printed."

"Tfu!" said Zagloba; "a pestilence on this place, where a man draws no air into his stomach but what is heretical! Lucifer might rule here as well as Radzivill."

"Gracious sir," answered Volodyovski, "abuse not Radzivill, for perhaps the country will soon owe its salvation to him."

They rode farther in silence, gazing at the town and wondering at its good order; for the streets were all paved with stone, which was at that period a novelty.

After they had ridden through the market-square and the street of the castle, they saw on an eminence the lordly residence recently built by Prince Yanush,--not fortified, it is true, but surpassing in size not only palaces but castles. The great pile was on a height, and looked on the town lying, as it were, at its feet. From both sides of the main building extended at right angles two lower wings, which formed a gigantic courtyard, closed in front with an iron railing fastened with long links. In the middle of the railing towered a strong walled gate; on it the arms of the Radzivills and the arms of the town of Kyedani, representing an eagle's foot with a black wing on a golden field, and at the foot a horseshoe with three red crosses. In front of the gate were sentries and Scottish soldiers keeping guard for show, not for defence.

The hour was early, but there was movement already in the yard; for before the main building a regiment of dragoons in blue jackets and Swedish helmets was exercising. Just then the long line of men was motionless, with drawn rapiers; an officer riding in front said something to the soldiers. Around the line and farther on near the walls, a number of attendants in various colors gazed at the dragoons, making remarks and giving opinions to one another.

"As God is dear to me," said Pan Michael, "that is Kharlamp drilling the regiment!"

"How!" cried Zagloba; "is he the same with whom you were going to fight a duel at Lipkovo?"

"The very same; but since that time we have lived in close friendship."

"'Tis he," said Zagloba; "I know him by his nose, which sticks out from under his helmet. It is well that visors have gone out of fashion, for that knight could not close any visor; he would need a special invention for his nose."

That moment Pan Kharlamp, seeing Volodyovski, came to him at a trot. "How are you, Michael?" cried he. "It is well that you have come."

"It is better that I meet you first. See, here is Pan Zagloba, whom you met in Lipkovo--no, before that in Syennitsy; and these are the Skshetuskis,--Yan, captain of the king's hussars, the hero of Zbaraj--"

"I see, then, as God is true, the greatest knight in Poland!" cried Kharlamp. "With the forehead, with the forehead!"

"And this is Stanislav Skshetuski, captain of Kalisk, who comes straight from Uistsie."

"From Uistsie? So you saw a terrible disgrace. We know already what has happened."

"It is just because such a thing happened that I have come, hoping that nothing like it will happen in this place."

"You may be certain of that; Radzivill is not Opalinski."

"We said the same at Upita yesterday."

"I greet you, gentlemen, most joyfully in my own name and that of the prince. The prince will be glad to see such knights, for he needs them much. Come with me to the barracks, where my quarters are. You will need, of course, to change clothes and eat breakfast. I will go with you, for I have finished the drill."

Pan Kharlamp hurried again to the line, and commanded in a quick, clear voice: "To the left! face--to the rear!"

Hoofs sounded on the pavement. The line broke into two; the halves broke again till there were four parts, which began to recede with slow step in the direction of the barracks.

"Good soldiers," said Skshetuski, looking with skilled eye at the regular movements of the dragoons.

"Those are petty nobles and attendant boyars who serve in that arm," answered Volodyovski.

"Oh, you could tell in a moment that they are not militia," cried Pan Stanislav.

"But does Kharlamp command them," asked Zagloba, "or am I mistaken? I remember that he served in the light-horse squadron and wore silver loops."

"True," answered Volodyovski; "but it is a couple of years since he took the dragoon regiment. He is an old soldier, and trained."

Meanwhile Kharlamp, having dismissed the dragoons, returned to the knights. "I beg you, gentlemen, to follow me. Over there are the barracks, beyond the castle."

Half an hour later the five were sitting over a bowl of heated beer, well whitened with cream, and were talking about the impending war.

"And what is to be heard here?" asked Pan Michael.

"With us something new may be heard every day, for people are lost in surmises and give out new reports all the time," said Kharlamp. "But in truth the prince alone knows what is coming. He has something on his mind, for though he simulates gladness and is kind to people as never before, he is terribly thoughtful. In the night, they say, he does not sleep, but walks with heavy tread through all the chambers, talking audibly to himself, and in the daytime takes counsel for whole hours with Harasimovich."

"Who is Harasimovich?" asked Volodyovski.

"The manager from Zabludovo in Podlyasye,--a man of small stature, who looks as though he kept the devil under his arm; but he is a confidential agent of the prince, and probably knows all his secrets.

According to my thinking, from these counsellings a terrible and vengeful war with Sweden will come, for which war we are all sighing. Meanwhile letters are flying hither from the Prince of Courland, from Hovanski, and from the Elector of Brandenburg. Some say that the prince is negotiating with Moscow to join the league against Sweden; others say the contrary; but it seems there will be a league with no one, but a war, as I have said, with these and those. Fresh troops are coming continually; letters are sent to nobles most faithful to the Radzivills, asking them to assemble. Every place is full of armed men. Ei, gentlemen, on whomsoever they put the grain, on him will it be ground; but we shall have our hands red to the elbows, for when Radzivill moves to the field, he will not negotiate."

"That's it, that's it!" said Zagloba, rubbing his palms. "No small amount of Swedish blood has dried on my hands, and there will be more of it in future. Not many of those old soldiers are alive yet who remember me at Putsk and Tjtsianna; but those who are living will never forget me."

"Is Prince Boguslav here?" asked Volodyovski.

"Of course. Besides him we expect to-day some great guests, for the upper chambers are made ready, and there is to be a banquet in the evening. I have my doubts, Michael, whether you will reach the prince to-day."

"He sent for me himself yesterday."

"That's nothing; he is terribly occupied. Besides, I don't know whether I can speak of it to you--but in an hour everybody will know of it, therefore I will tell you--something or another very strange is going on."

"What is it, what is it?" asked Zagloba.

"It must be known to you, gentlemen, that two days ago Pan Yudytski came, a knight of Malta, of whom you must have heard."

"Of course," said Yan; "he is a great knight."

"Immediately after him came the full hetman and treasurer. We were greatly astonished, for it is known in what rivalry and enmity Pan Gosyevski is with our prince. Some persons were rejoiced therefore that harmony had come between the lords, and said that the Swedish invasion was the real cause of this. I thought so myself; then yesterday the three shut themselves up in counsel, fastened all the doors, no one could hear what they were talking about; but Pan Krepshtul, who guarded the door, told us that their talk was terribly loud, especially the talk of Pan Gosyevski. Later the prince himself conducted them to their sleeping-chambers, and in the night--imagine to yourselves" (here Kharlamp lowered his voice)--"guards were placed at the door of each chamber."

Volodyovski sprang up from his seat. "In God's name! impossible!"

"But it is true. At the doors of each Scots are standing with muskets, and they have the order to let no one in or out under pain of death."

The knights looked at one another with astonishment; and Kharlamp was no less astonished at his own words, and looked at his companions with staring eyes, as if awaiting the explanation of the riddle from them.

"Does this mean that Pan Gosyevski is arrested? Has the grand hetman arrested the full hetman?" asked Zagloba; "what does this mean?"

"As if I know, and Yudytski such a knight!"

"But the officers of the prince must speak with one another about it and guess at causes. Have you heard nothing?"

"I asked Harasimovich last night."

"What did he say?" asked Zagloba.

"He would explain nothing, but he put his finger on his mouth and said, 'They are traitors!'"

"How traitors?" cried Volodyovski, seizing his head. "Neither the treasurer nor Pan Yudytski is a traitor. The whole Commonwealth knows them as honorable men and patriots."

"At present 'tis impossible to have faith in any man," answered Pan Stanislav, gloomily. "Did not Pan Opalinski pass for a Cato? Did he not reproach others with defects, with offences, with selfishness? But when it came to do something, he was the first to betray, and brought not only himself, but a whole province to treason."

"I will give my head for the treasurer and Pan Yudytski!" cried Volodyovski.

"Do not give your head for any man, Michael dear," said Zagloba. "They were not arrested without reason. There must have been some conspiracy; it cannot be otherwise,--how could it be? The prince is preparing for a terrible war, and every aid is precious to him. Whom, then, at such a time can he put under arrest, if not those who stand in the way of war? If this is so, if these two men have really stood in the way, then praise be to God that Radzivill has anticipated them. They deserve to sit under ground. Ah, the scoundrels!--at such a time to practise tricks, communicate with the enemy, rise against the country, hinder a great warrior in his undertaking! By the Most Holy Mother, what has met them is too little, the rascals!"

"These are wonders,--such wonders that I cannot put them in my head," said Kharlamp; "for letting alone that they are such dignitaries, they are arrested without judgment, without a diet, without the will of the whole Commonwealth,--a thing which the king himself has not the right to do."

"As true as I live," cried Pan Michael.

"It is evident that the prince wants to introduce Roman customs among us," said Pan Stanislav, "and become dictator in time of war."

"Let him be dictator if he will only beat the Swedes," said Zagloba; "I will be the first to vote for his dictatorship."

Pan Yan fell to thinking, and after a while said, "Unless he should wish to become protector, like that English Cromwell who did not hesitate to raise his sacrilegious hand on his own king."

"Nonsense! Cromwell? Cromwell was a heretic!" cried Zagloba.

"But what is the prince voevoda?" asked Pan Yan, seriously.

At this question all were silent, and considered the dark future for a time with fear; but Kharlamp looked angry and said,--

"I have served under the prince from early years, though I am little younger than he; for in the beginning, when I was still a stripling, he was my captain, later on he was full hetman, and now he is grand hetman. I know him better than any one here; I both love and honor him; therefore I ask you not to compare him with Cromwell, so that I may not be forced to say something which would not become me as host in this room."

Here Kharlamp began to twitch his mustaches terribly, and to frown a little at Pan Yan; seeing which, Volodyovski fixed on Kharlamp a cool and sharp look, as if he wished to say, "Only growl, only growl!"

Great Mustache took note at once, for he held Volodyovski in unusual esteem, and besides it was dangerous to get angry with him; therefore he continued in a far milder tone,--

"The prince is a Calvinist; but he did not reject the true faith for errors, for he was born in them. He will never become either a Cromwell, a Radzeyovski, or an Opalinski, though Kyedani had to sink through the earth. Not such is his blood, not such his stock."

"If he is the devil and has horns on his head," said Zagloba, "so much the better, for he will have something to gore the Swedes with."

"But that Pan Gosyevski and Pan Yudytski are arrested, well, well!" said Volodyovski, shaking his head. "The prince is not very amiable to guests who have confided in him."

"What do you say, Michael?" answered Kharlamp. "He is amiable as he has never been in his life. He is now a real father to the knights. Think how some time ago he had always a frown on his forehead, and on his lips one word, 'Service.' A man was more afraid to go near his majesty than he was to stand before the king; and now he goes every day among the lieutenants and the officers, converses, asks each one about his family, his children, his property, calls each man by name, and inquires if injustice has been done to any one in service. He who among the highest lords will not own an equal, walked yesterday arm-in-arm with young Kmita. We could not believe our eyes; for though the family of Kmita is a great one, he is quite young, and likely many accusations are weighing on him. Of this you know best."

"I know, I know," replied Volodyovski. "Has Kmita been here long?"

"He is not here now, for he went yesterday to Cheykishki for a regiment of infantry stationed there. No one is now in such favor with the prince as Kmita. When he was going away the prince looked after him awhile and said, 'That man is equal to anything, and is ready to seize the devil himself by the tail if I tell him!' We heard this with our own ears. It is true that Kmita brought a squadron that has not an equal in the whole army,--men and horses like dragons!"

"There is no use in talking, he is a valiant soldier, and in truth ready for everything," said Pan Michael. "He performed wonders in the last campaign, till a price was set on his head, for he led volunteers and carried on war himself."

Further conversation was interrupted by the entrance of a new figure. This was a noble about forty years of age, small, dry, alert, wriggling like a mud-fish, with a small face, very thin lips, a scant mustache, and very crooked eyes. He was dressed in a ticking-coat, with such long sleeves that they covered his hands completely. When he had entered he bent double, then he straightened himself as suddenly as if moved by a spring, again he inclined with a low bow, turned his head as if he were taking it out of his own armpits, and began to speak hurriedly in a voice which recalled the squeaking of a rusty weather-cock,--

"With the forehead, Pan Kharlamp, with the forehead. Ah! with the forehead, Pan Colonel, most abject servant!"

"With the forehead, Pan Harasimovich," answered Kharlamp; "and what is your wish?"

"God gave guests, distinguished guests. I came to offer my services and to inquire their rank."

"Did they come to you, Pan Harasimovich?"

"Certainly not to me, for I am not worthy of that; but because I take the place of the absent marshal. I have come to greet them profoundly."

"It is far from you to the marshal," said Kharlamp; "for he is a personage with inherited land, while you with permission are under-starosta of Zabludovo."

"A servant of the servants of Radzivill. That is true, Pan Kharlamp, I make no denial; God preserve me therefrom. But since the prince has heard of the guests, he has sent me to inquire who they are; therefore you will answer, Pan Kharlamp, if I were even a haiduk and not the under-starosta of Zabludovo."

"Oh, I would answer even a monkey if he were to come with an order," said Big Nose. "Listen now, and calk these names into yourself if your head is not able to hold them. This is Pan Skshetuski, that hero of Zbaraj; and this is his cousin Stanislav."

"Great God! what do I hear?" cried Harasimovich.

"This is Pan Zagloba."

"Great God! what do I hear?"

"If you are so confused at hearing my name," said Zagloba, "think of the confusion of the enemy in the field."

"And this is Colonel Volodyovski," finished Kharlamp.

"And he has a famous sabre, and besides is a Radzivill man." said Harasimovich, with a bow. "The prince's head is splitting from labor; but still he will find time for such knights, surely he will find it. Meanwhile with what can you be served? The whole castle is at the service of such welcome guests, and the cellars as well."

"We have heard of the famous meads of Kyedani," said Zagloba, hurriedly.

"Indeed!" answered Harasimovich, "there are glorious meads in Kyedani, glorious. I will send some hither for you to choose from right away. I hope that my benefactors will stay here long."

"We have come hither," said Pan Stanislav, "not to leave the side of the prince."

"Praiseworthy is your intention, the more so that trying times are at hand."

When he had said this, Harasimovich wriggled and became as small as if an ell had been taken from his stature.

"What is to be heard?" asked Kharlamp. "Is there any news?"

"The prince has not closed an eye all night, for two envoys have come. Evil are the tidings, increasingly evil. Karl Gustav has already entered the Commonwealth after Wittemberg; Poznan is now occupied, all Great Poland is occupied, Mazovia will be occupied soon; the Swedes are in Lovich, right at Warsaw. Our king has fled from Warsaw, which he left undefended. To-day or to-morrow the Swedes will enter. They say that the king has lost a considerable battle, that he thinks of escaping to Cracow, and thence to foreign lands to ask aid. Evil, gracious gentlemen, my benefactors! Though there are some who say that it is well; for the Swedes commit no violence, observe agreements sacredly, collect no imposts, respect liberties, do not hinder the faith. Therefore all accept the protection of Karl Gustav willingly. For our king, Yan Kazimir, is at fault, greatly at fault. All is lost, lost for him! One would like to weep, but all is lost, lost!"

"Why the devil do you wriggle like a mudfish going to the pot," howled Zagloba, "and speak of a misfortune as if you were glad of it?"

Harasimovich pretended not to hear, and raising his eyes to heaven he repeated yet a number of times: "All is lost, lost for the ages! The Commonwealth cannot stand against three wars. Lost! The will of God, the will of God! Our prince alone can save Lithuania."

The ill-omened words had not yet ceased to sound when Harasimovich vanished behind the door as quickly as if he had sunk through the earth, and the knights sat in gloom bent by the weight of terrible thoughts.

"We shall go mad!" cried Volodyovski at last.

"You are right," said Stanislav. "God give war, war at the earliest,-- war in which a man does not ruin himself in thinking, nor yield his soul to despair, but fights."

"We shall regret the first period of Hmelnitski's war," said Zagloba; "for though there were defeats then, there were no traitors."

"Three such terrible wars, when in fact there is a lack of forces for one," said Stanislav.

"Not a lack of forces, but of spirit. The country is perishing through viciousness. God grant us to live to something better!" said Pan Yan, gloomily.

"We shall not rest till we are in the field," said Stanislav.

"If we can only see this prince soon!" cried Zagloba.

Their wishes were accomplished directly; for after an hour's time Harasimovich came again, with still lower bows, and with the announcement that the prince was waiting anxiously to see them.

They sprang up at once, for they had already changed uniforms, and went. Harasimovich, in conducting them from the barracks, passed through the courtyard, which was full of soldiers and nobles. In some places they were conversing in crowds, evidently over the same news which the under-starosta of Zabludovo had brought the knights. On all faces were depicted lively alarm and a certain feverish expectation. Isolated groups of officers and nobles were listening to the speakers, who standing in the midst of them gesticulated violently. On the way were heard the words: "Vilna is burning, Vilna is burned!--No trace of it, nor the ashes! Warsaw is taken!--Untrue, not taken yet!--The Swedes are in Little Poland! The people of Syeradz will resist!--They will not resist, they will follow the example of Great Poland!--Treason! misfortune! O God, God! It is unknown where to put sabre or hand!"

Such words as these, more and more terrible, struck the ears of the knights; but they went on pushing after Harasimovich through the soldiers and nobles with difficulty. In places acquaintances greeted Volodyovski: "How is your health, Michael? 'Tis evil with us; we are perishing! With the forehead, brave Colonel! And what guests are these whom you are taking to the prince?" Pan Michael answered not, wishing to escape delay; and in this fashion they went to the main body of the castle, in which the janissaries of the prince, in chain-mail and gigantic white caps, were on guard.

In the antechamber and on the main staircase, set around with orange-trees, the throng was still greater than in the courtyard. They were discussing there the arrest of Gosyevski and Yudytski; for the affair had become known, and roused the minds of men to the utmost. They were astonished and lost in surmises, they were indignant or praised the foresight of the prince; but all hoped to hear the explanation of the riddle from Radzivill himself, therefore a river of heads was flowing along the broad staircase up to the hall of audience, in which at that time the prince was to receive colonels and the most intimate nobility. Soldiers disposed along the stone banisters to see that the throng was not too dense, repeated, from moment to moment, "Slowly, gracious gentlemen, slowly!" And the crowd pushed forward or halted for a moment, when a soldier stopped the way with a halbert so that those in front might have time to enter the hall.

At last the blue vaultings of the hall gleamed before the open door, and our acquaintances entered. Their glances fell first on an elevation, placed in the depth of the hall, occupied by a brilliant retinue of knights and lords in rich, many-colored dresses. In front stood an empty arm-chair, pushed forward beyond the others. This chair had a lofty back, ending with the gilded coronet of the prince, from beneath which flowed downward orange-colored velvet trimmed with ermine.

The prince was not in the hall yet; but Harasimovich, conducting the knights without interruption, pushed through the nobility till he reached a small door concealed in the wall at the side of the elevation. There he directed them to remain, and disappeared through the door.

After a while he returned with the announcement that the prince asked them to enter.

The two Skshetuskis, with Zagloba and Volodyovski, entered a small but very well-lighted room, having walls covered with leather stamped in flowers, which were gilded. The officers halted on seeing in the depth of the room, at a table covered with papers, two men conversing intently. One of them, still young, dressed in foreign fashion, wearing a wig with long locks falling to his shoulders, whispered something in the ear of his elder companion; the latter heard him with frowning brow, and nodded from time to time. So much was he occupied with the subject of the conversation that he did not turn attention at once to those who had entered.

He was a man somewhat beyond forty years, of gigantic stature and great shoulders. He wore a scarlet Polish coat, fastened at the neck with costly brooches. He had an enormous face, with features expressing pride, importance, and power. It was at once the face of an angry lion, of a warrior, and a ruler. Long pendent mustaches lent it a stern expression, and altogether in its strength and size it was as if struck out of marble with great blows of a hammer. The brows were at that moment frowning from intense thought; but it could easily be seen that when they were frowning from anger, woe to those men and those armies on whom the thunders of that anger should fall.

There was something so great in the form that it seemed to those knights that not only the room, but the whole castle was too narrow for it; in fact, their first impression had not deceived them, for sitting in their presence was Yanush Radzivill, prince at Birji and Dubinki, voevoda of Vilna and grand hetman of Lithuania,--a man so powerful and proud that in all his immense estates, in all his dignities, nay, in Jmud and in Lithuania itself, it was too narrow for him.

The younger man in the long wig and foreign dress was Prince Boguslav, the cousin of Yanush. After a while he whispered something more in the ear of the hetman, and at last said audibly,--

"I will leave, then, my signature on the document and go."

"Since it cannot be otherwise, go," said Yanush, "though I would that you remained, for it is unknown what may happen."

"You have planned everything properly; henceforth it is needful to look carefully to the cause, and now I commit you to God."

"May the Lord have in care our whole house and bring it praise."

"Adieu, mon frère."

"Adieu."

The two princes shook hands; then Boguslav went out hurriedly, and the grand hetman turned to the visitors.

"Pardon me, gentlemen, that I let you wait," said he, with a low, deliberate voice; "but now time and attention are snatched from us on every side. I have heard your names, and rejoice in my soul that God sent me such knights in this crisis. Be seated, dear guests. Who of you is Pan Yan Skshetuski?"

"I am, at the service of your highness."

"Then you are a starosta--pardon me, I forgot."

"I am not a starosta," answered Yan.

"How is that?" asked the prince, frowning with his two mighty brows; "they have not made you a starosta for what you did at Zbaraj?"

"I have never asked for the office."

"But they should have made you starosta without the asking. How is this? What do you tell me? You rewarded with nothing, forgotten entirely? This is a wonder to me. But I am talking at random. It should astonish no man; for in these days only he is rewarded who has the back of a willow, light-bending. You are not a starosta, upon my word! Thanks be to God that you have come hither, for here we have not such short memories, and no service remains unrewarded. How is it with you, worthy Colonel Volodyovski?"

"I have earned nothing yet."

"Leave that to me, and now take this document, drawn up in Rossyeni, by which I give you Dydkyemie for life. It is not a bad piece of land, and a hundred ploughs go out to work there every spring. Take even that, for I cannot give more, and tell Pan Skshetuski that Radzivill does not forget his friends, nor those who give their service to the country under his leadership."

"Your princely highness!" stammered Pan Michael, in confusion.

"Say nothing, and pardon that it is so small; but tell these gentlemen that he who joins his fortune for good and ill with that of Radzivill will not perish. I am not king; but if I were, God is my witness that I would never forget such a Yan Skshetuski or such a Zagloba."

"That is I!" said Zagloba, pushing himself forward sharply, for he had begun to be impatient that there was no mention of him.

"I thought it was you, for I have been told that you were a man of advanced years."

"I went to school in company with your highness's worthy father; and there was such knightly impulse in him from childhood that he took me to his confidence, for I loved the lance before Latin."

To Pan Stanislav, who knew Zagloba less, it was strange to hear this, since only the day before, Zagloba said in Upita that he had gone to school, not with the late Prince Kryshtof, but with Yanush himself,-- which was unlikely, for Prince Yanush was notably younger.

"Indeed," said the prince; "so then you are from Lithuania by family?"

"From Lithuania!" answered Zagloba, without hesitation.

"Then I know that you need no reward, for we Lithuanians are used to be fed with ingratitude. As God is true, if I should give you your deserts, gentlemen, there would be nothing left for myself. But such is fate! We give our blood, lives, fortunes, and no one nods a head to us. Ah! 'tis hard; but as they sow will they reap. That is what God and justice command. It is you who slew the famous Burlai and cut off three heads at a blow in Zbaraj?"

"I slew Burlai, your highness," answered Zagloba, "for it was said that no man could stand before him. I wished therefore to show younger warriors that manhood was not extinct in the Commonwealth. But as to cutting off the three heads, it may be that I did that in the thick of battle; but in Zbaraj some one else did it."

The prince was silent awhile, then continued: "Does not that contempt pain you, gentlemen, with which they pay you?"

"What is to be done, your highness, even if it is disagreeable to a man?" said Zagloba.

"Well, comfort yourselves, for that must change. I am already your debtor, since you have come here; and though I am not king, still with me it will not end with promises."

"Your princely highness," said Pan Yan, quickly and somewhat proudly, "we have come hither not for rewards and estates, but because the enemy has invaded the country, and we wish to go with our strength to assist it under the leadership of a famous warrior. My cousin Stanislav saw at Uistsie fear, disorder, shame, treason, and finally the enemy's triumph. Here under a great leader and a faithful defender of our country and king we will serve. Here not victories, not triumphs, but defeats and death await the enemy. This is why we have come to offer our service to your highness. We are soldiers; we want to fight, and are impatient for battle."

"If such is your desire, you will be satisfied," answered the prince, with importance. "You will not wait long, though at first we shall march on another enemy, for the ashes of Vilna demand vengeance. To-day or to-morrow we shall march in that direction, and God grant will redeem the wrongs with interest. I will not detain you longer, gentlemen; you need rest, and work is burning me. But come in the evening to the hall; maybe some proper entertainment will take place before the march, for a great number of fair heads have assembled under our protection at Kyedani before the war. Worthy Colonel Volodyovski, entertain these welcome guests as if in your own house, and remember that what is mine is yours. Pan Harasimovich, tell my brother nobles assembled in the hall, that I will not go out, for I have not the time, and this evening they will learn everything that they wish to know. Be in good health, gentlemen, and be friends of Radzivill, for that is greatly important for him now."

When he had said this, that mighty and proud lord gave his hand in turn to Zagloba, the two Skshetuskis, Volodyovski, and Kharlamp, as if to equals. His stern face grew radiant with a cordial and friendly smile, and that inaccessibleness usually surrounding him as with a dark cloud vanished completely.

"That is a leader, that is a warrior!" said Stanislav, when on the return they had pushed themselves through the throng of nobles assembled in the audience-hall.

"I would go into fire after him!" cried Zagloba. "Did you notice how he had all my exploits in his memory? It will be hot for the Swedes when that lion roars, and I second him. There is not another such man in the Commonwealth; and of the former men only Prince Yeremi first, and second Konyetspolski, the father, might be compared with him. That is not some mere castellan, the first of his family to sit in a senator's chair, on which he has not yet smoothed out the wrinkles of his trousers, and still turns up his nose and calls the nobles younger brothers, and gives orders right away to paint his portrait, so that while dining he may have his senatorship before him, since he has nothing to look at behind. Pan Michael, you have come to fortune. It is evident now that if a man rubs against Radzivill he will gild at once his threadbare coat. It is easier to get promotion here, I see, than a quart of rotten pears with us. Stick your hands into the water in this place, and with closed eyes you will catch a pike. For me he is the magnate of magnates! God give you luck, Pan Michael! You are as confused as a young woman just married; but that is nothing! What is the name of your life estate? Dudkovo, or something? Heathen names in this country! Throw nuts against the wall, and you will have in the rattling the proper name of a village or noble. But names are nothing if the income is only good."

"I am terribly confused, I confess," said Pan Michael, "because what you say about easy promotion is not true. More than once have I heard old soldiers charge the prince with avarice, but now unexpected favors are showered one after the other."

"Stick that document behind your belt,--do that for me,--and if any one in future complains of the thanklessness of the prince, draw it out and give it to him on the nose. You will not find a better argument."

"One thing I see clearly: the prince is attracting people to his person, and is forming plans for which he needs help." said Pan Yan.

"But have you not heard of those plans?" asked Zagloba. "Has he not said that we have to go to avenge the ashes of Vilna? They complained that he had robbed Vilna, but he wants to show that he not only does not need other people's property, but is ready to give of his own. That is a beautiful ambition, Yan, God give us more of such senators."

Conversing thus, they found themselves in the courtyard, to which every moment rode in now divisions of mounted troops, now crowds of armed nobles, and now carriages rolled in, bringing persons from the country around, with their wives and children.

Seeing this, Pan Michael drew all with him to the gate to look at those entering.

"Who knows, Michael, this is your fortunate day? Maybe there is a wife for you among these nobles' daughters," said Zagloba. "Look! see, there an open carriage is approaching, and in it something white is sitting."

"That is not a lady, but a man who may marry me to one," answered the swift-eyed Volodyovski; for from a distance he recognized the bishop Parchevski, coming with Father Byalozor, archdeacon of Vilna.

"If they are priests, how are they visiting a Calvinist?"

"What is to be done? When it's necessary for public affairs, they must be polite."

"Oh, it is crowded here! Oh, it is noisy!" cried Zagloba, with delight. "A man grows rusty in the country, like an old key in a lock; here I think of better times. I'm a rascal if I don't make love to some pretty girl to-day."

Zagloba's words were interrupted by the soldiers keeping guard at the gate, who rushing out from their booths stood in two ranks to salute the bishop; and he rode past, making the sign of the cross with his hand on each side, blessing the soldiers and the nobles assembled near by.

"The prince is a polite man," said Zagloba, "since he honors the bishop, though he does not recognize the supremacy of the Church. God grant this to be the first step toward conversion!"

"Oh, nothing will come of it! Not few were the efforts of his first wife, and she accomplished nothing, only died from vexation. But why do the Scots not leave the line? It is evident that another dignitary will pass."

In fact, a whole retinue of armed soldiers appeared in the distance.

"Those are Ganhoff's dragoons,--I know them," said Volodyovski; "but some carriages are in the middle!"

At that moment the drums began to rattle.

"Oh, it is evident that some one greater than the bishop of Jmud is there!" cried Zagloba.

"Wait, they are here already."

"There are two carriages in the middle."

"True. In the first sits Pan Korf, the voevoda of Venden."

"Of course!" cried Pan Yan; "that is an acquaintance from Zbaraj."

The voevoda recognized them, and first Volodyovski, whom he had evidently seen oftener; in passing he leaned from the carriage and cried,--

"I greet you, gentlemen, old comrades! See, I bring guests!"

In the second carriage, with the arms of Prince Yanush, drawn by four white horses, sat two gentlemen of lordly mien, dressed in foreign fashion, in broad-brimmed hats, from under which the blond curls of wigs flowed to their shoulders over wide lace collars. One was very portly, wore a pointed light-blond beard, and mustaches bushy and turned up at the ends; the other was younger, dressed wholly in black. He had a less knightly form, but perhaps a higher office, for a gold chain glittered on his neck, with some order at the end. Apparently both were foreigners, for they looked with curiosity at the castle, the people, and the dresses.

"What sort of devils?" asked Zagloba.

"I do not know them, I have never seen them," answered Volodyovski.

Meanwhile the carriages passed, and began to turn in the yard so as to reach the main entrance of the castle, but the dragoons remained outside the gate. "Volodyovski knew the officer leading them.

"Tokarzevich!" called he, "come to us, please."

"With the forehead, worthy Colonel."

"And what kind of hedgehogs are you bringing?"

"Those are Swedes."

"Swedes!"

"Yes, and men of distinction. The portly one is Count Löwenhaupt, and the slender man is Benedikt Schitte, Baron von Duderhoff."

"Duderhoff?" asked Zagloba.

"What do they want here?" inquired Volodyovski.

"God knows!" answered the officer. "We escorted them from Birji. Undoubtedly they have come to negotiate with our prince, for we heard in Birji that he is assembling a great army and is going to move on Livonia."

"Ah, rascals! you are growing timid," cried Zagloba. "Now you are invading Great Poland, now you are deposing the king, and now you are paying court to Radzivill, so that he should not tickle you in Livonia. Wait! you will run away to your Dunderhoff till your stockings are down. We'll soon dunder with you. Long life to Radzivill!"

"Long life!" repeated the nobles, standing near the gate.

"Defender of the country! Our shield! Against the Swedes, worthy gentlemen, against the Swedes!"

A circle was formed. Every moment nobles collected from the yard; seeing which, Zagloba sprang on the low guard-post of the gate, and began to cry,--

"Worthy gentlemen, listen! Whoso does not know me, to him I will say that I am that defender of Zbaraj who with this old hand slew Burlai, the greatest hetman after Hmelnitski; whoso has not heard of Zagloba was shelling peas, it is clear, in the first period of the Cossack war, or feeling hens (for eggs), or herding calves,--labors which I do not connect with such honorable cavaliers as you."

"He is a great knight!" called numerous voices. "There is no greater in the Commonwealth! Hear!"

"Listen, honorable gentlemen. My old bones craved repose; better for me to rest in the bakehouse, to eat cheese and cream, to walk in the gardens and gather apples, or putting my hands behind my back to stand over harvesters or pat a girl on the shoulder. And it is certain that for the enemy it would have been better to leave me at rest; for the Swedes and the Cossacks know that I have a very heavy hand, and God grant that my name is as well known to you, gentlemen, as to the enemy."

"What kind of rooster is that crowing so loud?" asked some voice in the crowd, suddenly.

"Don't interrupt! Would you were dead!" cried others.

But Zagloba heard him. "Forgive that cockerel, gentlemen," said he; "for he knows not yet on which end of him is his tail, nor on which his head."

The nobles burst into mighty laughter, and the confused disturber pushed quickly behind the crowd, to escape the sneers which came raining on his head.

"I return to the subject," said Zagloba. "I repeat, rest would be proper for me; but because the country is in a paroxysm, because the enemy is trampling our land, I am here, worthy gentlemen, with you to resist the enemy in the name of that mother who nourished us all. Whoso will not stand by her to-day, whoso will not run to save her, is not a son, but a step-son; he is unworthy of her love. I, an old man, am going, let the will of God be done; and if it comes to me to die, with my last breath will I cry, 'Against the Swedes! brothers, against the Swedes!' Let us swear that we will not drop the sabre from our hands till we drive them out of the country."

"We are ready to do that without oaths!" cried numbers of voices. "We will go where our hetman the prince leads us; we will go where 'tis needful."

"Worthy brothers, you have seen how two stocking-wearers came here in a gilded carriage. They know that there is no trifling with

Radzivill. They will follow him from chamber to chamber, and kiss him on the elbows to give them peace. But the prince, worthy gentlemen, with whom I have been advising and from whom I have just returned, has assured me, in the name of all Lithuania, that there will be no negotiations, no parchments, nothing but war and war!"

"War! war!" repeated, as an echo, the voices of the hearers.

"But because the leader," continued Zagloba, "will begin the more boldly, the surer he is of his soldiers, let us show him, worthy gentlemen, our sentiments. And now let us go under the windows of the prince and shout, 'Down with the Swedes!' After me, worthy gentlemen!"

Then he sprang from the post and moved forward, and after him the crowd. They came under the very windows with an uproar increasing each moment, till at last it was mingled in one gigantic shout,--"Down with the Swedes! down with the Swedes!"

Immediately Pan Korf, the voevoda of Venden, ran out of the antechamber greatly confused; after him Ganhoff; and both began to restrain the nobles, quieting them, begging them to disperse.

"For God's sake!" said Korf, "in the upper hall the window-panes are rattling. You gentlemen do not think what an awkward time you have chosen for your shouting. How can you treat envoys with disrespect, and give an example of insubordination? Who roused you to this?"

"I," said Zagloba. "Your grace, tell the prince, in the name of us all, that we beg him to be firm, that we are ready to remain with him to the last drop of our blood."

"I thank you, gentlemen, in the name of the hetman, I thank you; but I beg you to disperse. Consider, worthy gentlemen. By the living

God, consider that you are sinking the country! Whoso insults an envoy to-day, renders a bear's service to the Commonwealth."

"What do we care for envoys! We want to fight, not to negotiate!"

"Your courage comforts me. The time for fighting will come before long, God grant very soon. Rest now before the expedition. It is time for a drink of spirits and lunch. It is bad to fight on an empty stomach."

"That is as true as I live!" cried Zagloba, first.

"True, he struck the right spot. Since the prince knows our sentiments, we have nothing to do here!"

And the crowd began to disperse. The greater part flowed on to rooms in which many tables were already spread. Zagloba sat at the head of one of them. Pan Korf and Colonel Ganhoff returned then to the prince, who was sitting at counsel with the Swedish envoys, Bishop Parchevski, Father Byalozor, Pan Adam Komorovski, and Pan Alexander Myerzeyevski, a courtier of Yan Kazimir, who was stopping for the time in Kyedani.

"Who incited that tumult?" asked the prince, from whose lion-like face anger had not yet disappeared.

"It was that noble who has just come here, that famous Zagloba," answered Pan Korf.

"That is a brave knight," said the prince, "but he is beginning to manage me too soon."

Having said this, he beckoned to Colonel Ganhoff and whispered something in his ear.

Zagloba meanwhile, delighted with himself, went to the lower halls with solemn tread, having with him Volodyovski, with Yan and Stanislav Skshetuski.

"Well, friends, I have barely appeared and have roused love for the country in those nobles. It will be easier now for the prince to send off the envoys with nothing, for all he has to do is to call upon us. That will not be, I think, without reward, though it is more a question of honor with me. Why have you halted, Michael, as if turned to stone, with eyes fixed on that carriage at the gate?"

"That is she!" said Volodyovski, with twitching mustaches. "By the living God, that is she herself!"

"Who?"

"Panna Billevich."

"She who refused you?"

"The same. Look, gentlemen, look! Might not a man wither away from regret?"

"Wait a minute!" said Zagloba, "we must have a closer look."

Meanwhile the carriage, describing a half-circle, approached the speakers. Sitting in it was a stately noble with gray mustaches, and at his side Panna Aleksandra; beautiful as ever, calm, and full of dignity.

Pan Michael fixed on her a complaining look and bowed low, but she did not see him in the crowd.

"That is some lordly child," said Zagloba, gazing at her fine, noble features, "too delicate for a soldier. I confess that she is a beauty, but I prefer one of such kind that for the moment you would ask, 'Is that a cannon or a woman?'"

"Do you know who that is who has just passed?" asked Pan Michael of a noble standing near.

"Of course," answered the noble; "that is Pan Tomash Billevich, sword-bearer of Rossyeni. All here know him, for he is an old servant and friend of the Radzivills."

FOOTNOTES:

Footnote 1: Means "On the sea."

Footnote 2: Pereyaslav will be remembered by the readers of FIRE AND SWORD as the place where the Polish commissioners with Adam Kisel brought the baton and banner from the king to Hmelnitski.

Footnote 3: "Two-bridges." the Bipont of page 523, Vol. II.

Footnote 4: This word means technically "villages inhabited by petty nobles:" etymologically it means "behind walls,"--hence, "beyond or outside the walls," as above.

Footnote 5: This war was carried on by the Tsar Alexis, father of Peter the Great and son of Michael Romanoff. Set Introduction.

Footnote 6: The speech of the main body of the people in Jmud is Lithuanian to this day.

Footnote 7: Lithuanian forms, with nominative ending in *s* and *as*.

Footnote 8: The diminutive or more familiar form for Aleksandra. It is used frequently in this book.

Footnote 9: The diminutive of Andrei.

Footnote 10: A barber in those parts at that time did duty for a surgeon.

Footnote 11: Marysia and Maryska are both diminutives of Marya = Maria or Mary, and are used without distinction by the author. There are in Polish eight or ten other variants of the same name.

Footnote 12: It is the custom to put a watermelon in the carriage of an undesirable suitor,--a refusal without words.

Footnote 13: Deest = lacking.

Footnote 14: The name Grudzinski is derived from gruda = clod.

Footnote 15: See Daniel v. 25-28.

Footnote 16: Helena.

Footnote 17: The war against Russia.

Footnote 18: This Polish saying of striking out a wedge with a wedge means here, of course, to cure one love with another.

INDICE

Made in the USA
Middletown, DE
19 October 2018